D1613900

by Douglas Woolf

Hypocritic Days, 1955
Wall to Wall, 1962
Signs of a Migrant Worrier, 1965
Ya! & John-Juan, 1971
Spring of the Lamb, 1972
On Us, 1977
HAD, 1977
Future Preconditional, 1978
The Timing Chain, 1985
Loving Ladies, 1986
Hypocritic Days & Other Tales, 1993
Fade Out, 1959, 1996

DOUGLAS WOOLF

FADE OUT

BLACK SPARROW PRESS • SANTA ROSA • 1996

Black Sparrow Press books are printed on acid-free paper.

LIBRARY OF CONGRESS CATALOGING-IN-PUBLICATION DATA

Woolf, Douglas, 1922–1992
    Fade Out / Douglas Woolf.
      p.   cm.
    ISBN 0-87685-988-0 (cloth trade : alk. paper). — ISBN 0-87685-987-2 (paper : alk. paper). — ISBN 0-87685-989-9 (deluxe cloth : alk. paper)
    I. Title.
PS3573.O646F3   1996
813'.54—dc20   95-43350
                                                  CIP

To Robert Creeley

FADE OUT

ONE

Mr. Twombly was awake before Cynthia. Usually they slept only until the sun entered their room, and usually Cynthia woke first, woke him. Not today. Perhaps the sun had grown too weak for her or, hard to believe, would be in the room for too short a period to interest her. Yesterday it had been just twentynine minutes; this morning, although he was too late to time, he knew it would be a few seconds less. And Cynthia lay with her head pillowed by her hands, in sun and unaware. When he scratched her underside with his fingernail she stretched her long neck a little, opened her eyes to blink at him. Mr. Twombly did not really like to tease her, but he did not like to see her sluggish either. Shaking his head, he dropped her two breakfast flies. Some days he preferred not to watch her dismember and devour them, so he lay back on the pillow listening to her knock her rocks, and listening for Kate's snoring to stop, soon Ben's, little Gloria's. When finally that happened he knew, even more surely than when he felt the sun, that a day was here.

Mr. Twombly had been living with his daughter's family for only four months, but in that time he had had ample opportunity to learn the rules of the house. He had learned that Kate ran everything after a pattern, beginning with the order in which the family woke and continuing with the order in which they occupied the single bathroom: first came Kate, then little Gloria, then Kate's husband Ben (who required from twenty to twentythree minutes to shave) and then Mr. Twombly. On this, as on other mornings, Mr. Twombly sat waiting his turn on the edge of his bed, his short legs dangling high above the floor, and the minute he heard Ben's feet slap by in the hall he slid off the bed and hustled into the bathroom.

Standing on his toes in front of the bathroom mirror, Mr. Twombly stared shyly at his large, very porous face. It was a daily trial to him that, no matter how much he stretched his stooped back, it was a physical impossibility for him to bring the lower part of his chin into the mirror's range. It made shaving difficult, and the usual consequence was for Kate to remark that surely he was old enough to shave himself by now. Mr. Twombly decided to insert a new blade in his razor this morning, and he scraped blindly over the lower regions of his face four times before washing away the lather and dousing his wounds with cold water. In his apartment in Baltimore he had had a lower mirror.

The next thing for Mr. Twombly to do was to put on all

his clothes without omitting anything. He began by taking from his bureau drawer the things he would need, a shirt, underwear, socks, a fresh handkerchief for his breast pocket, and he placed them on the bed in the order he would need them, as Kate had suggested he do. After putting them on, he selected one of the three new ties from his tie rack and adjusted it neatly, taking pains not to crease his starched collar. Then he went to the closet and brought out his gray checked business suit. This he handled with particular care, because it was one of the few things of any value Kate had allowed, in fact encouraged him to buy with the money he had turned over to her upon his arrival at her home: it would hardly do for the neighbors to see him running around like a beggar off the streets.

Fully dressed in his coat, vest, and pants, with the white handkerchief peering cleanly from his breast pocket, Mr. Twombly examined himself in the bedroom mirror. He tugged the back of his coat a little until it rested neatly on his uneven shoulders. There, he thought, and he ran a comb through his sparse fluffy hair before leaving the bedroom.

Kate, Ben, and little Gloria were grouped around the kitchen table, as he had known they would be. Mr. Twombly stood with studied erectness in the doorway, waiting to be noticed.

"Well, here's Pop," Ben announced, his big, smiling mouth full of food. "Good to see you up and around so early, Pop."

Mr. Twombly, who had been awake fortyfive minutes longer than Ben, smiled and tried to say a cheery "Goodmorning, goodmorning." It was then that he realized he had forgotten something.

"Daddy, your *teeth!*" Kate squealed, half lifting herself from her chair. Little Gloria giggled.

Mr. Twombly raised one hand to his mouth, started to smile, thought better of it, and returned to his bedroom. He found his teeth in the bowl next to Cynthia's pan, where he had left them the night before. The slippery new plates were still awkward to him and he had to make several tries before he had them properly inserted. Then he opened and closed his mouth a few times, to be sure they wouldn't fly out the way they had at the supper table the day he got them.

Mr. Twombly hurried back to the kitchen doorway, where he stopped and said, "Goodmorning—good-morning, everybody," and tried to smile cheerfully.

Ben laughed. "Goodmorning, Pop."

"Goodmorning, Daddy," Kate said, her small black eyes peering narrowly at him from her full face.

Little Gloria didn't bother to look up.

Kate ordered, "Say goodmorning to your grandfather, Gloria."

Gloria bit into a piece of toast with her strong, young teeth. "Goodmorning, Grandfather," she said. It seemed to Mr. Twombly that in the four months he had been there Gloria had begun to look less like a cute, chubby little girl and more like Kate.

Mr. Twombly stood in the doorway, leaning forward a little, smiling.

"Well, Daddy?" Kate said. "Are you going out for your paper this morning?"

"Yes," Mr. Twombly said, still smiling. "I guess I'll go now."

"Bring me my pocketbook then. It's in the hall closet."

Mr. Twombly obediently fetched Kate's pocketbook from the closet and stood next to her chair while she searched in her change purse. "There we are," Kate said, handing Mr. Twombly a dime. "Will you put my pocketbook back on your way out?"

Mr. Twombly took the pocketbook in one hand and the dime in the other. "Thank you, Kate," he said. "Yes. I will." He smiled generally at the family and started out of the kitchen.

"And be sure to be back before I leave for the store, Daddy," Kate warned, "so that I can give you your breakfast."

"Yes. I will," Mr. Twombly said. He went down the hall, placed Kate's pocketbook where he had found it, and hurried a little as he neared the front door. But Kate's voice got there before he did.

"Don't forget your hat, Daddy."

"I won't, Kate."

Mr. Twombly returned to the hall closet. He had to stand on his toes to bring his gray felt hat down from the shelf. After adjusting it neatly on his large head, he left the apartment, closing the front door quietly behind him. Kate's was a secondstory apartment and Mr. Twombly held onto the railing on his way down the stairs, which he took one at a time. When he reached the sidewalk, he turned left down the hill, in the direction of the drugstore.

After Mr. Twombly had put several houses between himself and Kate's apartment, he allowed himself to relax a little, with the result that he felt the bony hump in his back more than usually prominent beneath his neatly tailored jacket. He moved steadily down the hill, past the little public park, not looking around him very much but feeling the warm sunshine. When he reached the drugstore he took a morning newspaper from the rack and went inside. He flipped the dime in his right hand a couple of times, to attract the attention of the young salesclerk behind the counter. Ordinarily Mr. Twombly's hands shook a little, but not when he handled money. He handled money like a man who was used to handling it. In Baltimore he had worked for a bank for almost fifty years.

"Goodmorning, Mr. Twombly," the bald young man behind the counter said. "Nice morning for a walk."

"Yes. It is." Mr. Twombly smiled and slid the dime across the counter. It came to rest exactly beside the young man's waiting hand.

The salesclerk smiled and rang up the dime. "Thank you, Mr. Twombly," he said. "I haven't seen your daughter Mrs. Mercer around lately. She all right?"

"She's all right," Mr. Twombly said, adding by way of explanation, "She's been working late at the store."

"Oh sure," the young man said. "Back-to-School-Days."

"Yes. That's it," Mr. Twombly said, tucking the newspaper under his arm.

"I guess there's plenty of work for Mrs. Mercer on Back-to-School-Days. She's at one of the big 5 and 10's, isn't she?"

"Yes," Mr. Twombly said, nodding and trying to remember the name of Kate's store. "It's one of the big ones all right."

"Hess's, isn't it?"

"Yes," Mr. Twombly said. "That's the store."

"Or is it the other one? Hesge's?"

"Something like that," Mr. Twombly said, transferring the newspaper to his other arm. "Well, I'll be getting along now."

He started walking rather quickly toward the sidewalk but slowed down when he heard the voice behind him.

"I guess you'll be going right home for breakfast, won't you, Mr. Twombly? Mrs. Mercer will be expecting you."

For just a second Mr. Twombly scowled. Then he smiled and straightened his shoulders a little. "Yes, I'm on my way."

Outside, he headed back up the hill, walking quickly at first but gradually slowing as he went. He passed the little park and had started across the street when he heard something, a giggle, and turned just in time to have the twins whoop out at him from behind a bush. Whooping, they circled Mr. Twombly, crowding him a little, forcing him back onto the sidewalk and toward the park. "Mush, Mr. Twombly! Come on, Mr. Twombly, mush!" Mushing obediently, Mr. Twombly turned himself around and half walked, half trotted into the park. His newspaper fell and one of the twins ran back to retrieve it. She brushed it off for him.

"Thank you, girls," Mr. Twombly said, tucking the newspaper in place again. He looked from one to the other of their pretty, snubby faces while they, waiting expectantly, hopped up and down.

"Guess, Mr. Twombly," they said. "Go on and guess."

Mr. Twombly looked more carefully into the duplicate faces, not so very much lower than his own. One of them had lost another tooth since Friday, but that of course did not help him much. "Becky," he guessed the one on his left, after a moment's pause, "and Berty."

They leaped on him, pommelling his back, congratulating him joyously as he reached inside his suitcoat for
the little green book he carried there. He found the book
and the green pen which some of the girls at the bank had
given him with his name on it, Mr. Twombly, but in the
excitement he had some difficulty turning to the page he
wanted. "Just a minute, girls," he said, and the girls
followed him to a park bench, where he sat down. After a
moment he found the page with the two columns of
numbers headed Yes and No. Under the Yes column he
crossed out the 28 and wrote 29 beneath. Then he returned
the pen and the book to his inside pocket and smiled at the
twins.

"What's your score now, Mr. Twombly?"

"29 to 26," Mr. Twombly said.

They cheered. "Mr. Twombly's winning! Good for Mr.
Twombly," they cheered.

Grinning, Mr. Twombly stood up. "You twins are
early today," he said.

The twins made identical pouting faces. "Ug," they
said. "School."

"That's right," Mr. Twombly said. "I almost forgot."
He tried to smile cheerfully, for he did not want them to
know that he had tried to forget.

"I wish you could go to school too, Mr. Twombly,"
one, Berty perhaps, said.

"No," Mr. Twombly said, adding quickly, "I'd like to
go all right, but I've already been."

"When? Tell us when."

"That was a long time ago," Mr. Twombly said.

"I wish we didn't have to go."

"We'll have to stay inside all day."

"We'll get soft."

"We'll forget our breathing."

They closed their mouths and breathed once or twice deeply through their noses.

"No no," Mr. Twombly told them. "You'll have your recesses and games."

"*Hop*scotch."

"Hopscotch is good for the coordination," Mr. Twombly assured them. "Good for the balance."

"Mr. Twombly! Why can't you come over during recesses, Mr. Twombly? We could meet you in the playground and you could train us there just like it was the park."

For a minute Mr. Twombly almost said yes, but "No," he said, "I don't think your teachers would want me there."

"Please, Mr. Twombly. They wouldn't mind."

Mr. Twombly patted the twins' heads. He pulled their braids playfully one at a time, but they still looked up at him with their squinty, serious eyes.

"What will you do all day, Mr. Twombly? Will you still come to the park?"

"Oh yes," Mr. Twombly said. "I'll still come all right."

But he hadn't made his voice hearty enough: "What will you *do*?"

Mr. Twombly looked around the empty park, at the trees, a little brown already, the graying grass, the empty benches. "Well," he said, "there will be children here. Your brother George will be here, won't he?"

"That *baby*! He's too young for you, you know that. He can't even run. He can't walk!"

"Well," Mr. Twombly said. They were looking at him

and he averted his eyes. He could not think what to say.

"You'll have your newspaper."

The twins giggled now.

"Yes," Mr. Twombly said, smiling and shifting his newspaper to the other arm. "I'll have my newspaper."

Looking at him, one twin nudged another. "We ought to go."

"Wait, twins," Mr. Twombly said, remembering. He reached into the watchpocket of his pants and took out his watch that he had received from the bank. This had his full name carved on back, Richard Stevenson Twombly, and the dates of his employment at the bank, 1908-1957. He transferred the watch to his left hand and then with two fingers of his right hand dug into the pocket for the pennies he had there. "One for you . . ."

"Berty," that twin said.

He fished some more. "And one for Becky."

"Gee, we didn't know you ever had money, Mr. Twombly."

"Oh yes," Mr. Twombly said. "When I worked in the bank I used to collect coins. I had quite a collection at one time, but I had to use most of them when I moved up here." What had really broken up his collection was when Kate had insisted that he give her his 1888 quarter to tip a delivery boy. Later the telegram had turned out to be for some other Mrs. Mercer down the street. "Those are Indian head pennies there. See the Indians on them?"

"Oh. Aren't these real pennies?"

"They're real pennies all right," Mr. Twombly assured them. "That's how they used to make pennies before they put President Lincoln on them. Those pennies are worth ten cents apiece."

They laughed at that. "Crazy, how can a penny be worth ten cents?"

"That's what they're worth," Mr. Twombly said.

"Gee. Then we can buy ten bubblegums."

"Well, no," Mr. Twombly said, explaining to the twins: "You'd have to take them to the coin shop to get ten cents for them."

"Where is the coin shop?"

"Well, there used to be one in Baltimore," Mr. Twombly said. "I don't know if they have one around here. I guess you'd probably have to mail them to a coin collector somewhere."

"Where, Mr. Twombly?"

"I don't know," Mr. Twombly said.

"Oh." The twins looked at Mr. Twombly and then they looked at one another. "What time is it?"

Mr. Twombly looked at his watch. "It's a quarter to nine."

"Well then, thanks for the pennies, Mr. Twombly."

"We'd better not be late."

"No," Mr. Twombly said, "we'd better not be late."

They stood there a minute and everyone was waiting.

"Shall we have a race for you, Mr. Twombly?"

"Run and find me a stick," Mr. Twombly said.

One of the twins brought Mr. Twombly a stick and he stooped to draw a line in front of the twins, across the dirt path. It was a rather uneven line, so he snuffed it out and drew another, straighter one. "On your mark," he said then, raising the stick in the air. The twins dug their brown and white shoes into the dirt and leaned forward on their hands with their backsides up in the air, as Mr. Twombly had taught them to do. They flexed a little back

and forth. "Get set," he said, and he could see the muscles
in their skinny legs grow tense. He paused, and before he
could say "Go!" the twins sprang off as though someone
had swatted both their backsides with a single board. That,
their impatience, was the one flaw in their form. Mr.
Twombly tried to call them back, but already they were
halfway across the park, shoulder to shoulder, their thin
strong legs flashing out in perfect stride, heads high and
braids floating, short skirts flapping wildly like partially
cropped wings that didn't quite permit them to fly. He
knew that their mouths were closed, and that they were
breathing deeply through their upturned noses. He
watched them race the length of the park on the other
side, giddily among the trees that bordered it, across the
street, around the stonewall corner, and they waved to
him as they passed out of sight. From where he stood at the
starting line he saw it as a tie.

It was very late. Kate's store was twelve long blocks
from the apartment house, and she liked to leave home not
later than ten minutes before nine in order to have time to
freshen herself in the powder room before the store doors
opened at nine-thirty. Mr. Twombly tossed the stick aside
and hurried out of the park. He had to wait at the curb for
a driver who stopped his car as though he was afraid Mr.
Twombly would step out in front of it if he drove by.
Mr. Twombly waited there until the man, shaking his
head from side to side, engaged his gears and fft-ffted
cautiously away. Then he hurried across the street and up
the hill. He was halfway up the stairs when he heard Kate
open the door for him.

"Daddy? Is that you, Daddy?"

"Yes, Kate," Mr. Twombly said. "It is." Coming

around the bend in the stairway, Mr. Twombly saw his daughter's mouth hang open wordlessly, as though she were unable to realize that he could be so late. "Hello, Kate." He smiled up at her, waiting for her to step back into the room and let him by.

"Daddy, do you know what time it is?"

"Yes, I do, Kate. I know it's late." Kate stepped back and he followed her into the apartment. "You'll have to hurry, Kate."

"I should be leaving now."

"You'd better hurry."

"Stop just standing there and telling me to hurry, Daddy," Kate said, confronting him. "Daddy, where have you *been*?"

"I stopped in the park for a few minutes, Kate."

"Stopped in the park? At this hour, before you've even had your breakfast, Daddy?"

Mr. Twombly did not really want to explain it all to Kate, but under her heavy gaze he found it difficult just to stand there without saying anything. "The twins were there. I stopped to talk to them."

"Daddy, those twins again?" Kate's hands went up, but her eyes stayed steady as they looked at him.

"They were on their way to school," Mr. Twombly said. "I won't be seeing them in the park much anymore."

"I guess that's something, anyway," Kate said. "Well, Daddy . . ." She looked at him as though she expected something more of him, and this made Mr. Twombly remember that he had not put his paper down. He took it from under his arm and placed it on the table beside the door. "Daddy, aren't you going to put your hat away?"

"Oh yes, Kate," Mr. Twombly said. Going to the

closet, he stretched himself to reach the shelf. His hat started to tip back off the shelf and he gave it little prods until it balanced there. If he pushed it any farther he would not be able to get it down again.

"Daddy, your breakfast is on the table, getting cold."

"All right," Mr. Twombly said. "Thank you, Kate."

"Gloria will be home to make your lunch at noon. She hasn't a key, so you'll have to be home to let her in."

"All right, Kate."

"You'll have to be sure to take the key with you if you go out. Do you think you can remember that, Daddy?"

"Yes, Kate."

Kate was putting on her hat. In the mirror she looked at Mr. Twombly doubtfully. "Maybe it would be better if you didn't go out this morning, Daddy. You could stay home and watch television."

"Don't worry, Kate. I'll remember."

"You could invite that big Whatsisname friend of yours."

"No, don't worry, Kate."

Turning, Kate still looked uncertainly at Mr. Twombly. She took the key from the table and brought it over to him. "Here, Daddy, unbutton your coat," she said. Mr. Twombly obeyed. Sinking to her knees Kate unhooked the keychain and fastened it to the belt loop next to Mr. Twombly's watchpocket. She pulled on it once or twice to see that it would hold, and then she tucked the key in his pocket beside his watch. On her knees, Kate had to look up at Mr. Twombly.

"Kate, I remember when I used to help you dress for school."

"Do you, Daddy?" Kate said, standing up.

Mr. Twombly nodded. "You were a pretty little thing."

For an instant Kate looked down at him almost with embarrassment. Then her wide shoulders pivoted to the right and she strode to the little table beside the door. He watched Kate tuck her short, tightly curled hair beneath her hat, above her broad white neck. "You used to have braids," he said.

Kate laughed a little. "You always used to yank them, Daddy."

"Did I, Kate?" he said, and: "Is that all you remember, Kate?"

Kate did not answer that, but at the door she turned to him. "Here I go."

"Goodbye, Kate," Mr. Twombly said. "Have a nice day at the store."

"Goodbye, Daddy," Kate said. "I'll probably be fired for being late."

"No, you won't," Mr. Twombly said to the closing door. "Oh, no you won't, Kate."

After Kate had left Mr. Twombly did not go at once to the kitchen. He went to his bedroom closet and brought out the white fur slippers which Kate had given him for his birthday in July. Kate called them his TV slippers, but he seldom watched TV. Furthermore, he knew that they had formerly been Kate's own slippers, for he remembered having sent them to her for her birthday several years ago. Going over to his bed, he shook the slippers until his old teeth fell out of one of them, and he tucked his new ones in their place. These old teeth of his certainly did look worn, but they fit comfortably and he could eat his food with them. Mr. Twombly put the slippers back in the closet, and going to the kitchen he whistled a little, for that was another thing his old teeth permitted him to do.

Mr. Twombly's toast and coffee, as Kate had warned, were cold. Mr. Twombly placed the toast on top of the coffee cup, turned the electric oven on. He placed his breakfast inside the oven, but left the door open so that the cup would not get too hot and break. He found it pleasant to be able to prepare his breakfast at his leisure, in his own way, without little Gloria there to watch how he did it all. Standing at the sink he drank his coffee slowly, absorbing much of it with large chunks of his warmed-over toast. When he had finished and rinsed his cup, saucer, and orange-juice glass, he felt so comfortable that he decided to go into the livingroom for an after-breakfast cigarette. Mr. Twombly did not really care much for smoking, but neither did he like Kate's asking him not to smoke when no one was home to put out whatever fires he might start. He selected a cigarette from the copper bowl on the television table (he knew which side Kate put the fresh ones on), tapped it on the television set, brushing the tobacco grains onto the floor. He lit the cigarette with Ben's silver lighter and after he had it going well he took a copper ashtray with him to his bedroom. He had not had a chance to look over his things in guaranteed privacy since leaving Baltimore in May.

Most of Mr. Twombly's things were stored in his wrinkled leather suitcase beneath his bed. There were not many things left inside. There were the remnants of his coin collection in a small lacquer box held closed by a web of assorted rubber bands which Mr. Twombly had brought home from the bank. He slipped these off and looked at the dozen or so coins, shaking them and turning

a few of them over to see the dates. Two 1917S dimes he
slipped into his watchpocket to give to the twins the next
time he met them in the park.

There was the large rolled photograph taken at the
farewell party which the bank had given Mr. Twombly
in May. Mr. Twombly put his cigarette down and spread
the picture on his bed, being careful not to disturb the
quilt. He could not make a bed as Kate liked it made, and
she had to make his for him every morning before she went
to work. The photograph had been taken at the moment
Mr. Wellington, President, had handed Mr. Twombly,
Retired, his watch; if you looked very closely you could
see the pen the girls had given him tucked in front of the
white handkerchief in the breast pocket of Mr. Twombly's
coat. You could also see the slight hump on Mr. Twombly's
back, and Mr. Twombly looked from that to the pretty
girls who were clapping and cheering him, Pat, Gertrude,
Jo, Muriel, he knew them all by name. At one time he had
known where they all were from, whether they were
married, and how many children they had had. Of course
he had known many, many young girls before them who
were now grown old or dead. The girls had been very
sorry to see Mr. Twombly go. They thought he was sweet,
they said. They said old First Trust and Savings wouldn't
be the same without Mr. Twombly sitting at his desk in
Personal Loans. Occasionally he received a letter from
one of them, written hurriedly on company time: "Dear
Mr. Twombly, the old bank just isn't the same without
you . . ." He kept these too.

There was a package of older letters and odds and ends,
including his marriage certificate, a lock of Kate's baby
hair, and a newspaper announcement of his wife's death

in 1941. Most of these were brown and tearing, and Mr. Twombly did not look at them today. He opened the large black picture album instead. This began with a picture of Mr. Twombly as a big-eared boy of ten, showed him leaning a little stiffly against the livingroom table in his parents' old home in Baltimore and staring at the camera with lively curiosity. The next picture was of the Twomblys on their wedding day, and here Mr. Twombly's curiosity was directed up at Jacqueline. With good reason, Mr. Twombly recalled, for at that time he had kissed Jacqueline only once, lightly, on the lips. And then there was Kate's first picture, taken by a professional photographer in Baltimore, showing her lying on a bear rug without her clothing on. It was Mr. Twombly's favorite picture, and he slipped it from its holders and held it up, returning Kate's little smile as he studied it. It seemed to him that Kate's smile was frank and tolerant.

Most of the other pictures Mr. Twombly had taken himself, on Sundays, and Kate was in all of them, alone, with Jacqueline, even in a few time exposures of the three of them in a family group. Sometimes, when Mr. Twombly looked at these pictures nowadays, it seemed to him that they represented the only time he had ever really had with his family, that he had used up that precious time laboriously recording it in smiling, always smiling, photographs. He wondered if they had ever smiled more naturally at other times, on cloudy Sundays, or on weekday evenings before Kate went to bed. He could not remember whether they had laughed. Probably he had done wrong to pull Kate's pigtails, since she remembered it. Kate's mother had always been rather strict with her, too strict it had seemed to Mr. Twombly, and tugging

Kate's pigtails had been Mr. Twombly's way of easing the constant tension in their home. Partly it had been his way of begging admittance to a kind of glum feminine conspiracy that had stubbornly excluded him. As Mr. Twombly tried to recall whether he had ever been let in, a spiral of acrid smoke rose from the ashtray to his face, interrupting thought.

Mr. Twombly snatched Kate's bear rug picture from the ashtray. He blew on it and waved it in the air until it had stopped smoldering, and then he looked at it. A large brown ring, darker than the faded film, had burned almost through the paper to Kate's backside. Mr. Twombly lay the photograph down gently, snuffed out his cigarette in the ashtray. Then he took the ashtray into the bathroom and dumped its contents into the toilet, flushing it. This was a subterfuge he had used as a boy at home, and it reminded him that he would have to open his window when he got back.

Mr. Twombly had started back, had got as far as the hall, when he heard a heavy step in the livingroom. A door banged closed. Motionless, he felt boards shake under him as steps approached.

"Pop. I didn't expect to find you home."

Mr. Twombly smiled. "Oh yes, I'm here," he said. Ben stood there as though he were waiting for some kind of explanation, as everyone always seemed to do, and Mr. Twombly said, "I was just getting ready to go to the park."

"What's that you've got there, Pop?"

Mr. Twombly looked where Ben was pointing, at his hand. He held it up trembling a little for Ben to see. "I was cleaning it in the bathroom, Ben."

Ben sniffed the air and grinned, or at least it seemed to Mr. Twombly that he grinned. Mr. Twombly could never be absolutely sure, for Ben's large yellow teeth were always in view no matter what his feelings were. "Good for you, Pop. Kate will be glad to hear how you're helping around the house." Now Ben glanced inside Mr. Twombly's room. "Well, what do you know," he said. He went into Mr. Twombly's room, and Mr. Twombly followed him. "Hell, Pop," Ben said, touching the suitcase with his shoe, "I didn't know you had all this junk. . . . What's this?" Ben had Kate's picture in his big hand, holding it up to the light, examining it.

Mr. Twombly reached for the picture. "Ben, don't hurt that."

Grinning, Ben turned to Mr. Twombly. He shook his head. "You really are a little queer, aren't you, Pop?"

"Ben . . ."

Laughing, Ben held the photograph beyond Mr. Twombly's reach. "I like that halo around her ass. Sexy, isn't it, Pop?" He winked. "Who is she, Pop?"

"That's Kate," Mr. Twombly said, his hand still stretched out to Ben.

"Kate! Oh, hey now," Ben said, and laughing he took the picture to the window for a better look at it. "Oh, hey now, that's wonderful. Really wonderful." When Ben turned back to Mr. Twombly, his teeth were wet with laughter. "Does Kate know you've got this, Pop?"

Mr. Twombly shook his head, but immediately he wished that he had not. Laughing, Ben stepped around Mr. Twombly to the door. Mr. Twombly hurried after Ben, and at the door he caught Ben's cuff. "Ben . . ."

"Don't worry, Pop. I'll give it right back to you as soon as she's had a look at it."

"Ben . . ."

Ben started through the door, but Mr. Twombly held on to him. Ben stopped and looked down at Mr. Twombly, all the way down at him. He seemed to be looking at him with his teeth as well. "Leggo me, Pop," he said quietly, and Mr. Twombly let go. He followed Ben to the living-room and watched him rummage in the desk drawer where he kept his sales accounts. He watched Ben take out some papers and wedge them in the pocket that held Kate's photograph. Ben looked up from the desk and grinned at Mr. Twombly watching him. "Big deal, eh Pop?" Then he came over to where Mr. Twombly stood in the hallway and he held out his hand to him. "We still pals, Pop?" When Mr. Twombly did not take the hand, Ben lifted it a little and patted the hump on Mr. Twombly's back. "Sure we are, Pop. Big pals," he said. Laughing he gave Mr. Twombly one last big pat and went out the apartment door.

When Mr. Twombly could no longer hear Ben's laughter on the stairs, he put the ashtray back and went to his room. He returned his things to his suitcase, locked and buckled it, pushed it under the bed again. There was just one thing more for him to do. Seated on a chair he took off his left shoe and removed the arch support from it. He took out the wad of travelers cheques, rapidly counted them. They were all there, $1,740 worth. Fitting the roll in his shoe again, he was reminded of the first money he had saved as a boy in Baltimore. It had been his runaway money, and he had cached it in a hole his doorknob had dug in the plaster of his wall. On the day his fund had reached an even dollar he had pushed it too far in, and it had fallen behind the wall. All that winter he had tried to get it out, using fish hooks, chewing gum, coat hangers, without success. He had never got over being troubled by the thought of that money probably still lying in there unused, never in fact had quite got over regretting that he had never run away. He stood up and looked at himself in the mirror now before he went out, straightening his narrow shoulders as best he could, but even with all those travelers cheques he slanted just appreciably to one side, his left.

Since he was going to be there a long time, Mr. Twombly settled himself on the park bench by stages, slowly. He did not throw himself down all at once, expecting to get his relaxation all at once. His hands he held palm down beside him on the bench, his newspaper tucked inside the stiff vise of his left arm, and although his highly polished shoes did not quite reach the ground they hung parallel to it, in walking position. Only as the sun-warmed bench seemed gradually to soften the tight knob in his back and take a little of the chill from it did Mr. Twombly begin to let go, as one does finally in a bath. He sighed and stretched himself. His back was a burden which he carried almost everywhere, a burden which he did not really think about until warmth relieved him of it. Even in his own state, in Maryland, the coldness had settled on him for three or sometimes four months during the winter, but looking up at the fading September sun Mr. Twombly felt that here in New York he would have it for six or seven months, and he did not know whether he could carry it that long. Thus his back absorbed the sunshine greedily, hoarding it in the permanent little knapsack there.

Actually, with all the children back in school, the sun was the only reason Mr. Twombly had left for visiting the park, that and Kate's reluctance to have him visit it. Kate felt that Mr. Twombly would be happier at home, saving his visits to the park for weekends when the apartment became too small for all of them; Kate was wrong. Kate's apartment house was cold. At the bank in Baltimore they had placed an electric heater behind Mr. Twombly's desk in Personal Loans, and after the initial surprise Mr. Twombly had come to enjoy having warm air blowing all day upon his back. In Kate's apartment the heat came from the ceiling, and there was no place Mr. Twombly could sit or stand and have it blow on him. It was especially designed that way. Furthermore, Kate's apartment was a shut-in place. It faced away from the street, toward another apartment house close by, and there was nothing anyone could look at except TV. The people across the way kept their curtains drawn. Thus neither Kate nor the opening of school did very much to alter Mr. Twombly's ways. Even without the children here, even without little Gloria around the apartment to spy on him, Mr. Twombly preferred the park.

A few benches down the path from him two babies were making something, roads probably, in the dirt. Mr. Twombly watched them for a while, but although he tried he could not become interested in what they were doing. He removed his newspaper from under his arm and unfolded it, opening first to the weather page. Yesterday's high temperature in Phoenix was 96, the low was 68. Mr. Twombly wrote these temperatures under the appropriate date in his pocket notebook, using the green pen the girls had given him. He did this daily, thinking he might find the information useful if he ever got out that way. Next, and prompted more by habit than by curiosity, he turned to the financial page. There he read the Dow-Jones averages, hmming a little over them as he had done every day for almost fifty years, but he did not record them in his book. He did not even make a mental note of them, as he had once felt obliged to do. He was impatient to get on to the human problems page, where he was pleased to see that Mary Mason had received three letters today. He unbuttoned the coat of his business suit, settling himself more comfortably. Mary's first problem was Mother Torn Between Love and Family. Tortured Mother wrote that she had been married sixteen years to a good provider twenty years her senior. He was a kind father to her two daughters by a previous marriage. They had been a happy couple until a few months ago, when Tortured Mother met a wonderful man a few years her junior. She had fallen in love for the first time in her life. What Tortured Mother wanted to know was whether she should leave her husband for this other man, at the risk of upsetting the happy life of her teenage daughters?

Mr. Twombly, after a little thought, decided that she should not, and Mary Mason at some length agreed with him. After pausing to wish a good goodmorning to Thankful Teenager and Petey Q, Mary went on to her next problem, Elderly Gentleman Victim of Loneliness. Mr. Twombly read this letter slowly. "My father is in his seventies," Worried Daughter wrote, "and he has always been a respectable citizen. After Mother died he lived alone for many years. Ever since he came to live with us he doesn't seem to be at ease with us. He doesn't seem to care much for his own grandchildren, but he likes to play with other children in the park, especially little girls. I feel that he pays them too much attention. Some of the mothers in the neighborhood have been acting a little strange lately too. Do you think there is anything to worry about?"

On this problem Mr. Twombly had no immediate opinion of his own, he did not know what to think. He was seventyfour years old, and he had come to live with Kate in May. He did not like little Gloria. He missed the twins. He was sitting in the park, and his back was cold. He read the letter again, and then he read what Mary Mason had to say. "It sometimes happens that elderly gentlemen, even those who have led exemplary lives, develop an abnormal interest in little girls. Often they are driven to this dangerous interest by boredom and loneliness. Old people need love and companionship as much as the rest of us. Try taking your father out for Sunday drives; take him with you when you visit friends who would not object to your bringing him; invite neighborhood ladies and gentlemen of his age over to your home to play cards or watch TV; if he hasn't a hobby, try to interest him in one. No matter what methods you use, I urge you to divert his attention from the park toward his own home."

Over the top of his newspaper Mr. Twombly looked around him at the park. His eyes rested on the babies digging in the path nearby with sticks, but he looked away from them. He noticed that most of the mothers had chosen benches at some distance away from his. It seemed to him that there was quite a sizeable group of mothers on the other side of the park, and sitting there on their benches all in a row they looked almost like a club. He had never noticed this before. On his own side there was the mother with the two digging babies, another lady sitting on a bench alone, and Mr. Twombly himself. He began to count the empty benches in his row. He was up to six, and still not through, when he turned to see Mrs. Kroll bearing down on him with the green-and-white perambulator. Returning Mrs. Kroll's wave, he watched her push the perambulator recklessly before her as though it were a basket of groceries which she was racing to check out, and when she braked it to a stop beside his bench he peered inside to see if little George was really there. He was, but he had lost his bottle and Mrs. Kroll gave it back to him. "Well now, Mr. Twombly, we're pretty quiet in the park this morning, aren't we?"

"Yes, we are," Mr. Twombly said. He could feel the sturdy bench sink a little as Mrs. Kroll sat down, and now his dangling toes brushed lightly on the ground.

"Ah, it must be lonely for you."

"Oh no," Mr. Twombly said quickly, looking away from Mrs. Kroll's kind, open face. Mrs. Kroll was wearing her hair in a scarf today, and it seemed to Mr. Twombly that this made her face look almost too kind, too open, if that were possible. "I'm having a fine time," he said.

"The twins are heartbroken," Mrs. Kroll said, and she laughed rather gruffly. "They told their mother they weren't going to school today. 'Mother,' they said, 'we're going to the park to see Mr. Twombly.'"

"They shouldn't have said that," Mr. Twombly said.

"But they did," Mrs. Kroll said with great good humor. "They said they wanted to come and race for Mr. Twombly. They're afraid they'll get soft sitting around school all day. Soft!"

"No, no, they'll have their recesses," Mr. Twombly said, and now he folded his newspaper up and tucked it under his arm.

"That's what I told them, but they wouldn't listen to me. They said they were going to lose their appetites too. Mrs. Alegard thinks they probably will, just out of stubbornness. She says their appetites have doubled this summer since you've been training them."

"She does?"

"She's quite anxious to meet you, Mr. Twombly," said Mrs. Kroll, "and find out what your secret is."

"Oh, there's no secret," Mr. Twombly said, shifting arms with his newspaper. "It was only play to pass the time."

"Well," Mrs. Kroll said, taking hold of the baby carriage and wildly rocking it, "I'm afraid it will be some time before this little fellow can run for you."

Mr. Twombly leaned forward to peer into the carriage with Mrs. Kroll. The baby had his finger in his mouth and he looked up at Mr. Twombly in that way, a little stupidly. Mr. Twombly waved at him.

"You see what I mean," said Mrs. Kroll.

"I guess I do."

"At least there's still the park," Mrs. Kroll said, raising her large bare arms above her head, "and the beautiful days."

Mr. Twombly sat back too, but he did not raise his arms with Mrs. Kroll's. "It's beginning to get a little colder, I think," he said.

Mrs. Kroll looked around the park contentedly. "Now that you mention it, I guess it is."

"It was 96 in Phoenix yesterday."

"96!"

"That's in Arizona," Mr. Twombly said.

"Ah, Arizona."

"I always think of the days as orange in Arizona," Mr. Twombly said a little bashfully, "and the nights are purple there."

Now Mrs. Kroll's eyes returned from their survey of the park to look at him. "Mr. Twombly, you make it sound real beautiful."

He turned to peer at her, but then aside. "I always thought I might live out there someday."

"Ah, Mr. Twombly, you'd be happy there. Just think of all that sunshine and oranges!"

"On August 23rd it was 112."

"112!" For a moment they were silent while Mrs. Kroll rocked and Mr. Twombly tried to imagine how his back would feel if it were basking in a temperature of 112. He could not, and Mrs. Kroll leaned forward to hold the bottle for George to drain: "I suppose you have plenty of money saved to move out there?"

"Oh, I have enough all right," Mr. Twombly said, but now he crossed his legs, adding, "My daughter Kate is keeping most of it for me."

"Mrs. Mercer is a fine woman," said Mrs. Kroll.

"Oh, yes," Mr. Twombly said.

"I'm sure she wouldn't mind you spending your money on a worthwhile cause."

"No," said Mr. Twombly, "I don't suppose she would."

"Children don't really like to have us live with them. I know. Mr. Twombly, would you believe I have a married daughter too? She was a very young bride, of course, but she lives in Gary and she has a little daughter. That's something else you probably didn't know." Mrs. Kroll paused to laugh, as though at her own surprise. "Yes, I'm a grandmother, Mr. Twombly. I went out to Gary to take care of my Sue when little Sue was born. I didn't stay there very long."

Mrs. Kroll looked at Mr. Twombly in an earnest, expectant way, and Mr. Twombly asked, "Didn't you?"

She shook her head. "Ah no, we know when we're not wanted, Mr. Twombly. I couldn't wait to get back to my own home and my work for Mrs. Alegard. I think we're better by ourselves, don't you? Well, not by *ourselves*. We need company, someone to look after us, don't you think so?"

"Yes, I suppose we do," Mr. Twombly said. The longer Mrs. Kroll sat the wider she seemed to grow, and he shifted over a little to give her room.

"I'll never forget how lonely I was when I lost Mr. Kroll," Mrs. Kroll went on. "It was only loneliness that drove me to that other brute. Oh, he was a real brute, Mr. Twombly," she said, shaking her bound head, "a real one. The things I could tell you! Do you know what the judge said when he gave me my divorce?" A hank of hair had slipped from Mrs. Kroll's scarf, and it hung there strangely, like a decoration on a melon of some kind. He did not remember Mrs. Kroll's hair being that dark or red before. "He said he didn't like to see a fine woman like me held down by a useless bum. He said the only reason he made my alimony just fifty dollars was because he knew a social dreg like that would never work hard enough to give me what I deserve. Oh, he was right all right. I'm usually lucky if I get the fifty. It's pitiable, Mr.

Twombly, a woman that's been married twice still earning her own living like I do."

"It certainly is," Mr. Twombly said.

"Now don't think I mind a little work, Mr. Twombly," Mrs. Kroll said quickly. "I can work as hard as the next woman, don't you doubt that. I've still got my health, I'm strong. My doctor says I've got the muscle tone of a woman of twentyfive." Mrs. Kroll looked out at the park and then behind the cover of the perambulator drew her skirt above her knee. "Just see." Mr. Twombly looked at the impressive woman beside him, at her impressive leg, then looked away as Mrs. Kroll laughed cheerfully. Putting her skirt in place, "The last time I went to my doctor, he said, 'Mrs. Kroll, you're a physical specimen.'"

While Mrs. Kroll beamed at him, Mr. Twombly looked down at his own thin legs dangling from the bench. He was aware that she waited, beaming, for him to speak. "I wouldn't kick you out of bed," he said.

It was as though some other man had said the words. He did not know where he had got them, whether from the almost forgotten past or from some more recent conversation overheard in the men's room at the bank. He heard Mrs. Kroll laugh, and he felt his face flush hot. He did not look up at Mrs. Kroll, but now her warm robust hand braced his back. "Mr. Twombly, you are a rascal, aren't you?" she said.

He tried to smile. "Oh, I don't know."

"What would Mrs. Mercer say if she could hear you talk that way?"

"I don't know," Mr. Twombly said.

"We'll talk more often, Mr. Twombly," Mrs. Kroll

said, and chuckling she stood up to leave. "You'll be here again tomorrow morning?"

"Well, I don't know."

"Try, Mr. Twombly, try."

"All right, Mrs. Kroll."

Releasing the carriage brake, Mrs. Kroll stooped close to him. "Grace."

"Grace," Mr. Twombly repeated, feeling her warm laugh on him. He watched Mrs. Kroll's strong back move swaying down the path, across the street, and then he looked away. The two digging babies were leaving with their mother now. Before he too left the park, he went over to see what it was that they had made. It was a road, all right. Lest someone should think he was escaping from the park, he took the long path that cut it in two parts diagonally. It did not matter much anyway, almost everyone he passed had her back to him. The others had interesting things to read. He passed morning papers uneasily, but all were turned to the comic page. Nevertheless he held his shoulders straight, for he could be sure the young man behind the drugstore counter had sighted him long ago. That was why they called it the Parkview Pharmacy.

The clerk watched Mr. Twombly's entrance in a worried way, as though fearful he might be returning to exchange his morning newspaper for a fresher one. But Mr. Twombly sidestepped the paper rack for the gayer rivalry of the candy stand. "Mints," he said, selecting a box of them.

Behind his counter the clerk was pleased. He looked at the mints admiringly. "Mints are good," he said.

"Yes. They are."

"Kind to the dentures too." The young man smiled, and it was as though he were putting his own on sale.

"These mints are for little Gloria."

Now the young man smiled more modestly, lowering his price by half. "Gloria sure loves her candy, doesn't she?"

"Yes," Mr. Twombly agreed. "She does."

The bald head shook admiringly. "I wish everyone loved their candy the way your Gloria does."

Mr. Twombly fished one of his dimes from his watch-pocket, flipped it in the air. It spun twice and came to rest against the polished thumbnail of the clerk's waiting hand. With a quick movement of his hand the clerk scooped it up before it could fall to the counter. In what seemed the same unbroken gesture he cast it into the cash register and whammed the drawer. He smiled at Mr. Twombly.

"You should have rung up fifty," Mr. Twombly said.

The clerk stopped smiling now. He looked at Mr. Twombly reproachfully, as though he did not deserve his lovely family, three fine customers like Kate and Ben and little Gloria. He said, "That looked like a dime you gave me, Mr. Twombly."

"That's right," Mr. Twombly said. "A 1917S."

"Ah." In one quick sidewise glance at the cash register the clerk took back his unkind thoughts. Then he banged the drawer open and fingered his dimes until he found Mr. Twombly's 1917S. He held it up, examining it. "I guess this is something pretty special, isn't it, Mr. Twombly?"

"Yes, it's a rare one."

"Worth fifty cents, you say?"

"Yes."

The clerk looked from the dime to Mr. Twombly, to the dime again. He held the coin in his palm, hefting it. "I'm afraid we can't . . ."

"That's all right." Mr. Twombly was looking at a strong black hair sprouting from the young man's forehead; he had had an unusually low brow in his day. "I don't expect you to."

"You understand, to us it's still a . . ."

"Of course it is."

"We have to take it at face value, you understand."

"Of course," Mr. Twombly said, and he turned to leave. The clerk called after him.

"Mr. Twombly, I wish we could have given you fifty for it."

"Nonsense," Mr. Twombly said, and at the door he waved his hand. "I just thought you might like to know." Walking out of the store he held his shoulders up, for although he had already made his purchase he felt that the young clerk's pale blue eyes still followed his back appraisingly.

Little Gloria was home now. Mr. Twombly could feel her on the stairs, shaking them one by one. As Mr. Twombly foresaw it, little Gloria would enter the apartment without knocking, hoping to surprise him at something, in some compromising activity, position, or mood. Here was what she would find: her grandfather partially hidden in the large, wing-backed easychair turned obliquely from the apartment door and facing squarely the television set, the television going, the shades drawn, and Mr. Twombly's dangling, slippered feet appearing to rest just comfortably on the TV stool. Mr. Twombly

would not turn to little Gloria at once but would wait long
enough for her to absorb fully the irreproachable temper-
ance of this scene, absorb it to perhaps later re-create
for her mother as evidence that Mr. Twombly had at
least not spent his entire morning running around town
and making a display of himself. Only then, after that
interval, would Mr. Twombly turn to the door and say
in pleased surprise, "Oh, is that you, Gloria?" and little
Gloria would make some nasty remark. Mr. Twombly
would not be offended. He would smile. He would try to
say something pleasant about little Gloria's appearance,
and then he would offer her the mints.

Gloria had reached the top of the stairs. Mr. Twombly
could feel her moving along the hall, passing the fire
extinguisher, feel her approaching the apartment door.
Almost. Now. There! Even though he had been waiting
for it, the abruptly opened door outraged his nerves with
the violence of a sprung mousetrap, with just that amount
of unprevisable shock. Mr. Twombly jerked forward in
his chair, but not so far forward that its wide wing failed
to conceal from his granddaughter's view the round lump
of his back, tingling unpleasantly now. Mr. Twombly
concerned himself with the television, chuckled at the fat
lady tossing peanuts into a monkey's gaping mouth. He
watched for a full dozen peanuts and then, shaking his
head as though admiringly, turned to the door. "Oh, is
that you, Gloria?" he asked.

Little Gloria dropped a great armful of books on the
slender table beside the door. "It isn't Queen Tut," she
said.

Mr. Twombly smiled. Seeing little Gloria wheel toward
the hall, he reached for the box of mints on the table

beside his chair, saying loudly to Gloria's back, "Gloria, you do look majestic with your hair up on top like that."

Little Gloria paused under the hall archway to bump her backside grandly in Mr. Twombly's direction. "Excuse *me*, Grandy," she said, swaying into the hall, "I've got to go to the john."

After Little Gloria had swayed out of sight, Mr. Twombly returned the box of mints to the table and once again faced the television set. Now the monkey was tossing peanuts into the fat lady's mouth, and Mr. Twombly looked away. His attention was caught by a flattering view of himself in the hall mirror, a limited view which framed his rather large oval head in a larger oval of somber light as in an early photograph, dishonest yet unretouched. His fluffy hair looked almost silver now; it was impossible to say where his uneven shoulders left off and the wings of his chair began. He saw that he was still smiling kindly for little Gloria. He held the smile and the pose, because little Gloria would have this view of him, although in a larger frame, upon her return to the livingroom.

And little Gloria was certainly on her way back. The bathroom door was open and the rushing water of the toilet seemed to accompany her along the hall, muffling her heavy progress. There she was now, filling the archway, her puffy, narrow eyes studying Mr. Twombly from the very position that his own deep-set eyes had looked back at him a moment ago. He returned her stare almost boldly, for he found it comforting to realize that never before had he known quite so nearly what it was she saw when she looked at him that way. He grappled for the chocolate mints. "Gloria, look what I've got for you."

Gloria came into the darkened livingroom and peered at the little box he held. She smelled strongly of flowers that never grew. "Thanks," she said, "I've sworn off the stuff."

From his chair Mr. Twombly watched little Gloria push through the swinging door to the kitchen, felt her wheel suddenly and push back through again. "Grandy," she said, holding the door with her strangely dainty hand, "where did you get those mints?"

"Why, I bought them at the drugstore, Gloria."

"Bought them, Grandy? How?"

"With money, Gloria!"

Now little Gloria released the door. She came over to Mr. Twombly's chair and stood looking down at him, her arms folded tightly under her bosom, at her waist. Pinched thus, her short skirt puckered up in front, revealing the starched lace border of her petticoat. The patent leather belt rounding the gentle curve of her waist ran uphill over her stomach to the little tin buckle there, then steeply down the other side and out of sight. Her eyes she held severely on Mr. Twombly's face. "Grandy, where did you get money?"

"I used a rare dime from my collection, Gloria."

Little Gloria's thin eyebrows sprang up from opposite directions, pushing her forehead into meaningless folds before them, like windshield wipers turned on by accident. Halfway up they stuck on accumulated flesh, fell back again. "I thought you didn't like to use your coins."

"Oh, I don't mind," Mr. Twombly said, and smiled.

The eyebrows swept up again, not so far this time. "I remember the stink you made when Mother told you to give one of your quarters to the telegram boy."

Mr. Twombly shook his head. "That, that was foolish-
ness. I guess we all grow up, don't we?" he said. "You're
growing up too, Gloria, you're filling out. You'll be a
lady soon."

"Well." Little Gloria looked down at herself. She un-
folded her arms, and everything settled into place again.
She ran her slender hands over her stomach, flattening it.
"Well, I suppose," said she.

"Sit down, Gloria," Mr. Twombly said. "Sit down and
have a mint."

"I really shouldn't."

Mr. Twombly opened the box, spreading the crisp
paper lining noisily as he held it out to Gloria. Little
Gloria looked at the dark mints aligned like eatable coins
enticingly in a row, and then she looked at the easychair
across the table from Mr. Twombly's higher one. The
smell of the mints had penetrated her eau de cologne.
"I guess just one won't hurt."

"It won't hurt."

Dogs were barking on the television now, and waiting
for them to stop Mr. Twombly and little Gloria sat
smiling across at one another from their easychairs,
nibbling mints. Gloria reached for another one, and Mr.
Twombly held the box for her. Silence came, surprising
them. They both began to speak at once.

"Excuse me, Gloria."

"I said, do you really think I am?"

"I was just going to say, Gloria," Mr. Twombly said,
"I've never seen you look so womanly before. I think
you're beginning to bloom," and now he realized that it
was true, something about little Gloria had changed. He
did not know what it was, but it had changed. In the four

months that he had lived here he had never before seen little Gloria so presentable, her eyes this far open, her complexion this nearly pure. He supposed it might be the light, but he wondered too if he had ever looked at Gloria as long and carefully before. "You really look much better," he said, offering mints.

Gloria accepted the compliment, as she did the chocolate mints, with terrible appetite. "That Bob Blakely," she said, settling the skirt more becomingly over her knees. "What a riot he is."

"He is?" Mr. Twombly asked. "What did he do?"

"Oh, nothing much," little Gloria said, examining her slender hands. "I was just going downstairs to the bookstore and as I went by the second floor he yelled right out, 'Hey, beautiful!' But I just kept on going as though I didn't know who he was talking to. He must have meant me, though, because I was the only girl in sight. Amy Richey was coming up, but Bob couldn't see her where he stood. Then he made some crack about getting the wrong number or something, and everyone laughed. Everyone but me, that is." Now Gloria did laugh, and it was a small, harsh laugh. "Maybe he won't be so fresh next time," she said.

Little Gloria looked up to shake her head, and Mr. Twombly shook his head too. They were both amused. Then, "You really do look better, Gloria," Mr. Twombly said.

Gloria looked at him. "So do you," she said.

"Ah, it must be the light!" Mr. Twombly stole a sidewise glance at the mirror, and he straightened his shoulders a little bit.

"But it's true," said little Gloria, tilting her head to

study him. "You do. You look more like grandfathers usually do."

"That's silly." Oh, it was true all right, he had taken another look. But little Gloria's view of him, Mr. Twombly knew, was not the one the mirror had. Under her close scrutiny he sank his back deeper into the easychair, turned his head until it faced her full. "No, no," he said.

Frowning now, little Gloria closed one eye. "I wish you had a large mustache."

"A mustache?"

"I don't suppose you could grow one, though."

Running a finger over his upper lip, he wondered if little Gloria could hear the rough noise it made. "Oh, I don't know."

"You could?"

"I might."

Frowning, "If you did, what color would it be?"

Now Mr. Twombly looked in the mirror more candidly. "Well, white, I suppose," he said.

"White!" Gloria took another mint, bit into it. "White," she said, narrowing her eyes more than she normally did, ecstatically. "White is my favorite color for you. We could have your picture taken then, and put it on the television the way other people do. Can't you just imagine it?"

Glancing at the television Mr. Twombly could, and blushed. "You'd like that, Gloria?"

"Like it?" Gloria asked. "Whenever my friends dropped over in the evening they'd want to know who the distinguished man in the picture was, and I'd say, 'Yes, that's my grandfather, he's a retired banker from Baltimore. Probably you've seen him in the park.' "

Somehow smiling, "You'd like that, wouldn't you, Gloria?"

Gloria leaned toward him. "Will you, Grandfather?"

"All right. I will," he promised her.

She threw herself upon him now, wrapping her arms about his head. She did not touch him with her lips, but he could smell the mints on them. "Grandfather," she whispered in his ear, "you'll really look like a grandfather now."

Patting her solid back, he said, "I just want you to be happy, child."

She leaned back so that they could look at one another, smile. Then, "I'd better make our lunch, I guess. If I don't hurry I'll be late to class."

"Can I help you, Gloria?"

"No, you sit right there and watch your television, Grandfather," Gloria said. She turned at the door to smile. "I'll call you when it's time to eat."

"All right, Gloria," Mr. Twombly said to her retreating back. "We'll save our mints for our dessert."

So he sat right there watching something on television, smiling at the busy kitchen sounds, until little Gloria came to the door. He knew she stood for a minute in the doorway, shaking her head a little, before she gently called to him. He looked up with surprise, and smiled. Then he picked up the mints and slid out of his chair to follow her. Little Gloria waited until he had reached the door, then softly said, "Grandfather, aren't you going to turn your television off?"

"Oh yes." Crossing to the television he could feel her fond smile on him. "There we go," he said.

Again little Gloria waited at the door for him.

"Grandfather, haven't you forgotten about your hands?"

Now Mr. Twombly smiled again. "I'll only be a minute, Gloria."

"All right, Grandfather."

On his way back from the bathroom, he did not forget the mints. Pushing into the kitchen, he took them to Gloria's place.

"Don't wait for me, Grandfather." Little Gloria was having some difficulty at the stove, and she did not turn to him.

"All right, Gloria." Mr. Twombly sat down before his tomato juice, his cream cheese salad, his unfilled coffee cup.

"Dig right in," called Gloria.

"All right." He shook out his napkin and tucked it at his neck; behind him something was boiling over onto the floor.

"Son of a bitch," little Gloria said, and squeezing past Mr. Twombly she scowled. "Sorry, son of a bumblebee," she said.

"There. You see, Gloria, you really are growing up," Mr. Twombly said. "You're not talking nasty anymore."

"Yes, Grandfather." Little Gloria's knees cracked sharply as she stooped for rags beneath the sink. A square of sunshine from the kitchen window fell on the back of her neck, lighting up red and yellow pimples. The other pimples on her plump bare arms extended from her elbows to her short, puffed sleeves, becoming deep purple near the corrugated rings the elastic made. In this frank light all her straps showed through. Mr. Twombly stared at his tomato joice, untouched. "Gloria, can I be of any help?"

"No, Grandfather. You just eat your lunch."

"All right, Gloria." Every time Gloria passed between
Mr. Twombly and the sink her large backside brushed
against his back. He was glad when she had the coffee
made, brought it over to the table in the heavy pot. Little
Gloria poured Mr. Twombly's coffee first, spilling a little
on his silverware, and then she poured herself a cup. She
glanced at Mr. Twombly, who winked at her. "Gloria,
you're that grown up?"

"Of course I am." Little Gloria sat down, clanking the
pot on the glass table top. She tucked her paper napkin
in the round neck of her collarless blouse, rubbing some
powder off. Watching her sip her black coffee Mr.
Twombly smiled at her.

"Good, Gloria?"

Little Gloria put down her cup. "Grandfather, do that
again."

"Do what, Gloria?"

"Smile."

Mr. Twombly smiled again for Gloria.

"Grandy, where are the new teeth Mother bought
for you?"

Mr. Twombly ceased to smile. He extracted a walnut
from his cream cheese salad, stirred sugar into his coffee
cup. "I changed them this morning, Gloria."

"For these old ugly ones?"

"These old teeth fit, Gloria. I can eat with them."

"Even so, what would Mother say?"

"Kate will never know, Gloria. I'll have the others in
when she gets home."

Little Gloria was watching him. Her eyes were almost
closed, and from the broad nose to the heavy jawbone

her puffy face was red. "Supposing I told her, Grandy," she said.

Mr. Twombly also stared. "Little Gloria," he said quietly, "if you do I'll tell her you put nuts in my cream cheese."

"Tell her."

Weakly he shook his head at her evil grin.

"Go on and tell," little Gloria said. "She puts them, too."

Again he shook his head.

"You're scared, Grandy," little Gloria said, with her tense grin. "You're trying to duck out of this."

"No, Gloria."

Little Gloria leaned across the table toward him. "Grandy, I think I'm going to tell on you."

"All right, Gloria." Little Gloria's red face was less than a foot away from Mr. Twombly's eyes, and he smiled at it. "Then I'll have to tell Kate that you wore your rouge to school."

For a moment nothing of little Gloria's appeared to move, although her eyes were so narrow he lost sight of them. Then her heavy arm swung out and her hand grasped Mr. Twombly's tie. Delicately she twisted the silk around her fist, as though testing it for wrinkles before buying it. Not satisfied, she lent weight to it, drawing Mr. Twombly's head slowly toward her until foreheads touched. Mr. Twombly closed his mouth to the flow of her warm breath, the sensation like stooping close to a pot of pink tapioca and finding it wildly fragrant with coffee, chocolate, mint. Gloria shook him a little bit. "You won't tell, Grandy," she breathed at him. "Oh no, you won't."

He wanted to smile; he wanted to speak but was

unable to. Little Gloria had taken another fold in his tie,
and he could feel it closing his throat.

"Well, Grandy?"

His mouth sprang open, but it was not to smile.

"Come again, Grandy," little Gloria said.

"Gloria . . .!"

Little Gloria shoved him back in his chair, and together
they watched his black tie unwind from her hand like an
injured snake. For a minute she sat looking at Mr.
Twombly as though she would speak, but then she flung
herself backwards to her feet, spilling mints and coffee to
the floor. Mints spun in lopsided circles over the linoleum,
and little Gloria went after one, soon caught up with it.
She squealed as it squirted out like a quashed pimple
beneath her toe, then spinning stomped on another one.
Red-faced she went from mint to mint around the room,
squealing whenever she squirted them. When she had
flattened them all, she squealed once shrilly at Mr.
Twombly and crashed through to the livingroom. Mr.
Twombly waited until he heard the bathroom door
before he stood up too. He stepped carefully among little
Gloria's tacky prints across the kitchen, the diningroom,
into the hall, turning off where they faded out at his
bedroom door. Taking his slippers from the closet, he
exchanged his teeth. He scowled at the mirror, and his
new teeth smiled back at him. Too large, too white, they
lent his face the fixed look of a skeleton. Turning from
the mirror, he smiled and they scowled at him.

Little Gloria met him in the hall. They glanced at one
another, and even in this dim light he was struck by the
nakedness of little Gloria's face. They stood for a moment
together under the archway before little Gloria ducked

ahead of him. He watched her pick her way across the
livingroom, gather books.

"I haven't time to clean this mess."

"I'll do it, Gloria."

"Do you know what to use?"

"Don't worry, I'll find something, Gloria."

"Well." Gloria turned from the door and came back
to him. She leaned very close, and now Mr. Twombly
could see how each naked pimple stood out clearly on her
face. "Try horsewater, Grandy," she said. She left quickly
then, and a moment later he could feel her on the stairs,
shaking them easily two at a time now because she was
on her way down, and late.

TWO

Outside the apartment house, Mr. Twombly turned down the hill. He let the sudden incline carry him along as though he were one of those little penguins with weighted feet from Kate's 5 and 10 cent store. A car passed him with a toylike quietness, turned at the corner uncannily. An airedale sniffed at him. "Down boy," Mr. Twombly said, and behind him a lady's wound-up voice called, "Lucybelle come here." Other housewives stood here and there on fadeproof lawns skillfully laid down wall-to-wall. Two model policemen were stationed at the corner, waiting for impossible trouble under the feckless sun. Mr. Twombly turned left before he got to them.

At the next corner he turned right again, and now he

was climbing up. Now real people were everywhere, real cars were noisier. Tiny babies, penned for play, howled hungrily while thrips and earwigs ate the lawns. Under the honest sun, bumblebees went mad and sidewalks swelled. No cops were here. Here most housewives could remain inside, relying on skinny signs to mark their distinctions for passers-by. Mr. Twombly kept on to the second Fitch, avoiding thus a mirthful error he sometimes made. But confronting now the blank front door he suffered the usual doubts. He gave the doorbell a tentative press, almost as though he could take it back.

He was right this time. The door swung in on little red Mrs. Fitch, the proper one, and she laughed at him. "Mr. Twombly, you did it!" she cried, and turning toward the interior cried: "Dad, guess what, Mr. Twombly has found us again!"

Mr. Twombly smiled modestly, acknowledging growls of applause from Behemoth Brown.

"Come in, come in," said Mrs. Fitch, and Mr. Twombly followed her little red figure through the hall to the darkened livingroom. "Behemoth, see . . ."

A hand was up: in this hybrid light it might have been a clump of bananas sprouting on top of a telephone pole. When it came down, it fell. On the screen a blonde was being strangled by a delivery boy, and Mrs. Fitch paused to watch it too. But Mr. Twombly as usual watched in admiration how Behemoth Brown sat his easychair, the long legs stretched out to take remote possession of the hearth, the great fists knuckled into the grassy rug on either side as though planted there, the shaggy, forward head not so much statuesque as simply rooted to the body through the massive neck. It was a proud, grand profession of immobility, the way Behemoth sat, and it seemed to lend the quality of permanence to the pasteboard living-room. As though nothing could threaten a room in which the Behemoth sat, for all the world was sterilized and served up to him under glass.

Now bloodless murder had been done, and Mrs. Fitch could laugh again. "Mr. Twombly, you're just in time to sell Christmas cards!"

"Christmas cards?" Mr. Twombly also laughed, but then looking at Behemoth Brown he stopped. His friend was looking for him. Pivoted sidewise in his easychair, one arm grounded over the back of it, he peered cordially into the gloom. Mr. Twombly knew that Behemoth was still seeing pictures everywhere. Now he seemed to have found the electric clock on the mantelpiece, and Mr. Twombly took a stance in front of it: Behemoth found the barometer. It was like trying to have one's portrait taken by a photographer with St. Vitus dance. Everything about Behemoth Brown was on massive scale except his eyes and nose, these were undersize. Worse, Behemoth called attention to his deficiencies by the use he made of them. He used them all at once, indiscriminately, so that whenever he looked at anything it was with a sniffing look. Thus he had a mannerism which one might expect to find in a lion raised by a mouse. Nor did his heavy black glasses do any good; they were simply a final absurdity. "Behemoth . . . Ed?"

Even as Mr. Twombly spoke, the hand went up again and Mrs. Fitch hissed at him. "He has to do in another blonde."

"I thought he already did that one?"

Mrs. Fitch violently shook her head.

"He didn't . . .?"

"*Twins.*"

Mr. Twombly sat down this time. Watching Behemoth bend hungrily to a new repast, Mr. Twombly shook his head. It always saddened him to see his friend use his eyes this way, or frightened him to think that if ever Behemoth lost his eyes there would be almost nothing left. Even now, it seemed to him, something vital in the big man was running out through them. He looked away, feeling superstitiously that if he were not watching it might escape less fast. Reaching aside for the movable dictionary stand, he rolled it to him and turned the tiny spotlight on. Behemoth ummed.

"Mr. Twombly's looking at your scrapbook, Dad."

"Um."

The title on the white leatherette cover was in flaking gold: TH FIS IC C REER OF ED (BE EMOTH) B OWN, and in smaller letters underneath: *The   oble Art o   Self- efence.* Figures in the lower left corner read 902-1916, and in the lower right W36,D5, 29. The book thudded loudly as Mr. Twombly opened it in half. The first half was fat with clippings from the daily papers and the *Police Gazette* in which Behemoth was variously described as an awesome giant, a freak, a two-legged hippopotamus, and during the reign of Jack Johnson a crowd-pleasing new white hope. Many of the stories here were written in foreign languages which Behemoth promised to learn someday. Mr. Twombly customarily opened Behemoth's scrapbook in the middle, for it was here the pictures began. Photographers had seldom troubled to take Behemoth's picture until the news reporters were already referring to him as a former contender for the heavyweight championship, a fighter who once beat so-and-so, a Goliath who was slipping fast. Thus most of the pictures showed Behemoth lying down. (Behemoth Brown Can't See Much, Down.) To Mr. Twombly it seemed an unkind representation of a man who had won more than half his fights, and it was not helped much by that other picture of Behemoth which the newspapers invariably ran on the eve of one of Behemoth's bouts. This picture showed Behemoth standing upright in defensive position, chin in and arms raised, his small near-sighted eyes peering apprehensively out over a glove from beneath lowered brow, seeming not sure what would come next but ready anyhow. For Mr. Twombly's part, whenever he saw that picture he knew pretty well what was coming next, and before he turned the page he would make a mental bet with himself about what the next page would hold. He was not always right. Every now and then he would come upon a picture of Behemoth standing fat-legged over a little victim and looking down at him with a kind of pleased surprise. Or occasionally he would be standing far off to one side scarcely watching the referee count a man out, as though he had nothing to do with it. On the other hand, it sometimes happened that Behemoth would be floored five or six times in a single fight, and it was then the photographers gave him his most complete coverage, with the knockdowns pictured in sequence above captions recording the counts and a brief description of the various blows that lowered him. Such a fight could use up as much as six or seven pages of Behemoth's book, which seemed to Mr. Twombly an uncalled-for waste.

But it was the very last picture in the scrapbook that always fascinated Mr. Twombly most. A large picture, so large that it took up the entire page and required the viewer to lean far back in order to coordinate and make some sense of the dots, it was captioned THE HIPPO TAKES HIS LAST PUNCH. The view was from the top of Behemoth's silk boxing trunks, and up. All that one saw of his opponent was one arm and glove, with the glove buried to the laces in the loose folds of Behemoth's waist. The photographer had caught marvelously the expression on Behemoth's face, an expression not so much of pain as of anxiety, and a fine sensitivity must have prevented his reloading his camera to take that final picture of Behemoth mortified. Mr. Twombly liked to think that Behemoth had once been a kind of hero to this photographer, and he could not entirely comprehend Behemoth's peevish manner whenever he caught Mr. Twombly turned to this last page, or Behemoth's growled complaint that "You'd think those guys could at least wait till a man was down."

Lights went on, and Mr. Twombly flipped quickly back to happier days, perusing them.

"Well, he didn't get away with it," said Mrs. Fitch.

"He should have used gloves," said Behemoth.

Mr. Twombly heard Mrs. Fitch's high laugh: he had almost knocked the book off its portable stand before he realized they were discussing the delivery boy. Now he turned pages in a diligent way, as though checking Behemoth's record against memory. He missed a page, flipped back again.

Another happy laugh. "Well, are you boys ready to go?"

"Dick's still reading my scrapbook, hon."

Mr. Twombly studied a report on the Comiskey fight. "Where are we going, Ed?" he casually asked.

There was a pause, and Mr. Twombly knew that

Behemoth too would be looking at other things. Then, "Like to help me sell some Christmas cards?"

Mr. Twombly turned a page. "Why, I guess so, Ed."

"You ever sell before?"

Mr. Twombly could feel Behemoth looking at him judiciously now, and he raised his eyes to return the look. "Well, Ed, I was in the money order window for seven years, if that means anything."

Behemoth turned to face Mr. Twombly more squarely, and he crossed his legs. "How did you do?"

Shrugging lightly, "I never had any complaints," Mr. Twombly said.

Behemoth nodded. "Like to try it again?" he asked.

"I guess so, Ed."

"Door to door, you understand?"

"Oh, yes."

"Forty percent of the purse, how does that sound to you?"

"Fine, Ed."

"I guess we're in business, Dick," said Behemoth.

Now Mrs. Fitch was on her feet, collecting things, pencil, streetmap, briefcase, Behemoth's hat. She handed these to Behemoth one at a time, and he made a little ceremony of finding the proper place for each, pencil in inside pocket of brown suitcoat, map outside, hat square on knee. The briefcase he took in his big hands to open and close it in various ways, testing its zipper under stress. He tested the leather's pliability, and blinking flapped it for Mr. Twombly to see. "Pigskin, Dick." He dropped the briefcase to his lap, shifted his gray felt hat to the other knee, glanced blinking shamefaced at Mrs. Fitch. Mrs. Fitch switched the TV off.

"Well?"

"I guess we're on our way," said Behemoth.

Mr. Twombly watched his friend. It always fascinated him to watch Behemoth raise himself. He did it by stages, carefully. First he dropped his hands to the floor and swung torso up and forward to edge of chair. He balanced so, readied his feet before putting weight on them. He bounced at the knees a little bit, limbering stiffened muscles up. Now his eyes were fixed on some stationary point directly in front of him, and grunting quietly he pitched toward that point, at the last moment fell back again. He always made it the second time. Mr. Twombly knew that if anyone had been counting, the count would have reached exactly ten by the time Behemoth gained his feet. "There we go," Behemoth said, ready for anything. He looked back at his chair, but his daughter was already plumping his pillows up. "Ready, Dick?"

"One minute, Ed."

Mr. Twombly had come upon Behemoth's publicity pose again and he turned the page to check his bet, then smiling rolled the dictionary stand away and flicked the light. "Just checking, Ed."

"Sure, Dick."

Mr. Twombly, coming from the flabby photographs, was impressed anew by the later Behemoth's more hardened look. His strong jawbone jutted more sharply than before, threatening to break through drier skin. His chest had sunk a trifle, and beneath his brown gabardine business suit his slightly forward shoulders were as wide and taut as those of his leather easychair. It was as though an ironic fate had waited until now to make an athlete out of a crowd-pleasing hippopotamus. Mr. Twombly went over to his friend, and they stood looking up and down at one another a bit uncomfortably, as they always did on first standing face to waist. Quickly adjusted now, they turned together toward the hall. Behind them Mrs. Fitch laughed happily. "You boys have fun," she said.

Behemoth turned to look with final anguish at the livingroom. "Hon, you're sure I've seen that picture on Channel 9."

"Twice."

"Well, then . . ."

Mrs. Fitch gave them a gentle shove. "Don't worry about anything. Think how you'll save your eyes."

"I'll be home for the five o'clock sportscast, hon."

"Fresh air will be good for both of you. Don't worry about the time."

Behemoth adjusted his hat, Mr. Twombly too. Side by side in the doorway they looked back at Mrs. Fitch, and she laughed at them. "Remember, no selling on Cherokee. Go somewhere else."

"All right, hon."

Together they stepped out the door, into the sun. They started down the path with Mrs. Fitch looking after them. Mr. Twombly had to run a little bit.

"Better go four or five blocks," called Mrs. Fitch.

They turned to wave at her, but they did not return her smile. Their faces were serious. They continued on down the hill, neither speaking nor looking at one another until they had turned left on Pinto off of Cherokee. Now Mr. Twombly glanced up and sidewise at his friend, caught Behemoth's glance at him.

"Dick, I want you to know this wasn't my idea," Behemoth said.

"I understand."

"What it really is, Dick, is just another way to get me out of the house."

"Oh now, Ed," Mr. Twombly said. "You know it's good for you. Think of your eyes."

"Ha." Behemoth tapped the briefcase nervously against his knee; in Behemoth's hand it looked like a pocketbook. "You know what that is, don't you, Dick? I'm supposed to buy new glasses with the money I make today."

"Oh, I see."

"Spencer. Spencer found the advertisement and cut it out, left it on my chair for me. Bought my briefcase too. But not a word from him—you'd think it was my idea from all the cracks he makes."

"Cracks, Ed?"

"Spencer doesn't think I'm the salesman type. He says down at the agency they use my type for showroom display. He says he'd put me behind the wheel in one of those cars on the revolving platform and have me watch one of his television sets across the room. That way he'd be advertising two features at once, the television's picture power and the car's four-way visibility."

Mr. Twombly chuckled, and Behemoth growled at him.

"Sorry, Ed. But he does have a flair, you know."

"Spencer thinks I'm punchy, Dick."

"Nonsense, Ed. We're all a little punchy by our age, Ed. We've been hit too often on the heart."

They were turning off Pinto now, onto Martinet, and here one cop was visible. Mr. Twombly was for crossing inconspicuously over to the park, but Behemoth disagreed with him heartily. Cops always attracted Behemoth; he seemed to assume they were all old fans of his and would not have it said he was too proud for them. "Hello, officer!"

This policeman looked at them warily, but then looking up at Behemoth he did have a kind of admiration, carefully measured, in his eyes. "Hello, men."

For a moment silence fell while Behemoth and the policeman exchanged questions and compliments with their eyes. Behemoth flapped his briefcase at his side. "Mr. Twombly here and I are out selling a few Christmas cards."

The policeman nodded at Mr. Twombly levelly; the impression was that he did have surprise, but in rigorously limited supply. "Well, Christmas cards," he said.

"Perhaps you'll be good enough to tell us, officer," Behemoth said. "Do we need a license or permit or anything?"

The policeman shook his head. He shook it more easily than he nodded it. "Not if you're just peddling to the doors," he said.

"We're working independently, you understand. We have no credentials of any kind."

"No need for that."

"I see, officer," Behemoth said. "We just thought we better check the law on this."

The policeman shook his head again. "There's no law," he said, "unless you get disorderly."

Behemoth nodded. "I know how it is, officer. I used to be in law enforcement myself."

The policeman eyed him steadily. "You belonged to the force?"

"No, not the force," Behemoth said, lightly touching his glasses. "By the time I hung up the gloves my eyes

were a little too weak for the force. I was in nighttime
protection, up in Buffalo."

"Ah, in Buffalo."

"Yes, one of the big warehouses there. Oh, we had our
share of trouble there."

"I bet you did all right," the officer said absently. He
was watching a fox terrier water some pansies on a nearby
lawn.

"More than our share, I'd say."

"I bet you did." The terrier had moved along now, but
the pansies remained under vigilance. "I bet you did."

Behemoth turned to Mr. Twombly now. "We don't
want to lose much time, Twombly," he said, and: "Thanks
for the information, officer."

"O.K., men." The policeman stepped smartly around
them to resume his beat. He was bearing in the direction
the terrier went.

"That was a nice officer," Behemoth said when he was
past.

"Yes. It was," said Mr. Twombly. It seemed to him
that in a world of officers and pugilists and television
stars he was used by Behemoth in much the same way
the human problems page was used by him, as a standard
against which one could measure one's own fortune and
usually come out ahead, so he said nothing else just now.

Behemoth flapped his briefcase thoughtfully. "Probably
I should have told him about that night at the warehouse in Buffalo. You know the one."

"Yes, Ed."

Behemoth chuckled. "When they shook that thug down
after the go they found he had two guns on him, a sawed-
off shotgun and a .38."

"He must have been a mean son of a gun," Mr. Twombly said.

"He was a sucker for a right cross though," said Behemoth, chuckling again. That fight at the warehouse in Buffalo, Behemoth's last, seemed to be the one he enjoyed remembering most. "I remember one of the officers that answered my call, said he couldn't understand why I wasn't on the force. He said, Who needs eyes with a right like that?"

"That must have been some go, Ed."

"That was a go, all right."

"Ed, there's something I've been wanting to know about."

"Shoot, Dick," said Behemoth.

"You won thirtysix goes, didn't you?"

"Thirtysix."

"Ed, why did the photographers take so many pictures of you on the floor?"

"On the canvas," Behemoth gently corrected him. "That's an easy one. The boys didn't have very good cameras then, they liked to wait until a man was motionless."

They were walking through the park now and mothers were everywhere. Mr. Twombly ducked ahead of Behemoth to greet a mother seated on a bench with her little girl, and the mother smiled back at him. "Ed, let's have a seat somewhere while we discuss our plans and our sales approach."

"Fine, Dick. I think I've got my instruction sheet somewhere here."

The bench they chose was not Mr. Twombly's customary bench but was centrally located so that most of the other

benches were turned toward it. Mr. Twombly let Behemoth sit down first, then slid onto the lowered seat.
Behemoth unzipped his briefcase easily, rummaged inside
a while. "There we go."

Mr. Twombly nodded at a mother on a nearby bench.
"Let's hear it, Ed."

Behemoth held the paper close to his eyes and nose.
"Dear Enterprising American," he read. "I call you that
because in answering our ad you have shown yourself to
be one who doesn't let Opportunity slip through the
fingertips. You are a first rate salesman, I know."

"Go on, Ed."

"The salesman has but one object," Behemoth read
hopefully. "To make a sale." He stopped again.

"Go on, Ed."

"There are three steps to entering a house." Behemoth
went back and read that again. "There are three steps
to entering a house: (1) Introduction (2) Statement of
Business (3) Entrance . . ." Behemoth was reading ahead
to himself. Thus when he read a paragraph aloud to Mr.
Twombly it came out rapidly, in fits. "(1) Introduction—
introduce yourself. Usually you can get the householder's
name from a mailbox or a sign somewhere, then politely
introduce yourself: 'Mr. or Mrs. Blank? I'm pleased to
have found you in, Mr. or Mrs. Blank. I'm Mr. or Mrs.
Blank.' If you're a man, take off your hat . . . (2) Statement of Business—this is your sales talk or spiel. A typical
sales talk might go like this: 'Mr. or Mrs. Blank, the
United States Postal Service has asked us to mail our
Christmas cards and packages early this year. If we obey
their directive little children will have their Christmas
Cheer on Christmas Day rather than a day or even a

month after. Postal employees will be able to celebrate Christmas Day with their families instead of *on the road.* You and I will enjoy Christmas more with the warm feeling that all our friends and relatives have already received our lovely cards. Do you realize that it's only blank weeks or months until Christmas (this should be figured ahead of time). I think you will thank me for showing you my samples and reminding you of this, Mr. or Mrs. Blank.' There's your sales talk."

Behemoth paused to adjust his glasses. Whenever he talked at any length his glasses were inclined to slip from his nose, for they had very little purchase there. Often he would keep on talking, finish a sentence before he pushed them back on his nose, so that at a glance he seemed to be gnawing on his glasses and making small mumbling noises of displeasure at their taste. "(3) Entrance—probably you will have accomplished (3) during the course of (1) or (2). You will have been waiting for your first opportunity to enter—and jumped at it. However, if you should still find yourself outside, this is the time for a well-chosen compliment. Glancing through the door, remark on something you see in there. 'What lovely wallpaper you have in your diningroom, Mr. or Mrs. Blank,' or 'Is that delightful sideboard an antique?' Anything will do. Even if you're already inside you can make use of this. (Politeness is always good.) . . . Now that you're comfortably inside seated facing your customer on the couch or chair," Behemoth went on in his omnivorous way, "show your samples. Your samples will do the rest. Remember to have your carbon paper turned right side up and remember to give the blue duplicate order sheet to the customer before you go. This is his or her only reminder of the sale. Ask for cash. Submit your orders to us by check or money orders only. No stamps, please. And remember the one object of the salesman is to make a sale. Take it from there—Good Luck!"

Behemoth folded the instruction sheet and returned it to his briefcase. This time the zipper caught, so he pulled it back and closed it savagely. Mr. Twombly glanced at his friend's blinking face, and it seemed to him that Behemoth was feeling ambition and disgust by such rapid turns that they became almost inseparable.

"Ed, have you got your carbon paper right side up? Be glad to check it for you."

With only a slight air of martyrdom Behemoth opened his briefcase and drew out his order book. He handed it to Mr. Twombly without a glance.

"Right as rain," Mr. Twombly said, examining it, "and right on top of your blue duplicate."

"Um." Behemoth returned the book to his briefcase, which closed all right. Things were looking a little better now. "Thanks, Dick."

Mr. Twombly had his green notebook out, studying it. "It's fifteen weeks before Christmas, Ed."

"Thanks, Dick."

Silence now, Behemoth was brooding still.

"Well, I suppose we ought to get started, Ed."

Behemoth drummed his briefcase with his fingertips. "Oh-oh, we haven't checked that streetmap yet." He took the map from his side pocket and together they unfolded it in front of them, Mr. Twombly holding the bottom edge, Behemoth the top. It took them a short time to find their park.

"Here's Cherokee, Ed," said Mr. Twombly, "and Martinet. Here's Quincy. Forgeus. Poe. We could try E. Beautyview."

"Count the blocks," Behemoth said. "How far is it from Cherokee?"

"Five blocks, Ed, and that includes the park."

"All right," Behemoth said decisively. "E. Beautyview's our territory."

Behemoth folded up the map. The streets were still showing when he got through, and he unfolded it and folded it again. This time the historic points of interest showed, but he crammed it in his pocket anyway. Mr. Twombly slid off the bench, stood waiting while his friend prepared to rise. With Behemoth umming hard, Mr. Twombly thought for just an instant he might not make it the second time, but, "There we go," said Behemoth upon his feet.

They left through the far side of the park, Mr. Twombly greeting a few ladies on the way, and walked without hurry the two blocks to Beautyview. There they stopped, looking left and right at their chosen territory. Except for them, Beautyview was a deserted street as far as they could see. Usually when they were out walking people seemed to be crowding them. Behemoth flapped his briefcase nervously. "How does it look to you, Dick?"

"Pretty quiet, Ed."

"Um." Behemoth raised his hand as though to view the sun, then flipped his wrist and read his watch instead. "We may have chosen a bad time, Dick. There's that movie on Channel 9."

"Um," Mr. Twombly said.

Together they looked up at the corner sign, Pinto-

E. Beautyview. Behemoth bent to read the hours on
the mail collection box, and blinking stood erect
again. "There's a mailman due by in a few minutes,
Dick."

"Hmm."

"Maybe he could give us some tips. Mailmen ought to
know where the good territories are, especially for
Christmas cards."

"He might not want to give out the information, Ed.
Mailmen don't like Christmas cards, you know."

"I guess that's true," Behemoth said. "In England a
mailman doesn't mind Christmas so much—they reward
him with Boxer's Day."

They looked up and down the street again, but still
there was no one to be seen on E. Beautyview.

"I guess we ought to get started, Ed."

"I guess."

Another dog was wetting the lawn before the corner
house, so they went on to the second one. Following
Behemoth up the walk Mr. Twombly felt pity for his
friend: anyone watching their approach might think
Behemoth was invading privacy alone. Yet Mr. Twombly
did not wish to trample pansies or the lawn. "The name
is Mr. or Mrs. Bell, an easy one," he said encouragingly
to Behemoth's back. "You ring, Ed."

Behemoth rang. His hand was shaking terribly. They
heard quick footsteps tap the floor inside, and Behemoth
ummed in agony. The door opened at first narrowly to a
girl's pretty face, but then it opened all the way. She had
a yellow kimono on, and her yellow hair was in curling
rags. Mr. Twombly took off his hat, Behemoth did the
same. "Yes?" and the girl smiled at them. "Yes?"

"Um, Mrs. Bell. I'm pleased to find you in, Mrs. Bell. I'm Mr. . . ."

Smiling the girl shook her head at Behemoth. "I'm sorry," she said to both of them, sounding truly so. "Mother won't be home until dinner time. She works, you see."

Mr. Twombly and Behemoth looked at one another, Behemoth frantically. Turning graciously to the girl, Mr. Twombly returned her smile. "Thank you anyway, Miss Bell."

"Yes, thank you very much," Behemoth said.

"I'm sorry," she said again.

"Don't mention it, Miss Bell."

"No, please don't mention it, Miss Bell."

Now they turned about to walk in single file back down the walk. Halfway to the street Behemoth turned to wave his hat at the watching girl. "Don't mention it, Miss Bell," he begged, and waving gaily back she closed the door.

Out on the sidewalk, they paused to put their hats back on. There was an elusive smile, at once proud and shamefaced, hovering around Behemoth's blinking eyes. He flapped his briefcase against his knee and looked at Mr. Twombly expectantly. "Well, Dick?"

"You were fine," Mr. Twombly said, lightly touching Behemoth's back. "You just ran into the wrong party that time, Ed."

"That's it, Dick. I think she would have bought Christmas cards if she had been Mrs. Bell."

"I think so too."

"It was good practice though." Behemoth lifted his head to sniff the sun, shook his arms and shoulders beneath his coat. He was enjoying outdoor exercise. "Dick, I think we're getting the hang of it."

"Mr. or Mrs. Basky next," Mr. Twombly pointed out to him.

"Check," Behemoth said. "Used to fight a fellow by that name."

"How'd you do?"

"Split," Behemoth said. "Two and two."

"Knockouts?"

"Some of them."

They had reached the door, that easily, and with a steady finger Behemoth pushed the bell. Hearing footsteps sound inside, they smiled obliquely with their eyes.

"Yeah?" The man in the doorway did not appear to be closely related to any heavyweights; he looked up at Behemoth with ill-humored disbelief. Then he looked at Mr. Twombly and shook his head at him, as one might at the owner of an exceptional Saint Bernard. "Yeah?" again.

"I'm glad to find you in, Mr. Basky. I'm Mr. Brown."

"Yeah."

Behemoth ummed underbreath. "The U.S. Post Office has asked us to mail our Christmas cards early this year," he began, and hurried on: "That way little children can get their things on Christmas Day. They won't have to wait." Behemoth paused now, but Mr. Basky only nodded. He seemed surprised that Behemoth could talk so well, and this made Behemoth gain confidence. "That way mailmen will be able to spend Christmas Day at home. They won't have to be *on the road* carrying mail."

"That's right."

It was Behemoth's turn to be surprised at Mr. Basky. "You aren't a mailman, by any chance?"

Mr. Basky shook his head. "I just feel sorry for the poor bastards, that's all."

"I guess mailmen don't like Christmas cards very much," Behemoth said.

"Hell no, they don't."

Behemoth had no comment. He was looking over Mr. Basky's head, into Mr. Basky's livingroom, and blinking he craned his head forward through the door. "That's a nice set you've got there," he said. "Watching Channel 2?"

"I'm damned if I know," said Mr. Basky, moving forward in the door until his head almost touched Behemoth's chin. "Something the kids are looking at."

Drawing back, Behemoth flapped his briefcase desperately. Mr. Twombly cleared his throat. "We're selling Christmas cards, Mr. Basky," he said strongly. "Mr. Brown has his samples in his briefcase there . . ." But Mr. Basky was already shaking no.

"It's fifteen weeks till Christmas," Behemoth said.

"That's right, pop. Lots of time, isn't there?"

"Um."

Mr. Twombly and Behemoth glanced at one another; their hats were on. "Well, thank you anyway, Mr. Basky," Mr. Twombly said, removing his.

"Yeah, thanks," said Behemoth.

"O.K., pops."

They started off the stoop.

"Hey, pop, if you'd like to come back around Christmas time," Mr. Basky called, "I might be able to use you for Santa Claus. Maybe I could use a reindeer too."

Not answering that, they settled their hats and continued

toward the street. Mr. Twombly walked squarely beside his friend, upon the lawn. Behemoth was switching his briefcase at imaginary flies, apparently missing them. "Ed, don't let him bother you."

From the sidewalk Behemoth switched a fly in the direction of Mr. Basky's house. "Must be a different Basky family," he muttered to himself or anyone. "The Buffalo Baker was a gentleman."

"Ah, the Buffalo Baker," Mr. Twombly said. "Now I remember him. He was a big one, wasn't he?"

"He wasn't any flyweight," Behemoth said, and then apologetically touched his briefcase to Mr. Twombly's back. "Sorry, Dick."

They had stopped to squint at a two-story apartment house, and Behemoth made his doleful noise again. The slanting sun glared off whitewashed brick and, in every second window, displayed the smug conformity of kitchen appliances. With four sets of windows facing the front alone, up and down, impossible to imagine what variety might be found in the livingrooms. Clearly a flexible strategy was needed here. "Ed, why don't we take turns at this."

Behemoth, jogging his briefcase against Mr. Twombly's chest, was cheered. "Your samples, Dick."

"No, you keep the briefcase." Mr. Twombly held his hands in front of him. "I'll do the talking, then you come through with the samples, Ed."

"Check, Dick. That's what we call a one-two punch." Behemoth's left fist gave Mr. Twombly a companionable tap on the chin, repeated with the other one.

Mr. Twombly smiled. "Don't knock out your mouthpiece, Ed," but Behemoth was too pleased to catch that one.

At least it was comforting to push unchallenged through the heavy door, enter the two-bulb hall. Moving past thinner doors Mr. Twombly peered at cryptic signs, Campbell Powell Sova Weir, while Behemoth whispered a brief analysis of each occupant's channel choice. Now returning past other messages, Padilla Boxer Loftfield Hertz, Mr. Twombly nodded toward the stairs and led the way. Here a small back window partially relieved the dirty bulbs, and Mr. Twombly did not have to strain so hard at the calling cards of Courtney Roether Weiden Davison, yet he did not slow down until he reached Merrywell. Hearing noise inside, he glanced at Behemoth enquiringly.

"Channel 6," Behemoth said. "I think that's stock reports."

Mr. Twombly rang the bell, but waiting heard no answering sound, only the serious voice on Channel 6. Whoever was listening was interested.

"Must be the weather," Behemoth judged.

Mr. Twombly touched the bell again, and this time the door opened before he could draw his finger back. As it opened only an inch or two, he found himself peeking in at a fragile lady of his own height who was peeking out through spectacles. Allaying fears, he removed his hat: the little lady nodded acknowledgment. Then her eyes went up above his head and she nodded once again, a startled nod: Behemoth pressing from behind had taken his hat off too.

"Mrs. Merrywell?" Mr. Twombly asked, and through the crack he glimpsed a nodded yes. "I'm pleased to meet you, Mrs. Merrywell. I'm Mr. Twombly, this is Mr. Brown." Mr. Twombly nodded at Behemoth. Now,

encouraged by a nod from Mrs. Merrywell, he improvised:
"Mr. Brown here needs new spectacles. You can see that
his eyes are weak." Tilting his head to bring Behemoth
into better view, "Notice how he blinks? This is because
his present spectacles are not strong enough," he said, the
little lady nodding constantly. "We thought if we could
get a little pocket money we would buy him a stronger
pair. Then he'll be able to watch the shows without
endangering his sight. Oh no, there are few more devoted
television fans anywhere than Mr. Brown." Mr. Twombly
paused to smile engagingly.

"That sounds like a nice set you've got there," Behemoth said. "A Commodore?"

Mrs. Merrywell confirming Behemoth's guess, Mr.
Twombly shook his head admiringly. "Didn't I tell you?"
he asked Mrs. Merrywell, and when Mrs. Merrywell agreed
with him: "What we're doing is selling Christmas cards.
Mr. Brown has his samples in his briefcase there. Care to
see a few?"

Yes. . . . Yes.

"May we come in and show them to you, Mrs. Merrywell?"

Mrs. Merrywell nodding agreeably, Mr. Twombly
smiled at Behemoth, pushed the knob. The door gave
partly, but then held fast. Mr. Twombly looked inside to
see what the trouble was. He thought perhaps the rug
was caught beneath the door, but it was not. Mrs.
Merrywell's foot was there. Higher up, he saw the
straining tendons of her withered arms. He looked
questioningly at her twisted face, an inch or two away, and
she looked back at his. Her eyes were immense behind
her spectacles, her head was nodding terribly. Mr.

Twombly felt himself pressed backward by the door as Mrs. Merrywell summoned surprising strength, and to save himself from being squeezed against the jamb he pushed equally hard. For a moment it was his strength against Mrs. Merrywell's, nicely counterpoised, and they stared at one another almost admiringly. But seeing Mrs. Merrywell's white hair fluttered by his heavy breaths, he graciously directed his breathing to one side. It was when Mr. Twombly's face was averted that Mrs. Merrywell found her voice. She shrieked.

"Don't," Mr. Twombly said, and Mrs. Merrywell shrieked again. Mr. Twombly let go the door and it slammed his head back against the jamb. Clamped there with his face pointing sidewise toward Mrs. Merrywell's Commodore, he heard activity in the hall which he could not see. A finger, Behemoth's size, prodded his back already sore from rubbing sharp wood so long. A voice, not Behemoth's, wanted to know what was going on in there. Mr. Twombly had nothing at all to say. He was watching the weather on Channel 6: tomorrow there would be some high thin cloudiness.

"Mr. Ponce, Mrs. Merrywell. You O.K. in there?"

Now Mrs. Merrywell released the door, and it was her turn to be rapped this time. Her spectacles tumbled to the floor. Mr. Twombly stooped to pick them up, and Mrs. Merrywell shrieked at him. A hand flung Mr. Twombly backward into the hall, against Behemoth flapping his briefcase there. Mr. Ponce made a threatening gesture with his arm, then stooped to retrieve Mrs. Merrywell's spectacles. He wiped them off carefully on his pants, and he helped replace them on her nose. Although of average height, Mr. Ponce took up as much lateral space as

Behemoth did, and even a simple thing like helping Mrs. Merrywell put her glasses on bulged muscles beneath his fuzzy polo shirt. Angrily, "What's going on in here, Mrs. Merrywell?"

Mrs. Merrywell's eyes were still too large, and her entire body was nodding ceaselessly. Mr. Ponce bent to hear her speak, but Mr. Twombly knew that they would have to wait for her. Beneath Mrs. Merrywell's mobile chin he could watch the nervous throat gulp down words as rapidly as the lips prepared for them. He looked away when she pointed her bones at him.

"Yes?" Mr. Ponce's voice served a two-fold function now, threat and encouragement. "What is it, Mrs. Merrywell?"

"These men tried to break in on me!"

"These men?" Over his shoulder Mr. Ponce glared at them rather doubtfully; he seemed to want them to deny Mrs. Merrywell's epithet but confirm her charge. "Well?"

"She said we could come in."

"Liar!" Mrs. Merrywell cried, pointing at Mr. Twombly. Her voice was so thin it pierced the eardrum dangerously. "I never, never did! They said they wanted money and spectacles. I think the big one wanted my Commodore."

Mr. Twombly shook his head, while Behemoth flapped his briefcase Mr. Ponce's way. "Christmas cards," Behemoth mumbled dismally. "We're selling them."

"Christmas cards?" Mr. Ponce might have laughed if Mrs. Merrywell had not been quavering so hard at him. "In September, dad?"

Behemoth tugged at his case, brought a sample out. "The United States Post Office has asked us to mail our

Christmas cards early this year," he said. "That way little children will get their things on time. Mailmen will be able to celebrate Christmas . . ."

"Oh, for mercy's sake, dad," Mr. Ponce said, taking the sample from Behemoth's hand. "Save the spiel for some other time." He held the sample up for Mrs. Merrywell to see, but frowning he took it back again. "Hello, buddy," he read aloud:

> Hello buddy, pal o' mine
> You know it would be dandy fine
> If you could be my Valentine.

"What's that?" Behemoth growled. He stepped forward to take the card from Mr. Ponce's hand. He held it up and blinked at it. Blinking he drew another sample from his briefcase now. He drew several others out and read them too. Then he turned his briefcase over and stood shaking it while red hearts and cupid bows and order slips cascaded at his feet. He held the briefcase upside down above his head to see if he had got everything: a savage slap dislodged a stubborn bit of paper lace. Without attempting to zip the empty briefcase closed, Behemoth flapped it hard for Mr. Ponce and Mrs. Merrywell to see. He showed them the writing on the back of it. "Pigskin," he said, and headed for the stairs. Halfway down he thought to look back for Mr. Twombly, but Mr. Twombly was beside his friend.

Breaking together through the heavy door, they turned left in front of the apartment house, ducked with eyes streetside past Mr. Basky and young Miss Bell, past the corner house. Mr. Twombly, trotting to Behemoth's savage pace, could no longer draw air through the nose alone. He nudged Behemoth's arm, and Behemoth slowed to a heartless plod, scuffing cracks and pebbles everywhere. Mr. Twombly dared not look up at Behemoth's eyes, at the shamefaced trinity, just now. "Shit, Dick," Behemoth said.

"Ah, Ed . . ."

"No, I mean it, Dick. Think what Spencer will have to say."

Now Mr. Twombly did look up at Behemoth's face, saw that Behemoth's eyes were dripping tears upon his cheeks. "The heck with Spencer, Ed. It's all his fault, he cut the ad. You thought you were selling Christmas cards."

"Spencer would have sold Valentines."

"Ed, in September, dad?"

"Spencer would," Behemoth said. "He gives them what he calls his two-way coverage. They've got a nice car, so he sells them a television set instead. Six months afterward he takes that television set as low down payment on a late model car. Now they're in the market for another television, a bigger one."

"Do they buy it, Ed?"

"Sure they do. They have no money left, but they've become such steady customers by now that Spencer can arrange easy terms for them."

Mr. Twombly shook his head. "That Spencer, you have to admire him, Ed."

"I have to live with Spencer, Dick."

"Ed." They were passing a wooded lot offered for sale by a reluctant realty. An aging sign attested that the price was high, another underneath warned the public off. Mr. Twombly led Behemoth along a well-trod path that went carefully around the sign, among stunted trees. He stopped in the thick of them, stopped Behemoth too. After assuring himself that he was everywhere invisible to passers-by, he sat on a rock and unlaced his shoe. Smiling at Behemoth's bafflement, he riffled cheques and brought out a ten, unerringly, without exposing the roll itself; he had much practice in privacy, but this was his first trial before an audience. "Presto, Ed."

Behemoth removed his glasses and wiped his eyes with a handkerchief. "Travelers cheque? Where did you get it, Dick?"

"At my bank in Baltimore," Mr. Twombly said as he laced his shoe. "There was no charge to us. I figured that was better than interest on a bond, and these are more readily negotiable."

"What are you going to do with it?"

"Banks are closed. We'll cash it at Saveway, Ed."

"What for?"

"For Christmas cards."

"Now Dick . . ."

"No. No arguments."

"But Dick . . ."

"Quiet there, Ed. Let's see your map." Spreading Behemoth's streetmap on the ground, Mr. Twombly traced a route to Saveway that avoided the park and Cherokee and Martinet. While Behemoth folded up the map, Mr. Twombly made a scouting trip. "All clear, Ed," he called quietly, waving Behemoth forward too. Emerging from the trees, they walked rapidly down Pinto, Poe, then right on Maplewood, not encountering anyone until Hagerty. And this lady had two small children in her arms, two more at her feet, and she did not

look at anything. From there on in to Saveway their way
was clear of pedestrians. The Saveway door sweeping
obsequiously aside for them, Mr. Twombly headed for the
glass cage where they kept the manager. He smiled at the
green eyeshade in there, and the manager looked out
harriedly. "Good afternoon, sir," Mr. Twombly said,
standing on tiptoe to reach the hole.

The eyeshade nodded acknowledgment.

"Ed, have you got that cheque?"

Beneath their visor, eyebrows went up. "Personal?"

"Travelers," Mr. Twombly said, filling out the cheque,
slipping it through the window slot to waiting hands.

The manager read the face of the travelers cheque,
every word and number there. He turned it over, but
there was little to read on the other side. He read the face
again, then looked up quickly at Mr. Twombly. "You're
Richard S. Twombly?"

"Yes. I am."

"May I see your driver's license, please."

"I don't drive," Mr. Twombly said.

"You don't?" This man did not believe just anything;
he waited for Mr. Twombly to retract his lie. Then,
"Have you identification of any kind?"

Mr. Twombly felt his pockets uselessly. "Just my notebook. And this." He held up his fountain pen, embossed.
Leaning forward as far as his visor would allow, the
manager read Mr. Twombly's name, then read the brand
name too. "Is that all you have?"

"No no. I have my watch." Unclipping his watchfob
from his belt, Mr. Twombly held his watch at eyelevel
before the window. They waited for its slow rotation to
cease, the manager impatiently. When it became clear

that the watch would not turn its back to the manager,
Mr. Twombly steadied it with his other hand. He held it
so while the manager read Mr. Twombly's full name this
time, the Richard Stevenson. Still skeptical, the manager
waved the watch away.

"I don't suppose you have anyone here who could
identify you, Mr. Twombly."

"Well, I have Mr. Brown here," Mr. Twombly said,
and turning saw Behemoth nod at him cordially.

The visor raised for a look at Behemoth. "I'm afraid I
don't know you either."

Mr. Twombly turned to Behemoth. "Ed, look around
and see if there's anyone who could identify you for this
supervisor here."

Behemoth blinked at the Saveway store, at the people
and canned goods and everything. "I don't think so,
Dick," at last.

The supervisor was tiring now. Shaking his head at both
of them, "I don't know either of you, you understand.
You have no papers or pictures of any kind. If you just
had a driver's license, now . . ."

"We don't drive," Mr. Twombly said.

Beneath the visor a chartreuse smile: anyone who told
him the same lie twice was out of his mind. But then he
threw the travelers cheque, a useless thing, into his money
drawer. He slipped a bill from his ten dollar pile, and
snapping it showed how crisp it was. When he slid the bill
under the window his fingers still clung to it, so that Mr.
Twombly had to use strength to capture it. Without
glancing at the bill he passed it over his shoulder to
Behemoth. "Here we go, Ed. We'll change it at the P and
P," and turning from the supervisor's chartreuse glare

they walked empty-handed past the courteous door. Mr.
Twombly smiled. "They ought to get a door that only
opens for visors and grocery bags." Their direction now
was north, but out of sight they headed east again.

"Dick, this isn't the way to the P and P."

"That was for sound effect. The P and P is no place to
celebrate—too bright in there."

"What are we going to celebrate?"

"Salesmanship. We just sold Saveway a travelers
cheque. You name it, Ed."

"How about a cool one, Dick?"

"A cool what, Ed?"

"Beer."

"Where, Ed? You name it."

"Well, there's a place over on Oakridge," Behemoth
said, "about a block from here. You've probably noticed
their Pilco as you passed by."

"Ah now, Ed. I thought we'd talk."

"Sure, Dick." Behemoth patted Mr. Twombly's back.
"I'll sit with my back to it." They were turning onto
Oakridge now, and suddenly it seemed warmer here.
Front doors and windows were opened wide, and flies
bumped into one another on patchwork screens festooned
with dirty cotton balls. Here and there a gray hose lay
rotting on a weedy lawn, its nozzle tantalizing a dying
shrub. Depraved old oak trees, their naked bodies em-
braced by countless generations of devoted boys, had
drawn in their dusty shade until school let out: were they
offended that nobody molested them? Here housewives
preferred to hide away, anonymous. No nameplates were
displayed, while cardboard signs spoke shamefully of bad
dogs and sleeping rooms with kitchen privs. Perhaps no

one was at home: on the corner a larger sign, a neon one, raved tipsily of BOB'S BLUE BAR AND G ILL.

"Dick,if you listen carefully you can hear that Pilco now."

"Why carefully?" They were at that unpleasant middle distance where it made a wampa-wampa noise, neither speech nor melody, like a tom-tom beaten by a one-armed idiot. They found themselves hurrying toward the noise. As they drew closer the theme became more complex, a little insane, a joyous anthem to broken homes and depreciated real estate. But now at the door sound was shattered into syllables, hushed then amplified, portending catastrophe. "Bad news, Ed?"

"I've already seen it, Dick. Rebroadcast of last night's game."

Holding the door for Behemoth, Mr. Twombly patted the preposterous back. "Who won, Ed?"

"The Buffalos, 3 to 2."

Inside a bartender and two customers in undershirts turned to stare or perhaps glare at them; it was too dark to read faces here. Behemoth waved them back to their game, and he stood behind them watching too. The announcer's voice was swept aside by the roar of the grandstand crowd: it looked and sounded like a waterfall. "Fifth inning," Behemoth whispered to Mr. Twombly, stooping low. "Score's 2 and 2."

Undershirts turning to them once more, they peered self-consciously around the bar. Difficult to say whether there were other customers, and if so where, for the room was illuminated only in furtive spots, by the television, the pinball, the shuffleboard. Mr. Twombly took Behemoth's arm. "Ed, shall we try to find a booth?"

"Check."

Groping they came upon high wooden booths running back to back along the wall, like bisected pews set aside for the worship of private, two-faced gods. Behemoth continued to the last of these and sat down with his back to the gentlemen's door. Mr. Twombly did not sit down. "You promised, Ed."

Grunting Behemoth heaved to his feet, and exchanging pews sat down again. "I've seen it anyway," he said.

"Sure you have, Ed."

A roar went up. Behemoth cleared his throat, and now his profile stood out against the glowing screen as he blinked at the waterfall. "Sixth inning: 3 to 2."

In the darkness Mr. Twombly shook his head. Even at the bank he had never known anyone with Behemoth's uncommon memory, his flair for the extraneous. "You would have made a good teller, Ed."

"Teller?"

"You know. Bank."

Behemoth's profile wagged. "Not interested."

"Neither was I." Mr. Twombly smiled; darkness concealed their disparities, permitting them to see I to I.

"Dick, I thought you were a bug on coins."

"Only rare ones, Ed. And speaking of rare ones, who's going to get those cool ones, Ed?"

"You want me to?"

"Your treat, Ed."

"Um." Mr. Twombly felt himself tilt backward toward the gentlemen's room, forward, then back again as Behemoth gained his feet the second time. The game was blacked out by Behemoth's back, but Mr. Twombly heard, without surprise, the announcer confirming Behemoth's estimate of inning and score in favor of the

FADE OUT   81

Buffalos. He heard an explosion, the announcer reporting catastrophe to the moaning crowd. Now moaning was lost in a roar, and on the screen there would be the waterfall. A little one, it dripped away, while in the brief silence Behemoth was umming dreadfully. A cash drawer whooshed, then whammed, and voices were loud with wonderment. "Hey, over there," one called past Behemoth's back. "Got anything smaller than this?"

Mr. Twombly started to his feet. "Do you mean me?"

"Dick." Laughter accompanied Behemoth over to the booth, and they laughed as Behemoth threw up his empty hands. "He wants to know what change you've got."

Mr. Twombly sat down again. "Ed, only a dime," and another explosion sounded in the Pilco set. The cash drawer whooshed.

"Hey, big man," the bartender called, and when Behemoth turned to him: "Hold out your hands." Quarters rang in Behemoth's palms, the bartender counting them as they fell. Mr. Twombly counted thirty-eight. "O.K., big man?"

"Um." Behemoth had been busy watching water fall. Amid laughter he dripped quarters into his side pockets, left and right, and glasses trembled on bottle necks as he turned away. Yet he reached the booth without incident. "There we go."

"Good job, Ed," Mr. Twombly said, steadying red and purple glasses in the light of the shuffleboard.

Behemoth squeezed jingling in. "I guess you heard what kind of change I got."

"Just the thing," Mr. Twombly said. "You've been out selling Christmas cards."

"All quarters, Dick?"

"You gave them a special rate, two or three for twenty-five."

"Hmm, Spencer would go for that."

"Those that didn't want Christmas cards you sold envelopes."

"Nice." Behemoth was only dimly visible, but Mr. Twombly could see Behemoth's bottle and glass. He liked the way he held them almost parallel to pour, then flipped them straight as the glass came full. Mr. Twombly tipped as Behemoth had, but conditions now were not the same. His bottle held mostly foam, there was too much yeast perhaps. "Dick, you're jumping the gun. A toast comes first."

"Sorry. You say, Ed."

"Mrs. Merrywell?"

"Mrs. Merrywell." In the darkness Mr. Twombly blew a foamy kiss to her.

"Ah, Dick," said Behemoth with smacking lips, "this is the life for us."

Mr. Twombly wiped his mouth. "Yes."

"Here's freedom, Dick."

"Fraternity, Ed."

"Equality."

"Money . . ." Mr. Twombly with a sticky hand put down his glass, moved his bottle to one side, and leaned over the table to his friend. "Ed, we could have it like this all the time."

"We could?"

"Ever been to Arizona, Ed?"

"I had a bout in Nevada once, but I think we went by way of Idaho."

"Like to go to Arizona, Ed?"

"I guess I would. When it comes to that, I'd like to go anywhere."

Mr. Twombly paused to lift his glass, and when he spoke his voice was low. "Why don't we go then, Ed? We've got enough money to."

"Nine-fifty, Dick?"

Mr. Twombly leaned into Behemoth's darkness, whispering, "There's lots more where that came from, Ed."

"Dick, there is?"

Mr. Twombly smiled at Behemoth's mistrust, then nodded invisibly. "Lots."

"Where'd you get it, Dick?"

"Been saving it for sunny days," Mr. Twombly said, and pleased with the phrase repeated it, "Been saving it for sunny days, you see." Was that foam beginning to work on him? "Ed, what do you say?"

"How would we get there, Dick?"

"By Bloodhound, Ed. Then when we got there we'd rent a little house, an adobe one. They keep out the cold, hold in the heat. We'd fix it up ourselves, live alone in it . . ."

"Dick, you have enough for that?"

"Oh yes. We could work part time to supplement. Maybe I could get a job as cashier in a drugstore, Ed. You could work on the day patrol."

"The what?"

"I don't know, you could find something, Ed. Maybe sell television door to door."

"Oh, Dick . . ."

"Well. You could find something, Ed. Promote some boxing bouts."

Behemoth started an um, but then his hand hit the table top: "Dick, I see the Indians have started their war dances again, they had them on Channel 4. Think they could use some more law enforcement there?"

"Sure, Ed. Anything." Mr. Twombly poured his beer, this time more cautiously. Sipping he waited for Behemoth, letting dreams sink in. He wanted Behemoth to catch up with him.

"Ah, Dick, Dick," Behemoth said, and now the entire booth seemed to tremble with eagerness. "No more Spencer then."

"No more."

"Think of the grapefruit and oranges."

"Think of the sunshine, Ed."

"The wild animals."

"Yes."

"They do have wild ones there?"

"Mostly cows and Gila monsters, Ed, I think."

"No buffalo?"

"Maybe a few."

"Ah, Dick," Behemoth said, his face glowing red in the nearer darkness now. "When do we go?"

"You name it, Ed."

"Wait." The booth tilted dangerously, fell forward hard, and Behemoth was on his feet, first try this time. "This calls for another round."

"Nice work, Ed." Mr. Twombly watched his friend stride to the bar, heard quarters slapped down with confidence. Listening he heard no laughter from watching undershirts, although they were turned from their game again. On the way back to the booth Behemoth's quarters jingled his delight, but Behemoth did not sit down at once. Placing bottles on the table top, he stood waiting at full height. Mr. Twombly also waited, apprehensively.

"Dick. We'll have TV?"

Mr. Twombly, sidling into Behemoth's shadow, smiled. "Of course we will, Ed, eventually."

Behemoth squeezed in mollified. He extended a hand to Mr. Twombly, five fine bananas, purple, red. "Pal," he said, "let's be on our way."

"Tonight?"

"Now."

Mr. Twombly smiled. "Easy does it," he said, pouring beer. "Not so fast. There are preparations to be made. We'll want to take a few things with us."

"Like what?"

"Underclothes, Ed, an extra shirt, socks, a few handkerchiefs."

"All that, in front of Spencer and everyone? I thought we were running away?"

"We are, Ed," Mr. Twombly said. "We are. We'll put our things in paper bags—you can use your briefcase— and hide them outside somewhere. Then we'll leave the house at night after everyone's gone to sleep. I've been keeping a record for three months, Ed. On an average night everyone's asleep at my house by eleven-twenty, twelve-ten on Saturdays."

"Dick, how do you tell? I could never be that sure."

"They all snore, Ed."

Silence now, while Behemoth considered this. Then, "At my house it would be later, Dick. We always stay up for the late show on Channel 10."

"When is that over, Ed?"

"Quarter to one."

"Hmm. Then they go straight to bed?"

"Straight. They're exhausted then."

"And straight to sleep?"

"I don't know, I imagine so."

"No snorers, Ed?"

"Only Spencer," Behemoth said. "But Spencer takes sleeping pills anyway. Mary always slept well when she was a child, but of course she was younger then."

"I see," Mr. Twombly said. "We'll play it safe, one-thirty, Ed."

"That should do it, Dick. Any particular night in mind?"

"Tomorrow night?"

"Check," Behemoth said, extending the warm clump again. But "Wait," he said, and drew it back, "tomorrow is fade out night."

"Fade out night?"

"Dick, where have you been! What have you been listening to? They want to find out how long it will take everyone to get out of town—everyone goes except prisoners, nightworkers, and invalids. No animals. Surely you've heard of it?"

"I don't think so, Ed."

"Dick, Dick, what do you do all day? Don't you ever watch TV? What will happen to you in case of an emergency? You'll be caught short, Dick, with the animals. It's dangerous."

"I did see that tomorrow there will be some high thin cloudiness, Ed. On Channel 6."

"Good boy, Dick."

"What time is this fade out going to be?"

"Eighty-thirty sharp at night. Anyone caught inside the city limits by nine gets a demerit slip."

"Good. Listen, Ed, you remember that vacant lot we stopped at on Pinto today."

"Yes."

"Meet you there at eight tomorrow night. Bring your briefcase, Ed, and your streetmap. From there we can make the city limits in an hour easily. Then we'll hike to the nearest Bloodhound stop."

"Eight it is," Behemoth said, and gay bananas dangled enticingly before Mr. Twombly's eyes. "Shake, pal," Behemoth said. Shaking they heard a new waterfall, the loudest yet, sweep over the frenzied voice of the announcer now submerged, now rising again. "Game's over," Behemoth said. "Four o'clock news is next."

"Let's get out of here."

They lifted beers. "To the fade out, Ed."

"To the fade out, Dick."

Banging glasses down they rose to their feet simultaneously, squeezed grunting from the rocking pew. Behind his rail the bartender coughed severely at them, infidels escaping before collection time, runners retiring before the plate was touched.

"Tip, Dick?"

"Hold on to your quarters, Ed," Mr. Twombly said, dropping his dime. "From now on we'll be practical."

Quickly past shuffleboards and undershirts, leaving bad news behind, they pushed through the scraping screen and found the light. The world was breathing more freely now. BOB'S BLUE BAR AND G ILL flapped languidly, and oak trees waved at little boys sprinting the last block home after loitering. Little girls who had already chalked their squares chanted folksongs as they hopped. Flies were being blown away and thankful dogs were waking up.

One mongrel sniffed at Mr. Twombly, slunk away when
Mr. Twombly blew his breath at him.

"Ed, we still have time to kill. What do you say we take
in the zoo?"

"Well, I promised hon I'd be home for the five o'clock
sportscast, Dick."

"Don't worry, Ed. Plenty of time for that."

Behemoth clapped Mr. Twombly's back. "Years," he said.

"That's right, Ed."

"We can get a line on those monsters you were talking
about."

"Gilas, Ed."

They were still on Oakridge, heading west, but only
the name of the street remained unchanged. Cotton balls
were whiter here, and spruce trees proffered no rooms for
rent. Dependable daily papers, pitched from new con-
vertibles by newsboys with twentyfive years' experience,
showed up nicely on evergreen lawns. Entire blocks
smelled like florist shops. Mr. Twombly and Behemoth
observed changes silently, for they were enjoying an
unequal contest between fresh air and their own sweet
fuzziness. As blocks went by, six or eight, new houses
gradually gave way to tiny lots already marked off by
far-sighted realtors for a coming generation of thousand-
aires. Through one of these a brook cut cheerfully: it
saddened Mr. Twombly for that was where the garage
would have to be.

"Nice walk, Dick," Behemoth said. "Brooks and
everything."

"Yes, Ed. Preview of tomorrow night."

"Of the next twenty years, God willing, Dick. Well,
fifteen."

Nodding, "I see the zoo."

"Where?" Behemoth was blinking eagerly, as though expecting to see the giraffe ahead.

"That spiked fence, Ed. The gate is south."

Turning left they followed the fence, pausing now and then to peer inside. Already they could hear the animals, yet the zoo had a rare quietness. There was place for the spoken voice in it. Now individual voices could be heard, the birds taking up where the lions stopped: it showed that they had been listening. When several voices sounded all at once, the effect was less din than harmony, tolerable in regard to decibels. Sudden silence came, and Mr. Twombly felt that had there been danger, thunder perhaps or flood, the animals would have heard before they took up their own thoughts again. Mr. Twombly tried to imagine how the world must have sounded before man learned to amplify his own voice above all the rest, how tranquil it must have been. He was going to broach this to Behemoth yet did not, for they were almost to the gate and Behemoth was devoted to electricity.

"What's the charge here, Dick?"

"More quarters, Ed."

The cashier looked askance at them as they headed for turnstiles past her booth, her look implying that they would only have to come back again. But Behemoth dropped quarters at random from his fist, and they clicked in. Now an attendant dropped his broom confoundedly, as a native might drop his blowgun in the heart of Africa, at such a sight. Ignoring him, they read metal signs aloud. Birds and reptiles were to the right, but Behemoth was already heading for large animals.

"Gilas are reptiles, Ed."

"Time for that later, Dick," so Mr. Twombly ran to catch up with him. Now it was not the noise one noticed but the smell, an unconcealed animal smell that one sniffed curiously and imagined certain far parts of the world must have. It seemed to saturate the ground at one's feet and give weight to the air; Behemoth blew his nose as they approached the bison pen. The bison glanced up and shook his beard, there were flies on it.

"Dick, that's a buffalo."

"I bet he wishes he could go with us, Ed."

The mangy beard nodding now, Mr. Twombly waved his hand a bit. "Sorry, we're going by Bloodhound, boy."

The elk were uninteresting. Approaching bears, Mr. Twombly stopped a few feet from the low stone wall that kept visitors from falling in the moat that kept the bears inside. A man in blue serge had his camera up. Hunching forward, moving his hips, he readied himself. On the other side of the moat a brown bear stood up on hind legs and spread his arms and opened his mouth wide for him. The man waited for the bear to get back down on all his feet, then snapped his shot. Smiling at Mr. Twombly and Behemoth, he wagged his chin at the performing bear: silly an-i-mal. He headed wagging for the bison pen. The brown bears, disgusted now, plodded off to their makeshift caves, although the polar bears did not appear to care about anything. "I wish we had brought peanuts, Ed."

"Don't like them, Dick."

"Don't bears?"

"Oh, bears," Behemoth said. "Probably."

They moved past passive lions and tigers, large sad-eyed pussycats, all seeming to ruminate on the camera-man. Even the elephants had their backs lined up. The giraffe must have fared best of all, for he looked down over his nose as though he owned the zoo and would see that nobody littered it. Stepping back a pace Mr. Twombly stared up at the haughty head, smiled when the giraffe turned his eyes away. But behind him Behemoth ummed unhappily. He had crossed to animals on the other side, and Mr. Twombly hastened to rejoin his friend, found Behemoth blinking hard.

"Dick, I don't look like that."

"No no, that's a rhinoceros, Ed."

"Um. Where are the hippos, Dick?"

A sign said they lived beside the rhinoceros, but looking in they found nothing but a plot of beaten dirt and a muddy, 8-shaped water tank. "They must be in the water, Ed. . . . Ah, there we go." An absurd head broke water noiselessly, held dripping there long enough for them to look at it, ducked again. Seconds passed before Mr. Twombly glanced up at Behemoth's blinking face.

Behemoth turned away. "Let's try the monkeys, Dick."

"Sure, Ed," Mr. Twombly agreed. "Monkeys are always fun."

"Um."

Mr. Twombly trotted at Behemoth's side. "I saw a smart one on television this morning, Ed."

"Good boy, Dick."

People were leaving the monkey cage. Mothers were prodding small children in front of them, young couples were talking in voices too loud, too quick. Old people were glum. Only a few stragglers remained; Mr. Twombly and Behemoth paused with them. Behind the bars, toward the front, a pair of baboons staggered in shameless love. Nearby a middle-aged couple stood, the lady with her back to the animal cage. Her plump companion talked to her in an animated way, all the while looking over her shoulder with shining eyes; his face was flushed. Mr. Twombly looked at the cage again. Except for that shameless pair, all the monkeys were scratching, dozing, swinging the bars, not interested. Mr. Twombly turned away from them. "Time for the reptiles, Ed?"

"Yes, Dick."

The reptile house lay long and low, of warping wood, a gray ugliness that seemed to writhe as it shed its skin. Its front doors stretched open, not invitingly. It was dim inside and clammy, cold. Along the walls ran glassfront showcases barely lighted and warmed by grimy bulbs, all snakes inside. Mr. Twombly and Behemoth slowed. They did not pass such showcases as easily as they might a department store. They began where the arrow told them to and looked into each window separately, letting those tortuous bodies spell out unspeakable things to them.

"No Gilas, Dick?"

"I'll ask this gentleman. Sir, we're interested in Gilas. Have you any in your zoo?"

The attendant shook his head. "I'm afraid you'll have to go to Arizona, friend."

"All right. Thank you, sir," Mr. Twombly said. He and Behemoth stood at the back door looking out. The sun was lower now, larger, colder, more noticeable. In Arizona it would be overhead. "Mind looking at the turtles, Ed? I'm interested." Fascinated, that was more exact. Mr. Twombly had been fascinated by turtles ever since he was a boy in Baltimore. Where other people measured their eras in cats and dogs, he measured his in turtles and tortoises. He could scarcely remember a time when he did not have a turtle of some kind beside his bed: Lucy, George, William, Myrtle, Cynthia, he fondly remembered all of them. He had waited hours for a turtle's move, finding more pleasure in his slow vitality than say the frantic scrambling of a guinea pig. A turtle did not seem to care much for the world, he never asked for anything, except to be left alone inside his shell. He seemed an introvert. But when a turtle moved it became more than a dumb victory over inertia, became almost a testament of faith, worth waiting for. His deity was the sun, and one of the greatest joys in Mr. Twombly's life was watching him stretch his neck to it. After fifty years' perfect attendance at the bank, Mr. Twombly believed he knew how god-forsaken the turtle felt in winter, all cloudy days, at night.

Today he was pleased, surprised to find that others loved turtles too. Several people were in the turtle yard, a crowd stood ten deep around the knee-high wall. Cryptic orders could be heard above the whispering of the audience. Mr. Twombly and Behemoth pushed through the crowd, up to the wall, and Mr. Twombly blinked as well as Behemoth at what they saw. White-shirted men with papers in their hands were scurrying among mobile cameras, cursing and barking nervous orders everywhere. One in a green beret barked most nervously, and nobody barked at him. In the center of the yard a blonde girl scantly clad in a white sarong lay full-length on the dirt, and five or six dirty, ill-kept tortoises stood facing her. A perspiring attendant stood behind each tortoise, shoving him, while the blonde lay giggling helplessly. She wore a clean white bathing suit beneath her sarong.

Behemoth stooped to whisper in Mr. Twombly's ear.

"Maybe these are our monsters, Dick."

"No, these are giant tortoises."

"What are they doing to them?"

"They're filming a television drama," a slender young man whispered over Mr. Twombly's head. "They're trying to get those turtles to snap at the heroine."

"Those aren't snappers," Mr. Twombly said.

"What's wrong with the girl?" Behemoth wanted to know.

"She twisted her ankle running away from the crazy zoologist who wanted to mate her with a kangaroo. She can't get up."

"Why doesn't she yell?"

"She's panic-stricken now. She'll yell as soon as the turtles start snapping her."

"Those aren't snappers," Mr. Twombly said.

The young man looked at Mr. Twombly and shook his head. He had yellow sideburns which he stroked with a dishwasher's immaculate fingertips. "This is a work of art," he hissed. "Didn't you ever hear of poetic license, friend?"

"Quiet!" Now the man in the green beret announced that he was ready to film. He asked the onlookers to cooperate. He asked them to take off their hats and look horrified. Gasps were fine, but no screams, please. At their murmured assent he smiled and said he had seldom seen a more convincing mob. Would they care to give him a preview before shooting began? Now? Holding his hat, Mr. Twombly looked horrified at the young man at his side. Each slender white hand held a great hank of yellow hair, twisting it painfully. In the pale, contorted face, nostrils and eyes were dilating in agony. Mr. Twombly reached out to help the boy, but convulsive shoulders shook him off: the director was approaching them. Without a glance at the unfortunate boy, the director stopped before Behemoth and Mr. Twombly. For a moment he studied them. Then tipping lopsided he patted their shoulders high and low, while everyone around them laughed. "I wonder if I could ask you two gentlemen to stand over here with me, behind the camera?" he asked.

"Certainly."

"Yes, certainly."

"In the interest of verisimilitude, you understand. Nothing personal."

"Certainly." Everyone laughed again, and looking back over his shoulder Mr. Twombly caught a blur of pale blond grinning agony. With Behemoth he moved around the wall, behind the cameras and the director's back. He smiled up at Behemoth, and Behemoth nodded bleakly down.

"Dick, thought we were going to be on television for a minute there."

"Me too, Ed."

"Quiet!" Now the director addressed his cameramen: "Men, wait until they give those turtles one last shove, then start shooting immediately while the men are getting out of the way. We can do our cutting later. With turtles like these, we can't afford to lose any of the activity. Honey," he said, with only a little more gentleness, "you move up closer to those turtles now. Let me see their feet on you. That's right, honey. Those turtles won't hurt." Giggling the girl inched toward lumpish feet that lay askew upon the ground like extra heads with broken necks, discarded now, while the tortoises watched in some surprise. One slowly withdrew his foot from her white thigh, but decided to leave it there when she inched forward again. "Splendid, honey. Now when you hear the cameras, you start screaming. Never stop. Start kicking as soon as you see a turtle move."

"Those tortoises won't move," Mr. Twombly said under his breath to Behemoth. "They should have done this earlier in the day, when the sun was warm. Last month would have been better yet."

"Shove, men!" the director cried, and perspiring men, heads low, feet slipping, churning sand, shoved their tortoises. Then they were scurrying left and right, the girl was screaming and cameras buzzed. For a moment all one could see was one white leg and the white sarong. When the dust settled, five tortoises were backing carefully away from the kicking, screaming heroine. "Cut!"

Silence fell. Nobody looked at the man in the green beret, and he looked slowly at everyone. "Get up, honey," he said with an unreal quietness, "and brush yourself."

The girl rose to her bare feet and began to brush herself. Then suddenly she turned her back to the director, hiding with her hands her averted face, but her bare shoulders and her backside were quivering. The director pushed himself from the low stone wall and took one quick step into the tortoise yard. He looked at the girl's dusty, quivering backside, then addressed himself to an attendant in immaculate white. He smiled, too pleasantly. "Doesn't anybody in this zoo know how to make a turtle move?"

Clean white sleeves flew up. "The reptile man isn't here today."

"Why isn't he here today? Didn't you have my shooting schedule three weeks ago?"

The attendant did not answer that, and the director's smile did not invite him to, dared him if anything.

In the distressing silence Mr. Twombly spoke to Behemoth. "I usually scratch their undersides."

Now the director turned slowly Mr. Twombly's way. He took that single step back to the wall again. He looked thoughtfully down at Mr. Twombly before he spoke. "What?"

"I said I scratch their undersides," Mr. Twombly said.

"Why?"

"I do it to stimulate their blood," Mr. Twombly said, "whenever the sun's not out."

"What do you scratch them with?"

"My fingernail. Then I set them down and they begin to run."

"Which way?"

"Sir?"

"Which way do they run?"

"Forwards," Mr. Twombly said.

The director looked at Mr. Twombly a little longer, but a little less carefully now, and then he turned to the attendant again. "Get me a hoe," he roared, and the attendant sprinted away. "Make that five hoes," the director roared after him. Glancing back at Mr. Twombly, as though to assure himself that Mr. Twombly had not run off, he walked over to his heroine. He brushed dust from her shoulderblades, and she turned to smile a dusty smile at him. Her gray cheeks looked fat with giggling. "I bet I look like hell," she said.

"You look wonderful, honey," the director said, and with his handkerchief he brushed a smudge from her pretty nose. "I think we may have those turtles licked this

time. Man over there seems to know what he's talking
about. I hope he does. You just lie down there again,
honey, and let me see them put their feet on you. If we
get any activity from them at all, I'll send the rescuers in
at once. That way we lose a little of the drama, but we
can't keep this up all night. You hear that, rescuers? Soon
as those turtles start to move, you run right in. No
loitering."

Some men stood up from the low stone wall to nod res-
pectfully, they understood. They sank back down again,
saving themselves for the ordeal ahead. Obeying a pat on
her backside the heroine dropped to the ground and
snuggled up to the tortoises. They seemed to be growing
used to her. A murmur went up in the crowd: the attendant was back carrying hoes. Trotting into the turtle yard
he presented them smartly to the director, handle-first,
but the director accepted them without a word. He
beckoned to his turtle men. When they trotted forward,
he passed stiffly along their file issuing hoes to them.
Shouldering their hoes, the turtle men waited attentively
for the director's command. The director stepped back a
step. "Men, you'll take your same turtles again. When I
give the word, scratch like hell. Then get out of there."

Nodding grimly, the men turned about and trotted to
their tortoises. They did not argue about which tortoise
belonged to them, there was no confusion of any kind.
Crouching low they poised their hoes, while everyone
waited expectantly.

"Scratch!" the director yelled, and five hoes went
down. In the silence one could hear them scratch the
tortoises' undersides. Then hoes went up and men ran
off amid buzzing cameras and heroine's screams. There

was less dust this time. This time one could see plainly
the heroine's yellow hair and her flailing legs, her white-
clad bust under tortoise feet. One could see black tortoise
heads turning, two to left and two to right. The tortoises
were not looking at the heroine, they were looking for the
turtle men. They seemed to want to be scratched again.
"Cut! Cut, cut, cut!"

First one, then the other camera stopped. The heroine
stopped screaming too, although her long legs were still
twitching in the sand. The director stood with his back
to the wall. He did not speak. He took off his green beret,
and Mr. Twombly was surprised to see that his hair was
gone. The director folded the beret and put it in his hip
pocket before he went over to the heroine. For a moment
he stood looking down at her. "Get up, honey," he said,
but the girl lay twitching there. Stooping he removed a
tortoise foot from her left breast, and grasping her bare
shoulders he yanked her onto her feet. The heroine toppled
into his arms, giggling hysterically, and he patted her.
Beckoning to the attendant in white, he waited for that
man to trot over to him. His voice was low. "Let's throw
her to the buffalo."

"The buffalo is mangy now."

"The elephants?"

"The elephants are all in must."

"Let's try the hippopotami."

The attendant was going to demur again, but he
changed his mind. "The hippopotami are not my department," he said, trotting off. "I'll get you a large animal
man."

The director waited silently for him to go, and then
supporting the girl and patting her he led her out of the

tortoise yard. His men went behind him wheeling cameras. The respectful crowd made way for them, then closed in again to follow them toward the hippopotami. Mr. Twombly and Behemoth were left alone with the tortoises. Five thick necks had stretched sidewise to watch the departing throng. Poised heads were motionless, and there was a trace of anxiety around the eyes, as though they looked hopefully for everyone to come back again. Then necks relaxed and heads one by one drew slowly in. Front feet went next, then hind. Five dusty shells lay in a row with unimaginable thoughts inside.

"Interesting animals, tortoises," Mr. Twombly said.

"Interesting reptiles, Dick," Behemoth corrected him.

"Check, Ed."

With this kind of understanding between them, they returned through the reptile house to the entrance gate. It was almost six o'clock. They had seen the zoo. They did not wish to arouse suspicion about where they had been this afternoon, where they would be tomorrow night. Thus they found themselves returning faster than they had come. It was cold besides. The sun was hidden behind trees half the time, soon behind houses permanently. Front doors were closed, and Mr. Twombly imagined that in many houses the heat was on. He buttoned his suitcoat all the way, buried his hands in his pockets, and hunched his shoulders up. Behemoth did not appear to mind the cold, yet he too seemed to have reasons for hurrying home, although he did not mention them.

"Then it's all set for tomorrow, Ed?" Mr. Twombly asked, twisting to look up at Behemoth's face.

"Eight o'clock, Dick?"

"Check, Ed. Don't forget to pack your briefcase and

hide it outside during the day. That way you can say you're going out for a short stroll at seven-thirty and nobody will notice you. . . . What is it, Ed?" Behemoth had stopped and his arms were flapping, disorganized. Shivering, Mr. Twombly looked up at him. "Cold, Ed?"

"My briefcase, Dick!"

"Where is it, Ed?"

Behemoth felt his pockets and his chest. "Dick, I must have left it in Bob's Blue Bar."

Mr. Twombly looked up and down the street. They were returning on Haversham. "The heck with it," he said, and his teeth were chattering. "We'll both use paper bags."

"What will Spencer say?"

"Ed, you don't have to worry about Spencer anymore."

"I will tonight."

"Tell you what," Mr. Twombly said, his hand on Behemoth's back. "I'll help you, Ed. You're on my way." He slapped encouragement on Behemoth's back and hurried on down Haversham, Behemoth after him.

It was almost dark when they reached Behemoth's block of Cherokee. Some lights were on. In the middle of the block a front stoop was bright, somehow ominous. At an um from Behemoth Mr. Twombly quickened his trot: the Fitches were expecting them. Even before they reached the path, the front door broke open and little red Mrs. Fitch stepped out. She did not answer Behemoth's wave, although her hand was up. Holding the door for them, she scarcely waited until they were inside to close it fast. She did not laugh at them.

"Hello, hon?"

Mrs. Fitch nodded her head, and her smile was destroyed by trembling lips.

"Spencer home?"

"He's in the livingroom."

"Um." Behemoth opened the closet door. He took off his hat and brushed its brim with his sleeve before placing it on the shelf. He turned it around, so that its front would show. He looked at it.

"Beemouth?" from the livingroom.

"Um, with you in a minute, Spence."

Behemoth took Mr. Twombly's hat and placed it on the shelf beside his own. He picked it up and put it on a lower one, neatly fronting it. Then he closed the door. Turning he patted Mr. Twombly's back reassuringly and guided him before him along the hall. Mrs. Fitch followed close behind.

Spencer Fitch sat in Behemoth's easychair. He had turned the chair a little to the left so that it faced obliquely both the television set and the entrance to the livingroom. The television was going, but the lights were also on. Spencer was watching Behemoth and beneath the disciplined curls of his dark hair his blue eyes did not blink at all. He wore a dark brown sport jacket, very wide, with a pale blue plaid in it. His sharp sleeves and clean white hands lay flat upon the arms of his easychair, light reflecting from stones in his big·rings. His polished shoes were off, yet ready beside his feet. "Where the hell have you been, Beemouth?" he asked.

Behemoth ummed the hair on Mr. Twombly's head. "Didn't hon tell you, Spence? Out selling a few Christmas cards."

Spencer did not smile, he merely showed that his teeth were bright. "Any luck?"

"Pretty good, Spence," Behemoth said.

"How much you make?"

Behemoth paused, and Mr. Twombly knew that he was blinking fast. "About nine, I guess."

"Nine what?"

"Dollars, Spence."

"Cash?"

Was Behemoth nodding yes?

"Let's see it," Spencer said.

Behind Mr. Twombly there was a doleful jingling, and Spencer's steady eyes grew wide as Behemoth's hands dug in and came out full.

"All quarters, Beemouth! What the hell did you two do, sell to a slot machine?"

Behemoth laughed heartily. "Nope, gave them a special rate, Spence," he said. "Three for twentyfive."

"And everyone bought three?"

"Not all of them."

"Then where are your order slips?"

"I . . ."

"Mr. Fitch, he has no order slips," Mr. Twombly said, and Spencer lowered his eyes to him. "He sold his samples instead, you see."

"Sold his samples?" Spencer asked, shaking his head almost admiringly. "Now there's a switch."

Behemoth laughed again. "Thought you'd like that, Spence."

Spencer raised his eyes to Behemoth, who clearly had gone too far this time. His right hand went up and smacked down hard on the arm of the chair, like a drawbridge operated by a maniac. Behemoth backed off floundering. "Bring me your briefcase, Mr. Beemouth Brown!"

"I can't."

"Can't?"

"I lost it, Spence . . ."

"Where?"

Behemoth had no answer at his command, nor could Mr. Twombly think of one. Spencer gave them a little while. Then, without taking his level eyes from them, he tipped forward and felt for a polished shoe, readily found the proper foot for it. "I guess you boys better get your hats again," he said quietly. "Mary, it might be better if you did that instead."

Mrs. Fitch said "Oh," then turned away. She hurried into the hall for hats, while Spencer covered the men with his eyes and laced. He was careful to get his laces straight, and he pulled them tight before tying them. He was working on his second shoe when his wife returned. Mrs. Fitch handed Mr. Twombly his hat without looking at his face. "Spencer, I couldn't get Behemoth's down."

"All right, Mary," Spencer said. "Let Beemouth get his own. Go with him, please."

"Oh." Mrs. Fitch glanced at Behemoth and Mr. Twombly, then went quickly before them to the hall.

"Hon?" Behemoth said following. "Where are we going?"

Not looking at them she opened the closet door. "We're going to take Mr. Twombly home."

Behemoth went into the closet and brought down his hat. He held his hat in both his hands, but he did not put it on. He faced his daughter inquiringly. "Hon . . .?"

"Shut up, Beemouth," Spencer said, in the hall. He went to the coat closet and got his hat himself. In the hall again, he spread his arms and pushed Mr. Twombly and

Behemoth toward the door. Mrs. Fitch was waiting there. She opened the door and went out first, Spencer last. Spencer snapped the doorlatch as though he were planning to be gone a while, and he slammed the door. He stepped quickly around Mr. Twombly and Behemoth, off the stoop. "Follow me," he ordered, heading toward the driveway and the garage. Mr. Twombly and Behemoth put on their hats and followed him. Mrs. Fitch brought up the rear.

It was quiet, cold. Spotlights cast them on the garage ahead, all four of them separately, Spencer broad and edges sharp, Behemoth close beside, immense, Mr. Twombly and Mrs. Fitch. Spencer threw the hanging door away, and their images broke up on the shiny grillwork of his new car. He opened a rear door, held it wide. "You two can sit in the back," he decided, briskly gesturing. Mr. Twombly stood aside for Behemoth, who stood aside for him. Spencer's gesture was more than brisk, it seemed to throw them together toward the door. "Just get in."

Mr. Twombly held his hat and scrambled in. Grunting Behemoth squeezed after him. Spencer slammed the door. He sat behind the steering wheel, and Mrs. Fitch closed the other door. Spencer started the motor up, sat listening to its quiet nnnn.

"Nice car you've got here, Mr. Fitch," Mr. Twombly said. "What is it, a Caddy or a Pack?"

Spencer did not answer him. He shoved the gear arm viciously and the car sprang from the garage onto the drive, left on Cherokee with howling tires; between swaying shoulders Mr. Twombly could read the glowing letters STUDEBAKE. He glanced at Behemoth and

Behemoth ummed. The car tipped howling onto Pinto now, and Behemoth sat forward to blink for streetsigns as they went. "Spence, we found a nice territory out on Beautyview."

"Shut up, Beemouth," Spencer said.

Mrs. Fitch turned to look over the seat at them. Only her head was visible. In the uncertain light her little red face seemed gray, and her eyes were like two great tears about to drop. Mr. Twombly and Behemoth stared curiously back at her. Each time she blinked it was as though tears had dropped, then formed again immediately. She dabbed them with a handkerchief, but it did no good. Shaking her head she whispered, "Why?"

Mr. Twombly and Behemoth turned to one another now. "Why?" Behemoth repeated, whispering.

"Why?"

They were still exchanging questioning looks, the three of them, when the car drew up in front of Kate's apartment house. Other cars were here. Never before had Mr. Twombly seen so many tenants home at once, all five floors were bright and shades were up. Yet no party noises could be heard. The entire apartment house had a watchful air, as though it waited for someone else to come. Spencer held the back door wide. "We're here."

It was Behemoth's task to get out first, and he ummed apprehensively. Car seats presented a special problem with which he did not normally have to cope. There was too little clearance overhead, he had to fold his body almost parallel. He had to plant his feet too far in front of his balance point. Although he rocked and heaved heroically, he had no room for leverage. Failing a fourth or fifth attempt, he sat back and blinked at Spencer

through the door and Spencer cursed. "Are you going to
get out, Beemouth?"

Behemoth tried another way. He squeezed forward on
the seat as far as he could go, then inclining sidewise
through the door heaved himself recklessly outside. Cursing Spencer broke his fall, leaned on him while he found
his staggering feet. "There we go," Behemoth gasped.

"Go to hell," Spencer said.

He slammed the door, and Mr. Twombly hopped out
the other one. Mr. Twombly hurried around the car to
Behemoth's side, allowed himself to be goaded with him
up the stone walk and steps to the apartment house.
Spencer held the door for them, and they went in after
Mrs. Fitch. The stairs inside were steeper ones; they
groaned beneath their carpeting. By the landing point
Mr. Twombly had little breath, some pain, yet he did not
stop to rest. He kept close beside his umming friend,
feeling Spencer's impatient prod at every step. Ahead of
them Mrs. Fitch climbed with an unnatural heaviness, as
though her new shoes were wet. When she reached the
second floor, she stopped and waited for Spencer to take
the lead again. Spencer rang Kate's bell.

Mr. Twombly could hear Kate's voice even before she
opened the apartment door, and closing his eyes he heard
her high thin "Daddee!" wail through the hall. There
was anguish in her voice, almost as though she had thought
him lost and was dismayed to find him back again. Slowly
he opened his eyes to her. "Hello, Kate."

"Daddy, what did you do to them!"

"Kate? Do to them . . ." but everyone was talking and
moving now. Spencer was cursing as he drove Behemoth
through the door, little Mrs. Fitch was still wondering

why. Kate strode up, and Mr. Twombly relaxed and let
her push him where she would. Kate's arms were strong.
He felt himself almost carried the last few steps into the
crowded room. Besides the Fitches, Behemoth, Kate, Ben
was there, little Gloria, a man in tan he did not know.
Here too the television set was on, yet everyone stood
looking at Behemoth and Mr. Twombly as if they were
something new. They all stood up, but there were no
introductions of any kind. What need to introduce an
audience? Little Gloria's impatient face was red, and her
eyes were opened wide enough to see. Even Ben did not
nearly smile; Mr. Twombly had never known he could
cover his teeth so well. Kate wailed once more, and the
man in tan stepped center stage. His tie hung loose,
pretending to have been up all night, yet his stiff white
collar was immaculate. The dark rings around his eyes
seemed painted there: for the next scene he would wipe
them off, and smile again.

"Mr. Twombly?"

"Yes."

"Then this will be Mr. Brown."

Behemoth was not watching television now; he blinked
closely at the man, then smiled companionably. "Aren't
you an officer?"

"Lieutenant Rudd."

"I'm pleased to meet you, officer." Behemoth held out
his hand, but Lieutenant Rudd had already turned to
Mr. Twombly again. His eyes were as steady as Spencer's
were, but they did not wish to sell anything. Theirs was
a more disquieting confidence, for it was the truth they
were going to rob him of: "Mr. Twombly, where have
you been this afternoon?"

Mr. Twombly braced himself, truth being a thing he gave away too readily. "Sir, out selling Christmas cards."

"All afternoon?"

Mr. Twombly nodded yes.

"Beemouth's got his pockets full of quarters," Spencer said. "They say they sold them three for twentyfive, or some such screwy thing."

The lieutenant was not surprised. "In what neighborhood?"

"Out here on Beautyview."

Behemoth stepped forward now. "That's E. Beautyview, officer. East, you know."

"What time was it when you started selling these Christmas cards, Mr. Twombly?"

"About two, two-thirty, officer, I guess."

"And you kept on selling them until the time you came home, about fortyfive minutes ago?"

Mr. Twombly nodded yes, but this time he felt his nod more weakly affirmative. The lieutenant was also feeling so, it seemed. "Then how was it," he wanted to know, "you were seen leaving some woods on the 900 Block of Pinto around three o'clock?"

"Well now . . ." Mr. Twombly glanced at Behemoth, but found no help in his rapid blinks.

"Mr. Twombly, well now what?"

"We did stop there a minute," Mr. Twombly said.

"Why?"

"To sit down and rest."

"You went all the way into the woods to sit down and rest?"

Mr. Twombly nodded yes. "It wasn't far," he said.

"And aside from that minute you sat down in the woods

to rest, you spent the entire afternoon selling Christmas cards on Beautyview?"

It seemed to Mr. Twombly that he was nodding far too much, so he said it this time, "Yes."

Lieutenant Rudd shook his head sidewise, showing Mr. Twombly how it was done. "Then when did you find time to have that drink?"

The next moment was a difficult one for Mr. Twombly. He did too much at once. He closed his mouth, not only to hold in breath but also to prevent Lieutenant Rudd's nose from entering, tried at the same time to close his ears to Kate's high wail in back of him, and looked slanting up past Lieutenant Rudd to Behemoth for help. But everyone else had more ideas than Behemoth did, his ums were lost in wails and mutterings.

"Daddy never drinks!"

"He doesn't?"

"No!"

"He's changed today." Lieutenant Rudd went up to Behemoth now. "Bend down," he said, and stretched to sniff. He shook his head. "You boys must have peddled your cards in a brewery."

"Daddee!"

"Why?"

Lieutenant Rudd returned to Mr. Twombly, but Kate meanwhile had usurped his space. She grasped Mr. Twombly's shoulders and shook him violently. Her face might have been a round loaf of homemade bread, perfumed, swelling yeastily even while Mr. Twombly looked at it. "Daddy, Daddy, what have you done to them!"

"Done, Kate? To what?"

Over Kate's shoulder Ben bared his teeth: "You
answer her, Pop. What did you do to them?"

"Do to . . .?" Mr. Twombly said, but the rest of his
words were lost. He felt his mouth fly open wider than he
had intended it to, saw the white gleam of his protruding
teeth below his nose, and powerless in Kate's strong grip
watched them spring out onto her bust and balance there
an instant before they toppled to the floor. Kate shrieked,
and looking down shrieked again. The dentures grinned
fatuously up at her. She released Mr. Twombly, stepped
back a step while he stooped to pick them up. Now Mr.
Twombly wiped his peccant teeth with his handkerchief,
much as Mr. Ponce had wiped Mrs. Merrywell's spectacles.
Fitting them in his mouth, he recalled now the pains
with which Mr. Ponce had adjusted the spectacles for
Mrs. Merrywell. He opened and closed his mouth several
times, making trials, and then he smiled. "I understand
you now," he said, smiling genially at all of them. "You're
talking about Mrs. Merrywell's spectacles."

"How's that?" demanded Lieutenant Rudd.

"They didn't break?"

"Daddee!" Kate gripped Mr. Twombly again, but
this time she did not shake so hard. "The twins! The
twins!"

"The twins, Kate?"

"The Alegard twins. What have you done to them?"

"Kate, I . . ."

Lieutenant Rudd clamped Kate's arms and she let go.
Now the lieutenant stood squarely in front of Mr.
Twombly, who watched the white, hairy fingers on the
lieutenant's tie slowly tighten it. "Mr. Twombly, the
Alegard twins have not come home from school," the

lieutenant said, spacing his words unnaturally. He looked at his wristwatch, as though he were rehearsing a speech and wanted to know how long it took. He waited a few seconds before he began again. "They should have been home almost six and a half hours ago. We have searchers out looking for them, but so far there isn't a trace. We think you and Mr. Brown may be able to tell us where to look."

The lieutenant paused, and Mr. Twombly shook his head, shook it again against a sudden red dizziness. He reached out toward Kate, but steadied himself in time to keep from touching her. "I'd like to sit down," he said.

"Sit on the couch," the lieutenant snapped, stepping aside and turning to Behemoth. "You sit next to him."

"Daddee!"

"Why?"

Mr. Twombly moved past Kate's wail across the room. Dropping onto lumpy cushions he felt Behemoth sink in deep beside. Now everyone had to rearrange to face the couch. They did it in an oddly polite, almost orderly way, by rows, the short in front, the tall in back, so that all could see. Lieutenant Rudd alone was not in line. He stood a little forward with his back to the crowd, as though requesting air for the victims of a well-managed accident. Behind him Ben offered the morning paper to Spencer Fitch, but Spencer had already looked at it. Ben pointed to the page neatly folded open in a square, and Spencer moved over toward reading light. "Jesus Christ," he said, for it was Mary Mason's page.

Mr. Twombly closed his eyes. Now someone turned the television off, but Ben asked that it be turned on again, there might be news on it. Behemoth ummed, but he did not suggest what channel they try. He placed his great hand on Mr. Twombly's knee, and Mr. Twombly heard a squeal from the outraged couch as Behemoth leaned close to him. "Dick, who are these twins?"

"They're friends of mine."

"What was that?" asked Lieutenant Rudd close by.

Mr. Twombly opened his eyes. "I said the twins were friends of mine."

"So I've heard," the lieutenant said, impressed. "Close friends, weren't they? I understand you played with them in the park this summer everyday?"

"Almost every, yes."

"Taught them to run with their mouths closed, didn't you?"

"Yes."

"You met them in the park this morning on their way to school? Talked to them?"

"Yes. Yes."

"What did you talk about?"

"School," Mr. Twombly said. "They didn't want to go. I told them to."

"That's all?"

"They raced for me."

"You asked them to meet you after school?"

Mr. Twombly shook his head.

"Or gave them money by any chance?"

Noses were almost touching now, and Mr. Twombly drew back to nod. "Yes," he said, "pennies from my rare coins."

"He gave me mints," little Gloria said, her sharp voice slicing in. "He made me spill them on the floor. You should have seen the mess they made."

Mr. Twombly looked past Lieutenant Rudd to little Gloria, her face. At night her purple pimples showed up more morbidly. "Gloria, I cleaned it up."

Little Gloria glared at him, but Lieutenant Rudd smiled in an amiable way. "What have you got, Mr. Twombly, a pretty good sized coin collection there?"

Mr. Twombly shook his head. "I used to have," he said, "but since I came to New York I've used most of it. I just have a few coins left."

"Those quarters of Mr. Brown's, they're part of your coin collection by any chance?"

Mr. Twombly shook no again.

"May I see one of those quarters, Mr. Brown?"

Behemoth heaved sidewise, came out with one. He handed it to Lieutenant Rudd, who frowned as he held it to the light, turning it. He flicked it with his fingernail. "1950. Is that a rare one, Mr. Twombly?"

"No."

Lieutenant Rudd gave the coin back to Behemoth, keeping records straight, and still leaning forward over the couch he placed his right hand on Mr. Twombly's shoulder, patted it. "What happened, Mr. Twombly," he asked quietly, showing sympathy, "did you and Mr. Brown play a little too rough with your little friends today? Did it make you scared? You had to quiet them?"

"No, sir!" Mr. Twombly tried to rise, but the lieutenant's arm shoved him rudely back. "Ask Mrs. Kroll," Mr. Twombly cried, clutching the lieutenant's hairy wrist in both his hands. "She'll tell you I wouldn't do anything to harm the twins."

The lieutenant shook his head at this suggestion.

"We've already spoken to Mrs. Kroll. She refuses to express an opinion about you, Mr. Twombly."

"Ah."

"She did say something though. She said underneath you are not the shy little gentleman you seem to be, but she wouldn't amplify. Now why do you suppose Mrs. Kroll would say a thing like that?"

Mr. Twombly did not say anything, nor look. He dropped his hands from the lieutenant's arm, for they were shaking it. His lowered eyes saw the hand on his shoulder tremble noticeably, or saw the stiff black hairs raked by the starched white cuff. It seemed to Mr. Twombly that the couch, the entire room, was being agitated by him, and he looked up. He looked from face to face for steadiness, but one by one they turned away. Not until Kate went to the door and opened it did he remember hearing the doorbell ring. A cop came in.

Lieutenant Rudd was the last to be interested. "Anything?"

"Not anything."

Mr. Twombly felt the couch quake sharply, but Behemoth did not attempt to rise this time. He leaned past Lieutenant Rudd to blink and wave at the uniformed officer. "Hello, officer! Remember us?"

The officer looked at both of them, and then he turned to Lieutenant Rudd and shook his head.

"This afternoon?" Behemoth asked, blinking less heartily. "Down on the corner here across from the park? We asked you if we needed permission to sell, permits or any . . ."

Again the officer shook his head for Lieutenant Rudd. "Um."

The lieutenant asked Behemoth what time that was.

"Well, about two-thirty, Dick?"

"Check it," the lieutenant said, and the officer went to the phone. The lieutenant leaned to Mr. Twombly, patted his shoulder as though apologizing for ignoring him so long. "Mr. Twombly, a while ago you started to say something about spectacles. I interrupted you."

"Mrs. Merrywell's spectacles. I thought maybe we had broken them."

"How?"

"They fell off while we were selling her Christmas cards. They looked all right when she put them on."

"Did you make the sale?"

"No."

"You say the name is Merrywell?" Preposterous. "I suppose she lives on Beautyview?"

"Yes."

"Remember her street number by any chance?"

"It was an apartment building, a whitewashed one. She lived on the second floor."

"Check it," Lieutenant Rudd said to the officer on the phone, and, "Find that officer they say they were talking to?"

"It was Sergeant Dowdy, lieutenant," the officer told him. "He thought they looked all right. Says he told them not to be disorderly."

Lieutenant Rudd laughed at a private joke, not a very funny one. "Well, we know what you were doing at two-thirty, don't we, men? Now all we have to find out is what you were doing between then and six. Suppose we talk about those quarters, Mr. Brown."

"If you ask me, lieutenant," Spencer said to the

lieutenant's back, "I say they hocked Behemoth's briefcase for them."

"Mr. Brown had a briefcase, did he?"

"He had a good one when he left the house. He says he lost it, they don't know where."

The lieutenant leaned over Behemoth now. "What have you got in your pockets, Mr. Brown? Any pawn tickets or anything?"

"Just quarters," Behemoth said.

"Suppose you stand up and empty them." Lieutenant Rudd could not know what a great deal he had asked of Behemoth, but something in his experience or training made him retreat a step or two as Behemoth handed his hat to Mr. Twombly and grunting prepared to rise. The big man was obviously tired tonight. It took him three heaves to make it all the way, and on his feet he seemed to feel that no self-congratulations had been earned. He emptied both his pockets, pouring quarters on the flattened cushion he had left behind. They made a fair-sized pile, which he covered with his handkerchief.

"Pull your pockets out," the lieutenant said, and Behemoth plucked them one by one. "Now undo your belt and shake yourself. Go on, go on."

But something was happening to Behemoth now. His shoulders hunched forward, his chin drew in. His hands went up in front of him, and his small eyes peered out, half wary, half dangerous. Mr. Twombly remembered, finally: Behemoth had assumed his publicity pose. For a moment Behemoth watched Lieutenant Rudd without a blink, but when the lieutenant stepped forward Behemoth slowly dropped his guard to his belt, unfastening. However, he did not shake himself.

"Shake it, Beemouth," Spencer jeered, and Behemoth cocked his head to look at him. Spencer grinned.

The lieutenant jabbed Behemoth's chest with his open palms. "Shake!"

Behemoth looked at no one now. Lifting his blinking eyes to the ceiling, holding his pants, he shook, rather gently at first, but soon with something like agony. To Mr. Twombly it seemed that Behemoth was shaking in spite of himself. It was as though a great tree were being rocked by winds too far aloft to touch the rest of them, and everyone there stood waiting hopefully in a circle around the tree, safely beyond the range of whatever inaccessible delicacies might fall from it. They all strained forward when something dropped, and Lieutenant Rudd stooped to pick Behemoth's glasses up.

"Aright, aright!" the lieutenant said. He waited impatiently for the wind to die before he reached up to balance the glasses on Behemoth's nose. While up there he ran quick hands under Behemoth's coat, over his shoulders, under his wide lapels. He turned away. "Now the shoes," he said. "First put those goddam quarters back."

While Behemoth stooped shaking to reload, the lieutenant snatched Behemoth's hat from Mr. Twombly and punched it inside out, unmercifully. He shook it, ran his finger inside the band, before he threw it down. He grabbed Mr. Twombly's hat and punched it too. Muttering he spun it to the couch, did not even wait to see it settle snugly inside Behemoth's hat. "Shake them, Mr. Brown."

Behemoth seated shook his shoes, size fifteens. Some leaves, a bit of sand fell out. Lieutenant Rudd grabbed

FADE OUT   119

the shoes and thrust his hands wrist-deep inside. "No arch supports?" Dropping the shoes at Behemoth's feet, he glared Mr. Twombly's way. Mr. Twombly had not finished repairing the damage to his hat. He touched the crease and held it up to look at it. He turned the hat around.

"Next!"

"I?"

"Who else?"

"Certainly." Handing his hat to Behemoth, Mr. Twombly prepared to rise.

"No, no, no," the lieutenant cried. "Let's get those shoes while you're sitting down."

"Certainly." Mr. Twombly bent forward to his shoes. He unlaced them, but he did not remove them yet. He glanced at Behemoth, and Behemoth blinked at him. "Lieutenant," Mr. Twombly said, "I think I remember where we lost that briefcase now."

"Where?"

"Try Bob's Blue Bar."

"Check it," Lieutenant Rudd said to the officer, but the officer was still checking Mrs. Merrywell. He turned the phone and a shrill lament stung Mr. Twombly's ear. The officer waited for it to break, then grunted soothingly and dropped the phone. Removing his cap he slapped his forehead noiselessly. "You boys must have had some afternoon," he said. "Lady says you tried to break into her apartment, steal her Commodore. Man there had to throw you out. Says you didn't even have Christmas cards, they were Valentines."

"Val . . . ?" Lieutenant Rudd strode to the door. There he turned to look at Mr. Twombly and Behemoth

pityingly, for they had lost his friendship now. His voice
was tired. "Come on," he said.

"Daddee!"

"Why?"

"For Christ's sake . . ."

"Valentines!"

Amid their cries Mr. Twombly bent to his shoes, and
tying them felt Behemoth's watchful anxiety. He stood up
quickly, and Behemoth joined him gruntlessly. Heads
bowed, hats in hand, they waited for everyone to step
out of their way, then passed between solemn files to
Lieutenant Rudd. Behind them Ben turned the TV off.

"Nice little Waldo you've got there, Ben," said Spencer
Fitch. "1952. They made a nice little set that year."

"Afraid it's beginning to feel its age, Spence," Ben said.

"Hm," said Spence.

At the door Kate threw herself in little Gloria's way.
"Gloria, you stay here and make supper. We won't be
long."

"Aw . . ."

"You heard me, Gloria."

Ben held a finger before little Gloria's nose. "Stay."

They entered the hall in single file, rather stiffly, each
looking at the feet of the person in front of him. Nobody
spoke, for behind doors slightly ajar tenants could be
heard straining to hear. Television sets were turned
down low, and small human sounds came through unnaturally. Odd to think of real people in all those rooms,
disquieting to find that they still blew their noses, belched.
Downstairs a tenant was in the hall, a rarity. She was too
busy to do more than glance at them. She opened her
mailbox with her key, peered in, felt all around, then

slammed the door with sharp disgust. Assuring herself that her box was properly closed, secure, she glanced outside as the crowd filed by. Maybe that mailman was late tonight.

The moon was out; Mr. Twombly somehow felt that it ought not be. It revealed his empty bench at the edge of the park, and with cool impartiality made legible the gold insignia on the patrolcar door. The uniformed officer stood waiting beside the car, and in this curious light the gun at his waist took on prominence. Ben's little gray coupé huddled miserably in shadow at the curb, Spencer's new Studebake grinning broadly down on it.

Mr. Twombly and Behemoth were to sit in the back again, this time without argument. They followed the pattern they had already rehearsed, Mr. Twombly taking the lead. Quickly inside they backed into corners and tugged the brims of their hats, sat squinting out under at the activity. Everyone was moving hurriedly now, as though running away. The officer slid behind the steering wheel, the lieutenant in the other side. Doors clicked shut, lights came on, and motors hummed. Ben's coupé stalled, farted up again. As the patrol car left the curb, Mr. Twombly looked up at the crowded windows of the apartment house, almost fancied he could hear Kate's wail in back of him. He glanced behind at the coupé and the Studebake, their little procession spaced so tightly that strangers could not enter it, like a funeral. He looked more carefully, for it occurred to him that this was exactly how long his own would be. Then he looked at Behemoth, finding some comfort in his blinking eyes. Behemoth was studying the ceiling; now his big hands spread out over the seat, exploring the upholstery. Mr.

Twombly too studied it, but he was less surprised to find it so clean, the dead were fastidious.

"Well, hell." A slow car was in their way, and the officer accelerated his motor threateningly. He did it again, but made no impression on the man ahead.

"Give him the siren," the lieutenant ordered.

It was as though Kate had started a wail but changed her mind, and the car in front seemed to jump to the curb. Mr. Twombly glanced into panicked eyes as they sped by. Once past, the officer did not slow down. They were in the business district now, a more challenging test of his driving skill. He reached the police station without using his siren again, and he scraped no fenders or pedestrians.

Lieutenant Rudd was already out of the car. As he held the door and beckoned them, Mr. Twombly saw that his tie was loose once more. Joining him Mr. Twombly turned to look worriedly at Behemoth, for this time the car was parked the wrong way for the sidewise fall. But Lieutenant Rudd had already figured this; he went inside and dragged Behemoth out, then stood him up. Now they were being prodded toward marble stairs, broken white globes above, slamming doors behind, high heels, and whisperings. The stairs were easy ones, but wooden doors closed on them heavily. Inside, such an official silence reigned that their echoing footsteps seemed felonious as they approached the desk where the probable sergeant sat with telephone balanced precariously on shoulder, murmuring. They lined up, all eight or ten of them, in front of the sergeant, who had to raise his eyebrows with extraordinary care, not wishing to dislodge the telephone.

"Sergeant, I'm booking these two men on the Alegard case," said Lieutenant Rudd.

The sergeant glanced at Behemoth and Mr. Twombly. He tipped quickly forward, catching the telephone in his hand, and shook his head. "Too late, lieutenant. The kids just came home."

Nobody spoke, nor wailed. The sergeant shook his head ruefully, as a father might. "They were at the zoo."

"The zoo?" asked Lieutenant Rudd, and Mr. Twombly and Behemoth asked it too.

The sergeant nodded. He grinned, and the lieutenant turned his back to him. The lieutenant looked at Mr. Twombly and Behemoth, not so much into eyes as hats. "Well, I guess you men can go now," he said at last, his reluctance undisguised. He threw up his open hand, not done with them. "We'll want to check that Merrywell complaint."

Kate stepped briskly out of line. "Thank you very much, Lieutenant Rudd."

"Yes, thanks, lieutenant," Spencer said.

The lieutenant nodded affably, but his voice was stern. "I don't want these boys to do any more selling," he said, "and I think it would be better if they stayed away from the park, until this thing blows over anyway."

"Thank you, lieutenant."

"Yes, thanks very much."

"That's understood?"

"Yes . . . yes . . . yes."

Putting hands in pockets Lieutenant Rudd turned away from Mr. Twombly and Behemoth, indicating that temporarily they did not interest him, there were more urgent cases to be solved. Strong sons and daughters took their arms and quickly led them off, with thanks. Outside, on the marble stairs, they paused and looked around as though making sure they had not forgotten anyone. They had not, of course. They moved on again.

"This your car, Ben?"

"Yes, Spence, that's my little beast."

"Well. We'll have to get together some one of these nights."

"Fine, Spence."

"You're in insurance, aren't you, Ben?"

"That's right, Spence."

"Here's my card," said Spence.

"Here's mine," Ben said.

Now everyone said goodbye. Mr. Twombly, watching Behemoth led away, lifted a hand for him. "See you, Ed."

"Check, Dick."

Mr. Twombly's place was in the middle of the seat. Squeezed there, trying not to interfere with Ben while not touching Kate, he watched Ben test his gears, fuss with the dashboard lights. Ben was waiting for Spence to start up his Studebake, but Spence was patient too. Ben stomped his car with both his feet, choked it viciously before it could stall. They lurched out on the street, and Spence nnned waving by.

"Well," Kate said, "I hope Gloria has supper ready, at least."

"She just better have," Ben agreed, and that was as much as anyone found to say before they stopped in front of the apartment house. There Kate wailed up at four dozen windows, unshaded, bright. "Ghouls," Ben said. They closed the car doors quietly, hurried quietly up the outside steps, shatteringly up the inside wooden ones. The apartment door opened well ahead of them, and little Gloria's head stuck out. "What happened, Ma?"

Kate lunged forward to bounce little Gloria into the livingroom, and Ben cursing slammed the door behind: "Gloria, can't you ever shut your big trap?"

"But Ma, what did they do to him?"

"They didn't do anything, Gloria. The twins came home."

"Came home!"

"They were at the zoo."

"The zoo? How come the zoo?" Little Gloria's face was slack with astonishment. "They didn't even take his fingerprints?"

"You shut your big trap, Gloria," Ben advised. "Go to bed."

"But Ma . . ."

Ben raised his fist to Gloria. "Gloria, will you go to goddam bed?"

For a moment little Gloria looked at Ben with pimply hate. Then she started toward the hall, but stopped. "Ma, you haven't heard about Grandy's teeth."

"Not now, Gloria."

"He had them out . . ."

"Bed, Gloria, bed!"

Wheeling slowly little Gloria waddled into the hall, and they all waited for her door to slam. Then Ben and Kate turned to look at Mr. Twombly, but when he smiled their looks shied up and met above his head.

Kate sighed. "Let's eat."

"I don't think I'm hungry," Mr. Twombly said, walking to the coat closet. "I think I'll just go right to bed." He opened the closet door and placed his hat upon the shelf. When he turned back to the livingroom, Ben and Kate were facing him.

"Well, Daddy, if you're sure."

"Yes. I'm sure, Kate." Mr. Twombly walked between them to the hall.

"Goodnight then, Daddy."

"Goodnight, Kate."

"Night."

"Goodnight, Ben."

Moonlight was in Mr. Twombly's room. It shone on the water in Cynthia's pan, and it was reflected by the mirror, the glass bureau top. Mr. Twombly closed the door, stood waiting there. He did not turn on the light. He was not eavesdropping, just not moving much.

"Well, I know where I'm going tomorrow, anyway."

"Do you?"

"To see that home we read about."

"Ah." A pause. "Kate, you didn't write that letter to Mary Whatsername . . . ?"

"No, Ben. But I could have though, the principle is just the same. That's what frightens me."

"Why, has Pop ever done anything?"

"He hasn't *done* anything, not yet. But whenever I meet one of the ladies in the neighborhood they say they saw Mr. Twombly in the park today. That's all they say, just *I saw Mr. Twombly in the park today. I saw your father in the park today.*"

"So you want to send him away."

"I think it would be better, Ben."

"Well. I don't imagine the old boy will be too excited about staying around here after all this."

"Then you agree?"

"I guess so, Kate."

Kate probably sighed. "All this has made a wreck of me. Let's eat."

"I'll wash," Ben said.

Although Ben entered the hall, he did not walk all the way along to the bathroom yet. He stopped in front of Mr. Twombly's door, and Mr. Twombly had time to slide under the covers before he opened it. Mr. Twombly could see Ben peer in, could watch Ben step quickly to the bureau and leave something there. As soon as the door had closed, Mr. Twombly left his bed. Kate's bear rug picture was propped right end up in the bottom of the bureau mirror, where Mr. Twombly could not have failed to see it in the morning when he combed his hair. Mr. Twombly turned the photograph to the moonlight. Ben had creased Kate's face, her arms, a little bit, but he had done no further damage to the burned halo around Kate's ass. Mr. Twombly took the picture to the door, stood with his mouth close to the crack of light from the livingroom. "Thanks, Ben," he called.

THREE

It came in slowly, first as the sound of his own harsh breathing, and other sounds less well defined, then as a first flickering glimpse of the room itself which he had to strain hard to make some sense of. There was no color, only a weak gray light, irresolute, that distorted the room vaguely, making it seem shrunken and oversimplified in black and white. For just a moment he thought that he had awakened too late to catch Cynthia's sun, but Cynthia looked sleepily up at him through her water without reproach. Stretching himself he looked out at a high thin cloudiness, and even as he watched the sun slid through: inside it was as though someone had switched color on, quickly off again. He whispered an apology to Cynthia

but made no effort to goad her into activity, for today she
would have enough of that. He too lay back, relaxed but
not asleep, waiting for Kate to stop snoring at seven
o'clock, then Ben and little Gloria at exact five minute
intervals. Now he sat dangling at the edge of his bed and
waited while they found their clothes, their hands and
feet, puffed one by one along the hall. They were puffing
right on schedule today, so far.

When his own turn came round, Mr. Twombly palmed
Cynthia and took her with him into the bathroom.
Turning on the light he set her down without warning
in the center of the bathmat, to see what she would do.
Cynthia looked around only a second, then headed fast
for the dark corner of the room, behind the tub. Pleased,
Mr. Twombly let her remain there while he shaved himself (four times again today, in case he had no opportunity
tomorrow) and then he palmed her back to his room.
There he sprinkled six flies in front of her, which would
have been twice her normal diet even in the heat of
summer, which of course anyway was gone. While he
dressed he prodded the flies toward her snub nose with
his fingertip, and one by one Cynthia tore them apart as
though understanding that after today they would not
float by so conveniently and in such quantity. Mr.
Twombly too was more than ordinarily diligent, so much
more that when he pushed through the swinging door to
the kitchen there was no question of his having forgotten
anything, and especially his teeth. Today he could smile
with confidence at the chewing family, say his good-
mornings without fear, and they in their turn greeted him
at once without even taking a moment to study him. Now
they did pause, chewing, to look at him, each expecting

the other to find something further to say. None did.

"Well," Mr. Twombly said, still smiling, "I guess I'll be on my way."

"I already got the paper, Daddy," Kate said, a fork half in her mouth. "I had to go to the drugstore anyway. You'll find it on the livingroom table."

"Well, thank you, Kate," Mr. Twombly said. He watched Kate withdraw the sticky fork from her mouth, set it daintily on the plate, before he turned to leave the room.

"Take a look at the front page, Pop," Ben called after him. "Little dohicky in the bottom righthand corner."

"All right, Ben. I will."

Mr. Twombly took Kate's paper over to the couch. He had no difficulty finding the little dohicky Ben was talking about, for it was in a black box with the words TOTS ELUDE COPS above: "Local police are sporting many a red face today, and not only because they spent all yesterday afternoon in the sun. When the Alegard twins, Becky and Berty, 7, failed to come home from school at noon, it was feared they had been abducted. All available policemen and more than 40 volunteer searchers combed the northeast section of town for six hours, but without success. Perhaps only another child would have thought to visit the zoo."

"Pop? Pretty good, isn't it?"

"Yes. Pretty good, Pop," Mr. Twombly called.

Mr. Twombly had little interest in the paper today, although he did turn briefly to the weather page to note with pleasure that the temperature in Phoenix had hit the hundreds again. He hoped it would stay up there for a few more days, but actually the nineties would do, the twenties. Folding the paper upon his lap, he sat quietly listening to their elaborately cautious voices swinging through the kitchen door to him, and today he admittedly was doing it, eavesdroppping:

"Ma, you don't honestly think you can keep him inside all day? Just wait until you go back to work, I mean."

"Why don't you shut up, Gloria."

"Well, you don't honestly think you can, do you?"

"Why don't you go to school."

"Honestly . . ."

Mr. Twombly raised his paper as little Gloria swung into the livingroom. Over the edge of it he watched her charge red-faced to her table of books, bunch them clumsily with her delicate hands, heave them up. "Have fun, Gloria," he called.

Little Gloria hugged her books. "Anyway," she muttered going to the door, "I have a prize excuse for not doing my homework last night." Then the door slammed and little Gloria was on her way to school, shaking them hard.

Mr. Twombly did not have to wait long for Ben. Passing, Ben smiled very quickly at him and went to the closet for his hat, a business man.

"Ben . . ."

"Hi, Pop."

"Ben, I want to thank you . . ."

"Later, Pop. I'm in a hurry now," Ben said, showing Mr. Twombly so. At the door he yelled goodbye, to anyone, and it was Kate who answered him.

In the kitchen now was the daily ruction between dirty dishes and Kate, this morning perhaps more brutal than on other days, and Mr. Twombly did not go in there until Kate called for him. Even then he did not go at once, but waited for her to call a second time. Tucking his napkin, he sat down before his place. He revolved his blue coffee cup half a turn, until the lipstick was on the farther side, and took a sip. Then he glanced up at Kate, watching him, and smiled. "You'd better hurry, Kate."

"I'm not going to work, Daddy, today."

"Oh?" Mr. Twombly said, tapping his toast on the edge of his dish. "Aren't you feeling well?"

"I feel all right. I just thought I'd take a day off today. Daddy, I thought we might all go for a ride this afternoon."

He swallowed an apricot. "Including me?"

"Yes, Daddy."

"At what time, Kate?"

"I don't know yet, Daddy."

He tried to look at Kate in a compelling way, fix her big face with a fatherly stare, but the thought that this face was in any way his seemed to him more than ever absurd. It might have been the full moon that looked down on him. Nevertheless he said to her, "Suppose you be sure to tell me, when you know."

"Don't worry, Daddy."

While Kate busied herself he bent to his food, eating the apricots, the toast, for energy, but leaving the blue coffee sitting cold. Somehow finished at last he piled his dishes and carried them to the sink. When he turned from the sink, Kate was standing wide in front of the door. For a moment they stood facing one another like two wild animals, say a woodchuck and a squirrel, each trying to decide whether he had anything to fear. Kate scratched her chin, without the necessity. "I think you better stay inside, don't you, today? Why don't we turn on the set?"

"Oh, I don't know, Kate."

"There are lots of little children on the morning shows," Kate said, showing him the way to the livingroom. Kate turned the dials, adjusted them for Mr. Twombly, and waited at the door until she was sure Mr. Twombly was watching, at least facing the set, before she opened it. "I'm just going to the drugstore, Daddy," she said. "I won't be long. . . . Promise me you'll be here when I get home?"

"Don't worry, Kate."

Kate smiled worriedly at him, and Mr. Twombly waited until he heard the door slam downstairs before he went to the telephone. He dialed the numbers rapidly from memory and without looking at the last three or four, a skill he had acquired at the bank. Too late he realized that he had forgotten to turn down the set, and plugging his ear he answered Mrs. Fitch's little hello. "This is Mr. Twombly, Mrs. Fitch."

"Mr. Twombly, how are you this morning!"

"I'm all right," Mr. Twombly said. "Mrs. Fitch, is Ed there?"

"No, Dad just went out a minute ago."

"He went out?"

"He said he had some rubbish to dump. He shouldn't be long."

"Oh, I see. Thank you very much, Mrs. Fitch."

"Shall I have him call you?"

"No," Mr. Twombly said. "Tell him I'll try to call him."

Mrs. Fitch laughed gaily. "All right, Mr. Twombly, I'll tell him you'll try."

In Mr. Twombly's bedroom Cynthia was floating in her
water sound asleep, but that was all right. He lifted her
out, shook her, and dropped her into his coat pocket as
soon as she awoke. The fact that there was no packing to
be done simplified her departure, although Mr. Twombly
would have felt better about it if she had had some way to
take along a small ration of flies. He could think of no
way, nothing practical, so he patted his pocket and hurried
out of the apartment without stopping for his hat. Downstairs he turned to his right and up the hill, away from the
drugstore, not by any means the direction he would have
taken had he had a choice, yet he was hopeful. At the
corner turning right, he was pleased to find that he had
remembered correctly the slight downward grade of this
street, perhaps steep enough to warrant the city's placing
a drain somewhere near. He hurried to the end of the
block, and there by good fortune was a drain, a surprisingly
new one. Stooping over it he did not talk to Cynthia as
he took her from his pocket, but turned her at once on
her side and slipped her between two of the bars. He had
to push a little to make her go down. He heard her land
on what sounded like mud, and from past experience he
knew that she had landed with everything tucked securely
inside. Peering through the new, almost shiny bars he
could not see Cynthia, could see nothing but darkness,
yet he did not have the sense of looking into a prison of
any kind. He knew that there was ample room down there
for Cynthia to wander at her will. She could sleep without
fear in the darkness, bask in warmth when the sun was
overhead. There would be flies. Perhaps soon rain would
come and carry her off to better places, places where
there was more warmth and more sun, perhaps eventually

to Phoenix itself. With this wild comfort, Mr. Twombly hurried toward home.

Turning the corner onto Martinet he saw Kate striding past the park, coming up, and he walked even faster because he knew Kate saw him. They did not speak as they met in front of the apartment house but hurried Kate-first up the outside stairs, the inside, to the apartment door, which Kate flung wrathfully in. "Daddy, you said you would be here when I got back."

"No. I said not to worry, Kate."

Flushing, "Where have you been?"

"Just up the street, Kate, letting Cynthia go."

"Letting her go? Why letting her go?"

"I thought she might be happier."

"Well," Kate said, "you may be right. Daddy . . ."

"Yes, Kate?"

"You remember that home we heard about when you first came to live with us?"

"Yes, Kate. I remember it."

"Well, Daddy, I called them this morning. They have room for you now."

"Have they, Kate?"

"Mr. Banting said the opening might be filled at any time—it's a very popular home—so I told him we would be there this afternoon."

"This afternoon!"

Kate flushed again. She drew back a step, stood looking down past the tip of her nose as though a finger were wagging there. She said "Yes," and then looked away as though aware it was not very much.

"Kate, why so soon?"

"I told you, Daddy, we don't want to lose that opening.

For one thing there's the evacuation tonight. You know
how crowded the car gets with all of us in . . ."
 "What time will we leave?"
 "I told Ben we'd be ready to leave when he comes home
at three."
 "At three."

 Mr. Twombly had his suitcase packed, his paper bag
inside and also packed, when little Gloria came home.
He heard her books land on the table beside the door,
heard Kate call out, "Come here, Gloria. Daddy, it's
time to wash." Now Mr. Twombly was supposed to
occupy himself for several minutes in the bathroom while
they whispered, and he did so obediently, scrubbing his
face three times in hot water and drying well. With large
pores such as his, travel brought blackheads and pimples
to the nose. In the mirror he smiled at himself, as much of
himself as he could see: a few days of sunshine would
purify him. He walked rather loudly through the hall,
coughing through the livingroom, broke banging into the
kitchen and little Gloria's hushed, excited "Doesn't he
care," Kate's homicidal gesture with the paring knife.
He said a friendly "Ah, Gloria" going to his place.
 "Hello, Grandy."
 "You eat too, Gloria," Kate warned. "You haven't
time to sit and talk."
 "Who's talking?"
 But Kate gestured threateningly, and little Gloria
gagged herself with romaine. They ate in comparative
silence then, Kate taking handfuls from the refrigerator
as she worked, helping them down with cups of coffee
from the stove. Over her spoon Gloria watched Mr.

Twombly separate the seeds from his salad, recool his tomato soup. He smiled at her, and it seemed to Mr. Twombly that she smiled behind her spoon, or winced. "Gloria, you remember that boy you were telling me about, the one who called to you in the hall?"

"So?"

"Did he call you again today?"

"Ha," little Gloria laughed at him. "I didn't even see him today."

Mr. Twombly looked aside. He smiled in little Gloria's direction, but he could not watch her face, for "Don't worry, Gloria," he was saying, "I think he will someday."

Little Gloria's chair fell back. For just an instant Mr. Twombly was fearful of her, but little Gloria was not looking at him. "I better go," she decided quickly. "Goodbye, everyone."

"Goodbye, Gloria," Mr. Twombly said.

Little Gloria went to the door. She started to push through the door, but then she turned to look back at Mr. Twombly, at him this time. "Goodbye, Grandfather," she said.

He sat listening to little Gloria leave, but from the kitchen he could not hear very much, could not hear her at all with her books, nor feel her progress on the stairs as more than a very slight trembling which he knew could not possibly have caused his blue coffee to spill as he raised his cup. Tugging his coat down over his pants, he poured the remaining coffee in the sink.

"Daddy . . ."

"Kate?"

"What are you going to do till it's time to leave?"

"I thought I might take a little nap."

Kate smiled. "That sounds like a fine idea," she said. "You'll probably be tired tonight."

"Yes, Kate. I will."

He already was. He lay down on the counterpane without removing his shoes, Kate would be washing everything anyway, and quickly, deliberately almost, moved into a more tranquil world, a world of quiet oranges suspended above him like a canopy from trunkless trees. And on every tree a big thermometer recorded extraordinary temperatures which he nevertheless felt only as a pleasant warmth, for wide flat leaves admitted the sun even as they shaded him in this endless stroll of his which was broken by no sound at all. Little Gloria was with him now, walking at his side, yet he was not displeased. This was a different little Gloria, a littler little Gloria such as he had imagined before he came to New York. She gave him her hand (they were friends) and he told her a wild, convincing story about sunshine and oranges, their importance for beauty and health. When he was through, little Gloria ran ahead of him laughing, leaping for oranges which she ate like grapes, in handfuls, whole and unpeeled. He ran after, wanting to caution her, but little Gloria ran too fast for him and soon was out of sight. Yet he ran on, faster than he could possibly run. After a very long while he stopped, gasping for breath, looking around from where he stood. He could not imagine where she was hiding, for in every direction there seemed no obstruction, no limit to his sight. He thought finally to look up, and there of course was little Gloria, her face, tremendous and wretched with its orange-size pimples, hovering between him and the sun. He cried out to her, but as he did so she faded sickly away,

as did everything now, into the weak gray light of his
room.

It was late. Mr. Twombly ran to the livingroom, the
kitchen,, the bedrooms and bath, calling and rapping on
doors, not looking for little Gloria now but for Kate, and
finding her nowhere he went to the phone. He dialed as
quietly as he could, whispered "Mr. Twombly" to Mrs.
Fitch.

"I'm glad you were able to call, Mr. Twombly," Mrs.
Fitch said, laughing. "I'll call Behemoth for you . . ."

"Dick?"

"Ed, can you talk?"

"Not very much, Dick."

"Is everything set, Ed, your paper sack and all?"

"Check, Dick."

"Listen, Ed. They're taking me away this afternoon."

"Taking you away!"

"Shhh. . . . That home I told you about."

"Oh hell, Dick."

"Now listen, Ed: I think I can make it anyway.
We're leaving soon, and they'll have to be back in time
for the fade out. They'll want to pick up little Gloria, and
eat. I think I can sneak away and get to our place on
time, Ed. I'll try."

"Try, Dick."

"Ed, I think I hear her coming now. . . . Wait for me
until eight o'clock, then hurry on home. You don't want
them to catch you on the streets."

"Check."

"Ed, take a nap this afternoon."

"Check, Dick."

"Good luck, Ed."

"Same, Dick."

Impossible to say which clicked first, the door or the phone: Mr. Twombly, although not easy, was safe. Stiff on his feet he watched Kate's puffed eyes study the room, looking for clues. At last the eyes shifted back to Mr. Twombly, for he was all she had to go on this time. "Daddy, I could have sworn I was hearing the set?"

"Just turned it off, Kate," Mr. Twombly said, unbending an arm and throwing it sidewise. "Three o'clock news."

"Well, Ben's home. He's down putting oil in the car. Are you all ready to go?"

"Any time, Kate."

Now Kate came toward him a step, tilting her head awkwardly to look at him. One hand stretched out, not far. Almost it was as though she were a little girl again, bringing home some wound or bruise for him to judge the seriousness of. "Daddy, you don't care?"

And he in his turn looked briefly concerned before his laugh reassured her that it was nothing at all. "No no, Kate, don't worry about that."

For an instant there was disappointment in Kate's eyes, even remorse, but years of practice helped her to continue looking steadily at Mr. Twombly until these feelings passed. It seemed to relieve her to hear Ben on the stairs, for she sighed. Mr. Twombly patted Kate's arm and went to the door. "Hello, Ben."

"Hello there, Pop!" Ben's voice, like his smile, was simply too strong. Inside, he stood looking at Mr. Twombly rather admiringly, impressed with how skillfully he was closing the door. When Mr. Twombly looked back at him Ben shook his head, for with old Pop gone things just wouldn't be done that way around here anymore. It was Mr. Twombly's smile, finally, that made Ben look over Mr. Twombly to Kate for help. "Well, the car's ready. I guess."

"Will you carry Daddy's suitcase down for him, Ben?"

"You bet."

Mr. Twombly followed Ben into the bedroom. He watched Ben heft his suitcase easily, set it down again with a shake of his head. "Sure got a load in there, haven't you, Pop?"

"Oh yes," Mr. Twombly said.

Ben looked around Mr. Twombly's room, but there was little else to see. "Anything else?"

"I guess only my hat," Mr. Twombly said, also looking around. "I guess Kate will dump Cynthia's water. I guess you can tell her to throw the flies away too."

"Sure, Pop."

Mr. Twombly went to the door. He stood jingling some coins in his pocket while Ben hefted the suitcase again, adjusting its weight. When Ben came to the door, Mr. Twombly drew a silver dollar from his pocket and held it out to Ben. Ben looked down at the coin, slowly letting the suitcase slip to the rug. "Pop, what's that for?"

"It's for Gloria," Mr. Twombly said. "Tell her to buy whatever she wants."

"Well, sure."

"Not whatever Kate wants."

"I get you, Pop." Winking, Ben pocketed the coin and went into the hall. Mr. Twombly followed Ben to the livingroom, where Kate smiled proudly at them both and held open the door. Taking the hat she held out to him, Mr. Twombly walked quickly past Kate without looking back. He did not look back at her following them, but kept close behind Ben on the stairs, which Mr. Twombly took briskly with alternate feet. Downstairs he ran ahead to hold the door for Ben, and Ben thanked him as he passed through. Mr. Twombly held the door behind him until he felt Kate take its weight, then let go. He hurried to catch up with Ben, and now while Ben put the suitcase away in the trunk Mr. Twombly opened the car door and slid in by himself. The young people soon joined him on either side.

"Well, we'll see if the beast wants to start," Ben said, stomping at once.

Kate looked grimly at the name of the car. "It better start."

But her voice was lost in the motor's heated debate, a seemingly hopeless dilemma which at the last moment was somehow resolved in favor of pro, and Mr. Twombly caught Ben's fierce smile as they lurched. "Nice work, Ben."

"Well, we're moving, anyway."

"How far is it, Ben?"

"Oh, say three, four miles."

"As close as that?"

"Sure, it's just down the road."

"What road, Ben?"

"Down Highway 8."

Mr. Twombly sat forward in the seat, looking past Kate, noting how Ben turned north on Pinto, east a few blocks on Haversham, north again on a street he did not know. "What's this one, Ben?"

"Beats me. Here's Highway 8," Ben said, so Mr. Twombly had to let that one go. "What ho, they lost someone else?"

Highway 8 was noisy with cops, coming in. They rode their new motorcycles very carefully, in pairs, with their heads held at regulation height, of course, but their eyes downcast on their handlebars. They were leading the way for the army trucks. In each army truck one skinny man, the driver, sat up front; in the back the fat soldiers stood propping one another and staring glumly at the driver of the following truck, who stared coldly at them. After the army came the cops again, but these cops were different from the leading ones. Perhaps because their cycles were older, they drove them in a manner much more relaxed, chatting, guffawing, turning their heads to meet the curious stares of the pedestrians. It was as though a parade had been called and they alone knew that it was scheduled for some other route, perhaps Highway 9, they and the bus driver who crept after the parade derisively hooting his airbrakes.

"What's that, Ben, a bus?"

"Looks like one to me, Pop."

Mr. Twombly looked through the back window at its emptiness. "Where is everyone?"

"He's probably going to his shed, Daddy," Kate said. "The busses aren't running toward town tonight."

"Oh." Mr. Twombly was forward again. "How far have we come now, Ben?"

"Call it four miles, Pop. There's the home on the right."

"That?" Mr. Twombly looked closely at the pink stucco house, but a sign over the door said "caretaker's hut." Behind the clean picture window a woman paused in her ironing to watch them pass through the gate. Now they were on a wide gravel drive that aimed straight up a hill to the home, also pink. On either side stretched a lawn shaded by young pines whose bottom branches were pruned, affording a fine view of the home from the fence, the fence from the home. Under each pine was a bench, but no one sat on them now. No one walked on the lawn, and the horseshoes and shuffleboard sticks hung in their racks. The only person in sight was a little lady camping on a stool in the gravel parking area close to the home, her ascetic face turned up to the high thin cloudiness as though to the sun. Ben parked the car and looked down at her, then he got out.

"Pardon me. We're looking for Mr. Banting, ma'am."

The little lady did not look at Ben; her compressed, cynical smile suggested that this was unnecessary, she knew him well. "What's the time?"

"Time? Quarter past four."

She nodded, for it was what she had known she would hear. "Banting's in the ladies' den at quarter-past-fours."

"Well, thanks." Touching his hat, a wasted gesture, Ben called to the car. "This way," he said, and Mr. Twombly and Kate slid out. They walked around the little lady's campstool to Ben. "We'll get Pop's suitcase later," Ben said under his breath.

Kate agreed, "Yes."

The home, a rectangular two-story building with no roof you could see, might have been anyone's home ten times enlarged. It even had its fluorescent five-digit number nailed over the door. Following Ben and Kate up the wide cement ramp, Mr. Twombly noted that all the pink shades in the downstairs picture windows were drawn. Upstairs shades were raised, yet no faces looked out. The bare hall too comforted him, for although its massive blue door opened wide to the drive no one was there to observe their approach. Smaller doors led off from the hall, some blue and some pink, each with its fluorescent title above. Ben waved toward the ladies' den, and Kate stepped up to listen, then rap. There were loud voices inside, but no one answering her rap Kate leaned on the door.

At first all Mr. Twombly could see was the set. Much larger than Kate's it was built into the wall, or rather into an imitation fireplace with a real mantel of knickknacks above and the bright picture where the fire would have been. The broom and the poker lay on the hearth, a hopper of magazines beside, and now peering in Mr. Twombly could see a boy in a white suit squatting close before the picture and toying nervously with the bellows while he watched. He could see how the ladies sat their low easychairs in rows four-deep behind the boy, how they sipped their tea with very long straws from metal glasses clamped to the arms of their chairs. There must have been twenty of them, and they all turned their heads to the light in the hall. The boy alone did not turn his head, until the ladies called out, and then he turned it reluctantly. But in the light of the set you could see the boy smile, could in fact hear his little laugh of pleasure as he scrambled to his feet and darted among the ladies on his way to the door, his fancy white suit showing up well. "Mrs. Mercer?"

"Yes," Kate said, backing off from the boy. "Is Mr. Banting around?"

The pleased laugh again. "Shall we go in to the hall?" He gave each of his syllables extra emphasis, as though trying hard not to say things too fast. He let company go first, and then in the hall he grinned quickly at Mr.

Twombly and tipped his head to the den: "La-dies
stuff." He was not a boy, but his plump cheeks were pink,
and his small hand felt very soft in Mr. Twombly's hand.
"You're Mister Twombly."

"Yes. I am."

"I'm John-ny."

Behind him Kate grasped Ben's arm and pushed him
forward a step calling, "This is my husband Mr. Mercer."

"Hello," Johnny said, but Mr. Twombly still had
Johnny's eyes and his hands. "Mister Twombly, have
you got a son?"

"Well, I have my son-in-law, Ben here," Mr. Twombly
said. "But no, not a son."

Smiling, squeezing softly, "You have now."

"Mr. Banting?" Ben said, but now a lady's shrill
voice came from the ladies' den, interrupting Ben's
thought: "John-ny. Tel-e-phone . . ."

"I'll be there in a minute, Mom," Johnny yelled at the
door. "Tell them to hold on." Johnny's full lips pouted
for Mr. Twombly as he squeezed, but suddenly they
smiled. "Heck, Dad Ingalls can show you around just as
well," he said, and he was talking too fast. "Dad Ingalls
knows more about our home than I do anyway."

Mr. Twombly watched Johnny run over to the gentlemen's den, softly open the door. In there too, before they
turned to the light, the men could be seen dimly sitting
their rows, sipping their coffee or tea, and leaning forward
to their imitation fireplace as though they hoped to have
the sense burned from their heads. When Johnny tapped
one on the shoulder, this man got at once to his feet and
followed Johnny into the hall. Johnny did not introduce
him to Ben or Kate, but lifted one of the man's big white

hands and carried it over to Mr. Twombly. "You'll understand each other. Dad Ingalls used to be a bank man too."

A portly man in a pure black suit, Dad Ingalls wore his pince-nez very high so that he had to hold his head up and back to look at anyone. Fat as was the area under his chin, there was a surprising leanness on either side of his jaw. He seemed conscious of the fact that he looked more like a retired banker than Mr. Twombly did. "Hello, Twombly," he said. "I understand you were with First Trust, in Baltimore. Lovely bank. I used to be with First Savings, in Schenectady."

"Oh, yes."

"I'll leave you two." Johnny pressed hands, and turning he whispered to Kate on his way out, "I think we're going to like our new dad."

Kate said nothing, but Dad Ingalls tipped back to look after Johnny with a stern, proud smile. "That boy is just like a son to all of us," he said, shaking his head. Turning from Mr. Twombly now, he introduced himself to Kate and Ben. "I think we're going to like Twombly too," he said, eyeing him through the pince-nez. "Twombly will be bunking with me, at any rate until he becomes acclimated to our ways. Shan't take long, I wager. He's found himself a family here. This is his home. You may have noticed the gate was open when you drove in? That's the way it always is here." He paused for comment, and Kate looked uneasily to Mr. Twombly for his.

"Sounds fine, Kate," Mr. Twombly said.

"Get Daddy's bag, Ben," Kate said.

"Room 21," Dad Ingalls told Ben. "You'll want to

remember that too, Twombly. But I guess you have a pretty good head for figures, hey?"

"Oh, yes."

Mr. Twombly and Kate followed Dad Ingalls up the escalator ("certified skidproof," Dad assured Kate) to the second floor, down the wide, well-lighted hall to Room 21. A sensible room of restful green, its picture window faced north so that no sun would shine in Dad Ingalls stood back to let them go first, then stepped past them to the low bed nearest the door. "This will be your bed, Twombly," he said, and his fist prodded it a time or two. "We have all foam nylon here. Wager you never had that before, Twombly."

"No, I haven't," Mr. Twombly said, resting his hat on the bed.

"No offense intended, Mrs. Mercer."

"Not at all."

Dad went to the low bureau now. "This is Twombly's bureau," he said. "If you keep the top uncluttered, Twombly, serve you two-fold duty as a desk." He threw back his head to see if there was anything else. "There's your chair." Clearing his throat he stepped to a door, placed his hand on the knob without turning it. "Lavat'ry," he said. "We all have our own lavat'ries here." He cleared his throat and now his voice was lower than before. "Twombly doesn't . . ."

"Oh no, not Daddy!" Kate said.

"Well now." Dad Ingalls folded his arms and tipped back to look at his visitors. "Have I forgotten anything?"

"I don't know," Mr. Twombly said.

"I think I hear Ben," said Kate.

Dad Ingalls met Ben at the door. "Fast work," he said.

He stepped over to Mr. Twombly's low chair, moved it a few inches out from the wall. "Goes right here. Nice leather," he said.

Ben put Mr. Twombly's suitcase on the chair, and they all stood looking at it.

"Daddy, shall I help you unpack?"

"No no, Kate," Mr. Twombly said in front of his suitcase. "I'll do all that."

Dad Ingalls nodded approvingly. "Independent chap, isn't he?"

"Well, then . . ." Kate looked at Mr. Twombly as though trying to smile. "I suppose we really ought to go."

"Yes, Kate."

Kate came over to Mr. Twombly, and leaning on his shoulders she pressed her cheek to his. Ben shook both Mr. Twombly's hands. "Daddy . . . Pop . . ."

Dad Ingalls stood at the door, his manner suggesting that these things were best done quickly. "Be able to find your way out, Mercer?"

"Yes, thanks anyway," Ben said, shaking Dad's hand.

From the hall Ben and Kate looked back a final look.

"We'll come see you, Daddy!"

"Sure will, Pop."

Mr. Twombly smiled at both of them. "Come soon," he said.

Dad Ingalls closed the door. Turning he looked down at Mr. Twombly and smiled almost kindly at him. "That a boy," he said. He went to the picture window, stood for a moment looking out. Gently then, "Help you unpack?"

"Thank you. I can manage all right."

"That a boy." Dad Ingalls turned from the window. "I

really ought to go down soon and see if Johnny is having
any trouble with the five o'clock sports."

"That's quite all right."

"Ah." Dad stood at the door. "Dinner's at five-thirty
sharp, Twombly."

"Check."

"Twombly?"

"Bully, Ingalls," Mr. Twombly said, and Dad Ingalls
smiled to himself as he went out the door. He closed it
quietly after him. Mr. Twombly went to the window,
stood as Dad had with hands clasped behind. The window
offered a clear view of the lawn in back of the home, but
there was no gate to be seen. Mr. Twombly stood for a
moment judging the height of the fence before he un-
strapped his suitcase, traded his teeth. There was a
knock on his door.

"Come in."

The man who came in was of Mr. Twombly's approxi-
mate size, but he looked somewhat shorter because he stood
very straight and his small ears were unusually low on his
head. Like Dad Ingalls he wore a black suit, although it
had spots in front. "Dick Twombly? Jack McKnight,"
and Mr. Twombly was astonished at the strength of his
grip. "I make a point of greeting all new brothers and
sisters when they arrive." They shook hands again, Jack
McKnight glancing at Dad Ingalls' low chair.

"Won't you sit down?" Mr. Twombly asked.

"For spite." Seated he grinned at Mr. Twombly,
saying, "I suppose you've been getting the propaganda,
Dick."

"The propaganda?"

"Look, Dick," Jack McKnight said, crossing his legs

and relaxing in Dad Ingalls' chair, "I want you to consider this a social call, not an official one. I want to know what you think."

Mr. Twombly sat down on the edge of his bed. "Think about what, Jack?"

"About all these dads, Dick."

"Well, I've only met Dad Ingalls so far."

"That's more than a plenty," Jack McKnight said. Now he leaned earnestly forward in his chair to tap Mr. Twombly's knee. "I like to get it straight from the people, Dick. What's your grassroots opinion of him?"

"Well, Ingalls seems a well-intentioned chap, fellow," Mr. Twombly said.

Jack McKnight sat back in the chair slowly shaking his head. Then he stopped shaking it to look thoughtfully at Mr. Twombly. "What would you say, Dick, if I were to tell you that they put all the new men in with Ingalls?" He paused to hear what Mr. Twombly would say.

"Do they, Jack?"

Jack McKnight was nodding now. "It's all part of a gigantic paternalistic conspiracy, Dick. They call it breaking a man in—I call it breaking him down. That's the size of it. Fraternalism before paternalism, I put it. Dick, am I right?"

"Check, Jack."

Smiling Jack McKnight leaned forward to tap once more. "Dick," he said, "there's work to be done, big work. That's what your union is for."

"My union?"

"That's right," Jack said, grasping Mr. Twombly's hand in his fist. "And I'm your elected president. Can we count on your help?"

"What kind of work do you do, Jack?"

"Well, Dick, we've been working most of this year on chow, periodical subscriptions, better reception, things like that. But that's only a start, Dick. We're working on something big now—town privileges."

"Town privileges?"

Jack nodded. "We want to be able to walk out of that gate once in a while, Dick."

Mr. Twombly stood up. "But I thought Dad Ingalls said the gate was always open."

Jack McKnight laughed. "Happen to notice the caretaker's hut on your way in, Dick? Notice a big picture window in front?"

"Yes, I did."

"By any chance notice anyone standing there, Dick?"

"Yes, I did," Mr. Twombly said.

"Well, you always will, day or night. That's what we're working on now. We call it the Caretaker's Night Off Fund. Our plan is to give him a paid night off, once a week. The entire family, that is—no baby sitters of course. It will be stated in the contract so."

"I see," Mr. Twombly said.

Jack McKnight stood up, very straight, and looked at Mr. Twombly. "Well, Dick, looks like you're on our side of the fence."

"Yes. I guess I am."

Shaking Mr. Twombly's hand, Jack McKnight glanced modestly at Mr. Twombly's suit and shoes. "Dues are only ten cents a month, brother," he said. He released Mr. Twombly's hand, and Mr. Twombly reached into his pocket for a quarter.

"This will pay me up for two and a half months, Jack."

Slipping the quarter into his vest pocket, Jack McKnight again grasped Mr. Twombly's hand. "If the bars weren't all closed tonight," he said, "I'd sneak you out for a beer."

"Thanks anyway, Jack." Withdrawing from Jack's powerful grip, Mr. Twombly went to the suitcase saying casually, "Little rubbish to dump."

"Dick." Jack stood behind Mr. Twombly with his hand on Mr. Twombly's arm. "I like to see a man step off on the right foot from the start. Rubbish falls under the maids' jurisdiction, you understand."

"Well." Mr. Twombly stepped hatless to the door. "Just this once, Jack."

Jack McKnight shrugged, after a decent pause. "I'll go down with you, Dick. Like to make sure Ingalls doesn't screw up that set."

"Fine, Jack."

They walked shoulder to shoulder in the hall, Mr. Twombly held fraternally by the arm, but at the escalator Jack McKnight waited for Mr. Twombly to go first. He stood on the stair above Mr. Twombly, his hand resting on Mr. Twombly's shoulder now. Downstairs he glided quickly to Mr. Twombly's side again, as Dad Ingalls approached them in the hall.

"Going somewhere, Twombly?"

"Just want to dump a little rubbish, Ingalls."

Dad Ingalls nodded approval on his way to the gentlemen's den. "Good man, Twombly."

Jack McKnight headed too for the gentlemen's den, calling loudly, "Have your card for you at supper, Dick, without fail."

"Check, Jack."

Mr. Twombly hurried out the open door. His only escape, unless he hurdled the low hand railing that ran on either side of the ramp, was straight down the ramp past the little lady still camping in the gravel parking area. Although he approached her from behind, the gentle grade and the sharp backward tilt of her head made it impossible for him to avoid her view. He paused over the startled backswept eyes, saying a cheerful, "Well, good afternoon!"

"Who are you?"

"Mr. Twombly," he said. "I have a little rubbish here. Can you tell me if there's a back gate to this home?"

She shook her narrow head, but then she tipped forward on the stool to point up at the sky. "There it is."

"There?"

"The moon," she said, and looking up Mr. Twombly could see for an instant the full gray moon appear through a hole in the clouds; at once it was hidden again. "Everything is all right now. He'll be here right on time tonight."

"He will?"

"Oh yes," she said, tipping her head back again and nodding it. "He's on his way now."

"Who?"

The little lady shaded her eyes as though the moonlight had been a little too bright for them. "He's Um, of course. Mayor of the Moon."

"Ah."

"I can see you haven't heard," the little lady said, looking compassionately at him. "Why do you suppose they're making everyone get out of town?"

"The fade out? Why, I thought that was rehearsal for enemy attack."

The lady gave him her wise, upside-down nod. "That's exactly what they want us to think. They know Um's their enemy, and they want us to think he's our enemy too. Um is Enemy of Evil, Saviour of Good." She closed her eyes, for the effort of explaining Um to Mr. Twombly had been vast, and Mr. Twombly took this opportunity to step around her campstool to the lawn. Moving quickly from pine to pine, he reached the back yard of the home without encountering anyone else, paused by the incinerator to catch his breath. There was no gate, no second one, and the spiked iron fence, cruelly tipped, rose over his head. Stooping he squeezed his paper sack between two of the bars, prodding it through with much the same feeling he had earlier prodded Cynthia, with hope. Turning, he saw a small child step from behind one of the pines. She had an ugly little face which she brought over to him slowly, like a threat.

Her voice was soft: "What's your name?"

"Darling, you'd better get away from me."

"What's your name?"

"Mr. Twombly. You better get . . ."

"I'm Beryl," the little girl said. "Do you like me?"

Smiling at her upturned face, he reached to tug a skinny braid. "Please, darling . . ."

"You like me," she said wonderingly.

"Yes. You better get away from me though."

"What did you put through the fence?"

"Just some rubbish, darling."

She put out her hands to stop him from passing. "I know something you don't know."

"What is that?"

"Lady bugs have orange eggs."

"Have they?"

Nodding, "Will you play with me everyday?"

"Well, I'm afraid probably not . . ."

"You said you liked me."

"Yes."

"Beryl!" Now a man in blue shirt and pants stepped from behind his pine tree close by. He held a hoe in his hand, and he swung it well at Beryl, just grazing her dirty white dress without slicing her leg. "Get home, Beryl."

Beryl looked back pinch-faced as she darted off, but still her voice was soft. "Remember . . ."

The man in blue stood over Mr. Twombly, staring at him, tamping the ground close to his feet with his hoe. He had "caretaker" stitched on his collar, in pink. "Who'r you?"

"Mr. Twombly."

The hoe came up in a slow arc, past Mr. Twombly's arm, his head, back onto the caretaker's shoulder. "We've heard about you here, Mr. Twombly. Stay away from the kid," and as the caretaker turned away Mr. Twombly had to jump back from the slicing hoe.

In the parking area before the home the little lady was just now folding her stool. It folded into a very skinny package, which she tucked under her skinny left arm with her right. She looked up at Mr. Twombly accusingly, as though he had watched something meaningful. He tried to make his smile a reassuring one. "Help you with your campstool, ma'am?"

The stiff left arm swept brusquely away. "What day of the week is it?"

"Wednesday."

She nodded her head, she knew, she knew. "We have

Sundays Wednesdays," she said, and Mr. Twombly followed her up the wide ramp.

Dad Ingalls stood rocking on his heels at the door to the diningroom, looking things over in his elevated way. "Afraid for a minute there you were going to be late, Twombly," he said, putting away his dedicatory watch. He took Mr. Twombly's arm in a strong yet friendly hand, guided him into the diningroom. The diningroom table was a circular one, at which the men sat around the outside edge and the ladies faced them, somewhat cramped, from the inside. "Johnny's eating with the moms tonight," Dad Ingalls said, and from between two moms Johnny gave Mr. Twombly a discreet, probably illegal little wave with his tips. "Think I best tell you, Twombly," Dad said, holding Mr. Twombly's chair out for him, "that the policy committee (I'm honorary chairman of that one) has recommended silence until dessert is brought in. Stimulates the digestion and the appetite."

"Suppresses free discussion of the food," Jack McKnight said, taking the empty chair at Mr. Twombly's side. "They gag us during the sloppy courses, then bring in the fancy dessert and invite us to talk. But we're working on that."

Dad Ingalls looked sternly past Mr. Twombly, at Jack McKnight. "McKnight, constructive criticism is one thing . . ."

"One thing that's not much encouraged around here," Jack McKnight snapped.

"That's not loyalty, McKnight!"

But just then the soup was brought in, and with a little crack of a smile in Mr. Twombly's direction Dad Ingalls deferred to policy, as did Jack McKnight with a nudge. Yet the meal was not an altogether silent one, although the soft meat stew was more in keeping with protocol than the split pea soup, the unsalted crackers, the warm milk. The hearts of lettuce salad showed very poor planning on somebody's part: or perhaps it was a calculated transition to conversation with dessert.

"Sundaes was right!" The little lady seated on her campstool across from Mr. Twombly nodded wisely at him. "I knew," she said.

"Yes, you did," Mr. Twombly said. Now he heard a small noise on his left, and under the table something was brushing his hand. It was his membership card. "Check, Jack."

"Twombly," Dad Ingalls said, after first taking a taste of his butterscotch, "I can appreciate a new man's anxiety to be popular with all elements. Altogether commendable, I feel. One doesn't want enemies, of course. One wants boosters. But nevertheless one wants to be cautious, not step brashly into embarrassing entanglements before he's had the opportunity to make sure of his ground. Am I right?"

Jack McKnight nudged Mr. Twombly's arm. "Dick, raincheck on that beer?" He leaned his little ear close to Mr. Twombly's mouth, for whispering.

"Twombly doesn't look like a drinking man to me, Jack," Dad Ingalls said, smiling benignly at Jack McKnight over a spoonful of ice cream.

"You weren't asked, Perry," Jack McKnight said.

Dad Ingalls flushed, but "Where were we, Twombly?" he asked. "Yes, I was saying that when our natural desire for popularity reaches so far as the lunatic fringe, well, that's tantamount to inviting the solider element to eye us askance."

"What's he mean?" Jack McKnight whispered. "Through the pance-nance?"

"We may seem a trifle crotchety to some elements, I warrant, Twombly," Dad Ingalls went on, "but that's one of the privileges of age, is it not? It's more than a privilege, it's a tradition, I'd say. Our crotchets are precious links with the past, and our nation thanks us for that. There are certain breaches of convention which we simply do not condone."

"Fraternalism before paternalism!" Jack McKnight, not very quietly, said.

Dad Ingalls shot a glance toward Johnny, saw thankfully that he was talking to a mom. "Think of the boy, Jack."

"That so-called boy is a grafter, Dick," Jack McKnight said. "He collects moms and dads the way you or I would collect dues, hoping they'll put his name in their wills."

"McKnight, that's tantamount to perfidy!"

Jack McKnight leaned past Mr. Twombly. "You just tantamounted once too often, Ingalls," he said, taking hold of Dad Ingalls by the pince-nez string. He pulled gently, drawing Dad's face slowly down, over his dish. He held it there for a full minute, while everyone watched. Then he gave it a little tweak, and the pince-nez was floating in butterscotch. Mr. Twombly, on his feet like everyone else, caught a glimpse of Johnny's round face, not pink now but white with shock, before Johnny was partially hidden by moms. And running to the hall he heard Johnny cry "Dad," yet he knew that Johnny was not crying to him. He knew that nobody in there would care that he was running through the hall, out the front door, down the wide ramp to the drive and the lawn. Even so he did not stop until he came to the fence.

Here he could see the pale glow of the caretaker's window, dimly see the figures moving inside, and in the obscure light of the sun or the moon could make out the face of his watch, the large hand just now passing the top. He wished Behemoth were here to say what they would be turned to this hour, how long the commercials would last. He waited five minutes and then started walking stiffly, as a fencepost might walk, close beside the fence to the gate, around the gate and back along the other side. He did not look behind, but neither did he hear any calls, any cries. So finally he did look back, to see that the dim figures were moving again. In the darkness he smiled to himself: Behemoth would be pleased with him.

He continued along the fence to his sack, then on around the other side, that anyone who might have seen him would .not do so twice. Now wide around the caretaker's hut, wondering how it was they did not have dogs, and a few hundred yards west of the home found Highway 8. Traffic was heavy, this time going out, but it moved slowly enough for Mr. Twombly to cut through its lanes. On the far side of the highway a few army trucks, without escort, were still rolling in; he stood off the road, with his thumb held toward their lights. Trucks did not stop. In the passing glare he could not see the little drivers, nor know whether they could see him. Not until someone stalled up ahead did the soldiers in the back of one of the trucks lean down to haul Mr. Twombly aboard. "Going the wrong way, aren't you, pal?"

"Have to meet a pal on Pinto," Mr. Twombly said.

He stood close to the tailboard propped by fat soldiers, helping prop them, staring with them at the next driver behind. But soon they all looked away when that driver turned up his bright lights. Now they looked at the canvas over their heads, at the sky beyond that. No one spoke except to borrow something, or curse. It was as though the only light in the world were shining on them, for inside the city limits all streets and houses were dark. Only the traffic signals were alight, and when their truck stopped at the second of these Mr. Twombly leaned out over the tailboard to see. "Must be getting close to Pinto now, wouldn't you say?"

"Damn if I know," a fat boy replied, "I'm from Arkansas." But he took Mr. Twombly under the arms and handed him down to the street. Mr. Twombly cut quickly across the outgoing lanes to the curb, stood there a moment looking for signs. In the glare of the passing cars finding nothing to read, he ducked off Highway 8 to a sidestreet going south. It was quieter here, terribly dark. Even the sidewalk looked black at his feet. Houses seemed deserted, yet here and there he could detect the guarded croak of a radio set. No cars passed by; he could hear them all honking one block to the east. He was wondering whether that could be Pinto when someone said "Hey."

"Me?"

A flashlight shone in his eyes. "What's your name, mister?"

"It's Stevenson. Richard Stevenson."

"You live around here?"

"No. In Baltimore."

"Don't you know you're supposed to get out of town tonight?"

"Yes, officer, I know. I have to meet a pal on P . . ."

"You'll never make it on foot, that's for sure," the officer said. A car was approaching now, and he waved his flashlight in front of it. For just a moment Mr. Twombly thought the officer would be overrun, but at last brakes howled as the huge old car shuddered, stopped.

"See your registration, please."

"Officer?"

The officer shone his flashlight on the steering arm. "You're Barney Woods?"

"Yes, he is, officer. I'm Mrs. Woods." The lady in the front seat was large, and she had three tiny bald babies in her arms.

"Got room for another passenger, a little one?"

"Well . . ." Mrs. Woods said.

"Glad to have him, officer," Mr. Woods said, leaning past his wife. "He can hold one of the babies for Mrs. Woods here."

"Sure he can," the officer said. "Name of Stevens, I believe." The officer held the door and Mr. Twombly squeezed past Mrs. Woods to the tremendous back seat, where some children made room for him. He set his bag between his feet, and the officer slammed the door. He had to slam it again. "You better get an early start," he said.

"Officer?" Mr. Woods shifted his gears and the car shuddered slowly past the officer. "Give the man the baby, honey."

"Which one?"

"Honey, do I have to tell you everything?"

As the car jumped into high gear, Mrs. Woods swung herself around to lift a baby to Mr. Twombly's hands. "He's dry."

"That's all right," Mr. Twombly said, making a little cradle of his arms. "Ah, I'm supposed to meet a pal on Pinto Street . . ."

"Well . . ." said Mrs. Woods.

"Plenty of room for him, friend," Mr. Woods said, turning cordially to Mr. Twombly. "What did you say your name was again?"

"Stevens," Mr. Twombly said. "That's the 900 block of Pinto."

"Sure."

"There's a vacant lot out there."

"Know it well."

"Keep your eyes on the road, Barney," Mrs. Woods said.

Mr. Woods turned back to his wheel. Resting the baby on his lap, Mr. Twombly squeezed out his watch. He waited for a car to bring light: it was only a quarter after seven, and smiling he tucked the watch in his vest pocket this time. Feeling the children straining to see him, he took the baby in his arms again, patted the little bald head. He could not see well in the darkness, but he felt that the little fellow was asleep. Mr. Twombly too closed his eyes.

"This isn't the way to Pinto," Mrs. Woods said.

"Not yet, honey," Mr. Woods agreed. "I'm trying to find that Mexaco gas."

"You mean you didn't get gas yet?"

"Honey, I forgot."

"I notice you didn't forget your whisky bottle though."

"That's all right," Barney Woods said. He pressed his acceleration pedal, and the car went a little faster. He turned left, then right, then left again. "That must be it now," he said.

"Where?"

"That line ahead."

Mr. Twombly leaned forward between Mr. and Mrs. Woods. Cars were lined as far as he could see, a block or more, and they were motionless. "Mr. Woods, it's about twenty after now."

"I know what time it is."

Already other cars had pulled into line behind Mr. Woods, and by their lights Mr. Twombly could see the Woods all at once. He looked at the little one in his arms, asleep, the watchful children at his side. They all looked bald, or nearly so, like Mr. Woods. He could see the bright perspiration rolling on Mr. Woods' scalp whenever he tipped back to drink, and he could see Mrs. Woods shake her hairy head whenever Mr. Woods offered the bottle to her. But soon she was shaking it all of the time, whether or not the offer was made. It took them twenty minutes to reach a pump.

Mr. Woods turned in his seat. "Got any loose change with you back there?"

Mr. Twombly put the baby down to search. "I'm afraid only fortyfive cents."

"Just what we need."

When Mr. Woods asked the attendant for a dollar-fortyfive worth of gas, the man wiped their windshields very slowly. The pump was empty when he walked back to pump their gas, and it took them a few minutes to reach another one. The gas came slowly, and the attendant took Mr. Woods' money in a leisurely way. He found his tiny flashlight, counted Mr. Twombly's nickels and dimes in its thin beam. They were on the road at ten minutes to eight.

"Now for Pinto," said Mr. Woods. He gunned his motor a little bit, causing his car to backfire. He seemed to know where he was going, for he stopped to read no street signs as with a policeman's carelessness he swung left and right. The neighborhoods they passed looked unfamiliar in the dark, but Mr. Twombly was not surprised until Mr. Woods slowed down the car. "900 block, right on the nose," said Mr. Woods.

"Here?"

"This is South Pinto," said Mrs. Woods.

"Ha? The man forgot to specify."

"So what, you're so smart. That's no vacant lot, there's a skyscraper on it."

Mr. Woods looked out his side next.

"That's a waterworks there," said Mrs. Woods.

"That is? Must be new." Slapping his gear here and there Barney Woods reversed his car by an S-turn in the middle of the block, headed north on Pinto at shuddering speed. No one spoke until he stopped in front of the vacant lot.

"It's a quarter past eight," Mrs. Woods said.

"I know what time it is, honey."

This time Mrs. Woods held the front door open wide, far enough for Mr. Twombly to jump past her out of the car. He ran at once. Halfway to the woods he stumbled over the real estate sign, fell, scrambled to his feet calling, "Behemoth . . . Ed?" He stopped at their rock; already he knew. Behemoth was not standing anywhere there. It was very dark in the woods, but Behemoth would have been visible up in the sky. "Ed?" Mr. Twombly called to the trees, but he expected no answer from them. He stooped to a white spot on their rock. He held the folded paper up to his eyes, although he did not need to see what it was. Tucking Behemoth's streetmap into his coat he softly called "Ed" a last time, and then he turned from the woods. He hoped that his friend had not waited too long, that he had somehow got through the streets without being seen, that by now he was sitting safely at home. At least Behemoth would have the lights out, he knew.

"What's the matter, pal didn't show?"

"He had to leave," Mr. Twombly said. He walked around the car, and Mrs. Woods held her reluctant door for him. Squeezing into the back, he took the baby again. Either his baby had wet himself while Mr. Twombly was gone, or Mrs. Woods had given him another one. Mr. Woods took one more drink before they got under way. Highway 8 was dense with cars leaving town, and Mr. Woods had to hold up traffic a few minutes while he maneuvered his big honking car through their lanes. Now they were going south toward town, away from the home, and for a while Mr. Woods could keep his car swinging along at comfortable speed. It was not until they reached the street bisecting the town that they found traffic again. Here the cars were lined end to end, either way, and voices had to be raised over sirens and horns.

"You should have gone north," Mrs. Woods said. "At least we were nearer the city limits there."

"I know where the city limits are, honey," Mr. Woods said. He waited until a few inches of space appeared in the line before he moved in. Soon he had his car aligned with the other cars, and now there was nothing he could do but sit back and drive at normal pace. He was not so much driving as simply gunning his motor every minute or so, to prevent it from stalling on him. He used his whisky in a similar way. Occasionally he would move the car forward a couple of feet, spanking the bumper of the car next in line.

"We'll never make it," Mrs. Woods said.

Mr. Woods held his bottle up to the light, took a drink. "It's that stop at Pinto that did it," he said.

"Now don't let's start that!"

"Well, what was it then?"

Mr. Twombly said quietly, "It was that Mexaco gas."

Mr. Woods took the bottle away from his lips. He turned very slowly to Mr. Twombly; in the yellow glare of the following cars his perspiring face might well have been a round soggy sponge from which dirty things dripped down on the seat. "Drop dead," he said, and some of the children squealed their delight. The cars in back were honking more loudly now, and he turned to see that the driver immediately in front had moved a few feet. Engaging his gears, he rammed bumpers with him. As bright tail lights blinked in alarm, he rammed once again.

Now the driver of that car got out. He walked slowly back to them, looked in the window at Mr. Woods. The man looked again, and his slender nose quivered as he turned back to his car. "Why don't you look where you're going," he said.

While Mr. Woods had a loud drink on that, Mr. Twombly closed his eyes and leaned back on the seat. He could feel dampness seeping through his vest, and he turned the baby over on his other side. The horns now were a constant, almost a soothing noise, yet close by he could hear the children breathing hysterical things. Now and then the car bucked forward a few feet, stopping with thuds, but mostly it sat shuddering quietly. Mr. Twombly must have been half asleep when the officer came to their car, for the first thing he saw was the flashlight pointed at Mr. Woods' head, and the officer already knew Barney Woods' name.

"You'll have to walk if you expect to get out of the city limits by nine, Mr. Woods."

"Officer?"

"A walk will do him good, officer," Mrs. Woods said.

"We'll have the roads patrolled for looters," the officer said, "but you better roll your windows and lock your doors, if you can."

"Don't worry, officer," Mr. Woods said to the light, "we'll take everyone along with us."

"Better leave that bottle behind."

"Officer?"

The officer watched them get out of the car. He took Mr. Twombly's baby from his arms, handing it to Mrs. Woods. Mr. Twombly followed her, a child at each hand. They were quieter now. Mr. Woods staggered ahead, clearing wide paths. The crowd was less thick off to either side, but Mr. Woods preferred to stay close to the road. He knew where the city limits were. He led everyone right to them, arriving there at exactly one minute after nine. A few feet beyond he sank gratefully to grass under a tree, and already he was making noises in his sleep. Mr. Twombly said goodbye to the children and went on.

He supposed the time had come now for a triumphant chuckle, and he tried. He found it easier, a moment later, to chuckle at the sob he'd heard. Perhaps dying would be like walking at night, cold-chested down a black straight highway, escaping from an unfriendly home, with sirens going. With similar distractions: things following, snakes sliding in the weeds on either side, fiends lurking everywhere behind billboards, antennas toppling on power lines, shrieks and wails, sirens, sirens, and somewhere ahead a bottomless pit with jagged walls, most of which invented by the traveler himself to make his parting appear a reluctant one. Otherwise he will have ended up as indifferent as he began, the mark of a full life being a fear of death and this his last chance to do a thing properly. Yes or no, such a walk at night became crowded with uncertainties. Crowded. Even though he clearly remembered leaving the bald-headed children at the city limits, Mr. Twombly still felt their peevish tugging at his hands: they had been asleep and they did not like him much for waking them. Their hands were cold. On his part, he could not welcome them. The one at his right hand was called Memory, the one at his left was Guilt. He preferred all billboard fiends.

Kate had been a pretty child and sometimes gay, with a flair for making tiny things. She had made him a party for his birthday once, his thirtyfifth, of button dishes and thimble cups, needles and pins for silverware. All this fastidiously set out on a cardboard tray. She had brought it to him at dinnertime, in her excitement tipping it sugared water and all on his city suit. Her mother had of course been furious, and loyally he had too. But tonight, leaving the past behind, he questioned his loyalties. In a cruel way that even now he only halfway understood, they had used Kate to cement their fragile marriage, puttying her between the cracks in it. There in the kitchen, watching Kate pick up her little utensils and return them to the sewing box, they had felt closer to one another than they usually did. (This was not the only time, perhaps not the worst.) And when Kate had gone to her room, quietly to bed, she had left tokens of her party behind, tiny napkins of toilet paper, individually initialed and edged with delicate floral designs. It seemed to Mr. Twombly now that these were the earliest paper napkins he had seen; perhaps Kate had invented them. With encouragement she might have become a fashioner of useful eccentricities, led a useful life. She might have married a creative man rather than a salivorous fear-sucker that, given Kate, one had to feel sorry for. Kate quite aside, Mr. Twombly still could have felt sad for Ben, as for any middleman who did not have the parasitic appetite. He had had plenty of time to develop such sympathies in the teller's cage, as smiling representative of the grimy, perfumed statesmen and general-presidents.

What he would like to have been was one of the ologists, one of the outdoor kind who spent their days in the sunshine digging warm history from the sand. He had a strong sense of the past lying everywhere thinly buried beneath his feet, and it depressed him to know that he had lived seventyfour years without ever finding it. He would have liked to have got his hands on it. As an historian he saw himself with a great cordon of children surrounding him, all clear-skinned and eager and helping him dig. He heard himself in the evening, warm beneath the stars, not lecturing but suggesting to them the continuities, relating the stone ax to the flintlock, to the radio. He fancied them listening. For he was leaving them a view of how the world had been, a view of the future too.

What he had left was a can of flies, a daughter stupefied beyond all hope, a granddaughter fiercely impatient for a wedding night which would climax her wretchedness. What he had brought with him was a cold spot about the heart where the baby had wet on him, and a queer new sense that at any moment life might end with a blast inside his head. He peered at the passers-by, noted that they were fewer now. Their greetings were fewer too. Couples broke abruptly on each side of him, single walkers followed scuffing a step or two before hurriedly passing around. He tripped on something stiffish-soft, a dead dog or a cat perhaps, and righting himself knew that no one would stop for him. He would have no warm hand to hold, no one he could tell what the cold was like. Almost he was ready to turn around, but the city was empty too.

It was a heavy dark, broken only here and there by glowing orange window shades. The high thin clouds let only the brightest stars shine through, and the declining moon was at antenna height. Mr. Twombly walked with lowered eyes, hugging his chest against a stiffening breeze, using the occasional cars to show up the dead pets ahead. He wished he had thought to bring a flash along. He had not even brought a match to light a fire, if he could have permitted himself to light one with all those sirens going. Yet they were in the tolerable distance now, their wails almost reduced to the innocent annoyance of children's toys. He judged that he had walked at least three miles, the last without being flanked by anyone. Looking behind he saw two lonely lights searching the clouds, or forlornly beckoning, wanting people back. Ahead, one traveler alone was answering them. He faced the city, on the illegal side of the road, stumbling and staggering at a reckless pace. Passing beams caught the rims of his spectacles, their groundward tilt, and lit up the huge white paper bag that flapped at his side. Mr. Twombly stood utterly still, voiceless with doubt, waiting for the big man to run over him. Seconds later he lay on his back beside the road, pounding the ground with elbows and heels, laughing so hard that his chest felt warm.

FOUR

"ED, ED! Where are you going!"

"Dick?"

"Where have you been?"

"Dick, I've been looking for you!"

"Turn around, turn around! Wrong way, Ed!"

Behemoth helped Mr. Twombly onto dancing feet, dusted him off with his rattling bag, pommelled his hump without apology. "I found you, Dick." They stood now peering at one another, up and down, and Behemoth adjusted his glasses straight. Passing cars let the tears gleam through, and Mr. Twombly was laughing more quietly. "Dick, your paper bag?"

Mr. Twombly tapped his vest. "Your map as well."

"Ah, I thought they had you, Dick," tapping there too.

"No no, I was delayed, that's all."

"I thought so, Dick."

"I thought you would have been home in bed long ago."

"I did start back, but Spencer was out hunting me. He was hunting on E. Beautyview, caught me on Martinet. He brought me straight out to the limits with him."

"What time did you get there, Ed?"

"Quarter to nine."

"Beat me by just sixteen minutes, Ed."

"No demerit slip?"

"No no. But how did you ever get away from Spence?"

"I told him I had to do business in the woods. By that time Spence was too disgusted to follow me."

"Ho, you just walked away from him?"

"I was running, Dick."

Gently, "You gave up though?"

"Well." They were walking now, and Behemoth flapped his bag at the darkness ahead of them. "I thought I had missed you, Dick. I was tired of stepping on all those dogs, besides."

"I understand, Ed. I almost turned back too."

"Ah." A brief silence now. "Good thing I gave up before you did, Dick. I might never have found you otherwise."

"Check. We work well together, don't we, Ed?"

"Dick, we do."

Among other things, they gave off heat. Together, they almost forgot how cold it was and dark. Perhaps their brushing arms made sparks, or their sidewise slanting glances of delight. Perhaps their marching feet. For all Mr. Twombly knew, it was something Behemoth carried in his white bag, the newest thing, sacked heat perhaps. In any case he looked up at the big man with unprecedented confidence, feeling that with Behemoth next to him he could keep walking, south, all night. Behemoth, however, clung to realities.

"Dick, what time is it?"

"One minute, Ed."

"Dick?"

"I'm looking, Ed." His was a daytime watch, and passing cars were no longer reliable. But Behemoth rummaging in his bag brought out a kitchen match, cupped a torch for him which the wind sniffed out. "My watch has stopped."

"Stopped? Try winding it."

"It's tight."

"Shake it a little bit."

"No good, Ed."

"Ah, Dick . . ."

"No no. Time is unimportant now. Think I'll try to turn this in for a speedometer."

"Hm."

"Perhaps a thermometer."

"Mmm. Sun set tonight at 6:24, but that doesn't do much good."

"It's interesting."

"Rises tomorrow at 5:20, Dick."

"There goes that moon. Happen to know what time the moon sets, Ed?"

"Dick? I'll have to study that."

In silence they watched the broken moon fall toward the ground. Difficult to say just how high it was, there were no antennas out here to measure by. And even as they watched the moon appeared to bounce up again, no doubt having left Um behind.

"Dick, what time did it stop?"

"At nine."

"Nine." Was Behemoth shivering? "Wish we had that speedometer now. How far do you judge to the next Bloodhound stop?"

"Well, just consider it, Ed. Look at all this space they've let go to waste. It can't be far to the next settlement." A slow car went by, lighting up the road for them. "Didn't I tell you, see those billboards, Ed?" The car stopped now, its bright eyes reading up on a hotel of the family type, children and television at regular price. "See that one, Ed?"

"That's Spencer, Dick!"

"Ed, how can you tell!"

"Who else but Spence has eight rear lights?"

Mr. Twombly counting them, four red, four white, saw that they blinked closer now. "He's backing up!"

"Run for it, Dick! He's got a spot with a three-quarter-mile beam on it."

"Three-quarter, Ed!" Taking off from the road through difficult grass they saw the beam cut the darkness over their heads. It was much lower the next time past.

"Ed, lie down!"

The beam raked the grass at their feet this time.

Grunting "Too late, Dick," Behemoth was straight again and thrashing east with flailing arms.

"Make for the billboard, Ed. Spence will never think to look in back of it."

The beam was ahead of them now. Behemoth veered to the north, away from it, but rushed back when Mr.

Twombly cried "Ed!" to him. Mr. Twombly had fallen down; one-handed, Behemoth righted him. Together they ran after the light, a losing chase, saw it double back as they dove together behind the sign. They lay gasping there, peering out through latticework. As Mr. Twombly had guessed it would, the spotlight swept the billboard reading style, top to bottom, left to right, then turned away well satisfied. Flipping up, it showed them darkness three-quarters high. With one last flash, goodbye, Spence's spotlight blinked out and Spence's Studebake nnned cityward.

"Thought he had us, Ed."

"Did you, Dick?"

They lay watching Spence's eight rear lights blur into two, then one, fade out of sight. A little later they got to their feet, Behemoth finally with the help of the lattice-work, and brushed themselves. Behemoth still had his paper bag. He slapped it against the billboard rather fractiously. Then he walked away, Mr. Twombly follow-ing.

"Dick. Spence didn't look very hard for me."

"Ah, Ed. We outsmarted him."

"You don't outsmart Spence, Dick, he just makes it look that way. You do what Spence wants you to."

Mr. Twombly reached Behemoth's side. "You know what I think, Ed? I think Spence has gone to get the cops to help."

A considering pause. "You thınk ʝo, Dick?"

"I do. I think we better stay off the highway, stick to the grass a while."

"Well, we don't want to get lost," Behemoth said.

"We won't stray far. Anyway, it seems lighter now."

In fact the weak clouds were gone, stars were bright, and
the erratic moon was traveling high. Mr. Twombly could
even see the gleam of Behemoth's skeptical skyward look.
"Um."

"Ed?"

"Nothing. I hear dogs ahead."

"Probably they belong to that gas station across the
highway, Ed. They won't bother us, and we won't them."

"Well, I wish we had a compass, Ed."

"Ed, a great idea," congratulating Behemoth's back.
"We'll buy a compass first chance we get, head due south-
southwest by it."

Behemoth stopped; Mr. Twombly could feel his friend
looking down on him. "Don't you ever get sleepy, Dick?"

"Sorry, Ed, of course I do. I must be a little excited
tonight. Let's rest a while."

"Out here?"

"Behind this billboard, Ed. It has latticework."

On his hands and knees Mr. Twombly cleared a space
behind the sign, raking bottles and cans away. He sat
down with his back to the latticework, patted the damp
earth invitingly.

"Here, let me show you how. That's no good,"
Behemoth said, sighing to his knees at Mr. Twombly's
side. "You've got to think of your contours, Dick." He
chose a tin can and began digging the area Mr. Twombly
had cleared, heaping the dirt in a pile a few feet away.
He did not stop until he had a good-sized hole and pile,
which he patted firm with the palms of his hands. Next
he waved Mr. Twombly aside and dug a second hole, a
smaller one. Mr. Twombly's dirt he threw in a separate
pile, not so far off this time. Now he leaned back to

examine his work, leaned forward for a final pat or two. Obviously pleased, he turned himself over and settled himself snugly into the larger hole. Reaching for his white paper bag, he placed it behind his head and pillowed himself on his pile nearby. Looking Mr. Twombly's way, he sighed. Mr. Twombly now drew his paper bag from under his vest and settled himself exactly as Behemoth had. He also sighed, with some surprise. He was comfortable.

"Ed, where did you learn all this?"

"Took a fancy to the Boy Scout Hour."

Closing his eyes, Mr. Twombly lay quietly listening to Behemoth's sighing breaths. Somehow he supposed the big man to be blinking hard. "Ed?"

"Um?"

"How's this: as soon as we get to Phoenix we'll trade my watch in as down payment on a good used set."

Behemoth was stirring now. Mr. Twombly opened his eyes to see his friend sitting erect, his blinking face latticed by orange light. Mr. Twombly also turned, "What is it, Ed?"

"Sounds like a Bloodhound, Dick."

"It's slowing down. It's going to stop at that station, Ed."

"Check."

Quickly out of their holes, not forgetting their paper bags, they made for the highway fast. A step or two off the pace, Mr. Twombly was pleased to hear that Behemoth carried his quarters still. The bus was already moving when they came abreast, but Behemoth reached up and rapped the window glass hard and high. Doors wheezing open, they lunged inside, stood smiling thanks to the driver while they gasped for breath.

"Boys going someplace?"

"Dick?"

"Sir, are you heading south? Or west?"

The driver swiveled sidewise a few degrees, better to study them. He appeared to have been driving many miles: his waist had settled so well to the front and sides that it almost obliterated his silver changer, his puncher and keys, and his hand-tooled belt. His new boots were neat beside his chair, and he toed his pedals with green knit socks too long for him. Yet these harmonized with his polaroid sun glasses restfully. His big shirt pockets sagged with pencils and pipes, his side pockets were fat with newspapers and magazines, and his cigarettes and matches he carried in the band of his driver's hat. No doubt that left both hip pockets free for storing his joke-books in. "Suh, we're headin' straight for the Masin-Dixin line." A shriek was muffled behind his back, and he looked in his big mirror at the shaking girl. "You gentlemen care to try our rockin' chi-ars?"

"Give him your quarters, Ed," Mr. Twombly said, to further shrieks. "We'll go as far as we can with him."

The driver did not remark on Behemoth's jingling fare, but took off his hat and extended it hole up, polite. When Behemoth had dripped all his quarters in, the driver shook his hat gently, spreading the coins so that he could examine them under his dashboard light. "That all you got?"

Behemoth searched his pockets fruitlessly.

Now the driver extended his hat to the passengers. "Anyone else," he asked, "got beer money for a hard-driving man?" He winked at cracks of laughter in the dark, and at the quaking girl who dropped a penny in. "Thanks, Hysteria."

"I'm Dorabeth!"

Swiveling back, he lifted his waist folds off his belt and slipped his changer out. That was how he managed that. He counted Behemoth's quarters aloud as he racked them up, then ejected a dime and a nickel, Behemoth's change. He gave him Hysteria's penny too. Burying his changer again, he scribbled on tickets which he drew from his boots. He issued their tickets individually, first Behemoth's, Mr. Twombly's next. "You gents are on your way to Baltimore."

The bus was already rolling south, but it stopped at a stifled shriek: Behemoth had fallen all over that girl trying to give her her penny back. The driver swung half-circle to look at them. "You all right, Hysteria?"

"Doooorabeth!"

"Now, you want to take it easy, gents. You've got a long hike ahead of you."

The bus flew out from under their feet, and Behemoth lurched wildly north, umming apologies. Mr. Twombly staggered after him. They stopped beside seats from time to time, but always bodies stirred and they hurried on past groans and snores. It was on the wide back seat that they at last found space between a sleeping girl and a peeking man, sank gratefully whispering there with paper bags between their feet.

"Ed, looks like everyone's still leaving town."

"It looks that way."

"I didn't think they were going to take it so seriously."

"We must have missed some last-minute bulletins . . ."

Mr. Twombly nudged Behemoth still, for one row ahead an aged pair were staring hard through spectacles. Perhaps it was the bus's unlicensed speed that made their heads bob on their thin necks in such a wild and knowing way; Mr. Twombly had to avert his eyes.

"Did I hear you say you were going to Mexico?"

Mr. Twombly looked cautiously to his left. "No, Phoenix," he said, "by way of Baltimore."

"You'll fry," he heard. "I know, I used to punch cows out there."

"In Phoenix, Arizona, you say you did?"

"Sure, and Phenix City, Arkansas."

Mr. Twombly looked again. This narrow-eyed passenger filled his corner up, his head was deep in shadow, high, but the reflected moon revealed not so much a man as a large boy with a gray mustache. Was that gray in his sideburns too? "How hot does it get out there, in Phoenix, Arizona, I mean to say?"

"Hotter than hell," the large boy said. "I've been there too."

They fell silent now, while the bus jostled them wantonly in their rocking chairs. Looking forward Mr. Twombly could dimly make out how the driver drove with his back to the road, conversing with Hysteria. But he did not watch long, for the wildly bobbing couple still had their spectacles trained on him.

"What time is it?"

Mr. Twombly felt for his watch.

"Don't bother," the large boy advised disgustedly. "Your watch has stopped."

Reaching out both hands, "Where did you get that!"

"Right here, pop," the large boy said, tucking it back in his vest for him.

"You're a . . ."

"Not professionally." The large boy folded his arms. "I

just pick up my travel expenses that way. What I am is a lobbyist."

His eyes on the boy, Mr. Twombly transferred his watch to the far side of his vest. He saw the large boy flip back one of the very wide lapels of his overcoat; he kept his ticket in a pocket there, behind his knife. "See there—D.C. The Parental Responsibility Act comes up in the House next week. I represent the juveniles. What we hope to effect is a compromise. We'll pay all expenses and indirect costs for our misdeeds, our parents will get the time. Do you know the name of your congressman?"

Dumbly Mr. Twombly shook his head.

"I'll send it to you first thing Monday morning, c/o General Delivery, Phoenix, Arizona. Also Arkansas," the large boy said. "I got your name from your watch. All you have to do is write him a postcard saying you support the Keely Amendment to Bill 38. Tell your friend to too." In the darkness he jotted something on the back of his ticket before returning it to the pocket behind his lapel. Now he folded his arms again, sat staring out the window broodingly. "Hope that old lady wasn't in any hurry to get to Washington. Well, maybe next time she'll know better than to doze in a public place, or at least not buy her ticket until she's wide awake. Anyway, I think I left her enough money to get another one if she really has business in the capital." He paused to massage his upper lip; his gray mustache had a hinge on it. "Oh, I have other sources of income," he explained. "I write some copy on the side. You've probably seen the one for Ammo-dent: 'Sweetens Your Breath While It Sharpens Your Teeth.' That's mine. Also, 'On That Difficult Man Who Has Everything, Try the Handy New Stillet-o-

Blade.' I could go on, but you've heard them all." The
large boy was in a mood again, his narrow eyes looked
around the bus for something that might inspirit him.
Presently he switched on a small light above his head: he
was reading Mr. Twombly's green memo book. For the
most part he seemed to find it tedious stuff. "What are
all these numbers, cash?"

"No, temperatures."

"I was going to say," the large boy said, "you two must
have something in your bags besides underpants."

He switched off the light and returned the notebook to
the inside pocket of Mr. Twombly's coat, patting it in
place. He wished to assure Mr. Twombly that he had
nothing to fear from him. For his part, Mr. Twombly let
a long minute pass before turning to Behemoth casually.
"Care to change seats for a little while? I've seen everything on this side, Ed."

"Dick, let's wait until this bus slows down or stops."

"Please, Ed," and Mr. Twombly stood swaying up.
"Thatta boy," as Behemoth listed with the bus. Quickly
claiming Behemoth's place, he thought he saw where the
big man's reluctance lay, in part. He looked at the sleeping
girl admiringly, at her pouting mouth, her pale moonlit
skin, and her dark shining hair that sprawled over her
upturned coat collar in a somehow undressed way. Even
as he watched, her cheek slipped from her hand onto the
slobbered windowpane. Her body stirred uneasily and
she turned his way, laying her head against his arm and
tucking her silken knees against his thigh. Now he could
see her other side, her swollen eye protruding above a
mottled, purple cheek, and her thick, bruised mouth
which even heavy lipstick could not set straight. It was as

though they had found a new type of bomb which left its victims only half destroyed, that they might not forget what they once had been. Somehow it permitted Mr. Twombly to take her hand in his, press it gently beneath her coat. She was sobbing in her sleep besides. "Why did they do it?" she asked, and "Why?" He made himself perfectly still for her, at seventyfour a man does not need much oxygen.

"I was all-weight champ of Canada," the large boy was telling Behemoth, "but I moved to Mexico."

One row ahead the bobbing heads were still concerned, but even they looked up as sleeping bodies gained their feet and staggered frontward in the bus. The driver took one glance at them and swiveled to face the road. He applied his brakes just in time to skid broadside off the highway before a closed wire gate guarded by an all-steel sentry box. In both directions, farther than one could see, ran a high wire fence, barbed and probably electrified. The bus door puffed open and sleeping bodies stumbled out murmuring curses and graveyard jokes. The armed soldiers frisked them as they staggered single-file through the half-open gate, sent them on their way with hearty claps. When the last had gone, the bus door sprang shut again. Now all who remained were Hysteria, that couple, the mutilated girl and Mr. Twombly, Behemoth and the large boy of course.

"Ah yes, I used to script that show. Just now I don't recall which nom de plume I used."

"E. E. Hummingway?"

"That's the one."

The door huffed open to let a passenger in.

"Get a load of this fat-assed gob," the large boy said,

"trying to hitch rides at one a.m. I bet he's been farting all night to keep him warm."

They watched the sailor bounce past Hysteria down the aisle, all the way, stopping at last to toss his pregnant overnight case onto the luggage rack. He pressed past Mr. Twombly and wedged himself into the corner beside the sleeping girl.

"I used to be one," the large boy said, peering narrowly across at him. "They didn't keep me long, of course."

The girl, stirring in her sleep once more, withdrew her hand from Mr. Twombly's. She turned on her other side, resting her head on the sailor's arm. Mr. Twombly watched her resnuggle her knees, saw how her black hair fell loose on the sailor's sleeve. Only the skirt of her coat was touching Mr. Twombly now; he removed his hand from under it, for he was feeling jealousy. He let his head drop back against the seat, and breathing deeply closed his eyes.

"What finally made me leave Arizona was the oranges. They make warts on me."

"Hm."

"I can eat grapefruit though."

Before going to sleep Mr. Twombly firmly crossed his legs, his right over his left at the knee. His uneasy dream was of bobbing, watchful oranges, warty and mustachioed. Their narrow eyes dripped thick syrup onto their cheeks as he pierced them one by one with a stiletto blade. But it was their mournful sobbing that soon brought him back to reality. "I don't know why they had to do this to me— I never did anything to them."

"That's what you get for messing with the army, kid."

"I know I'll get a beating for this," Mr. Twombly

heard the poor girl prophesy, "but I know I'll never, never leave Georgia again."

"Kid, try to sleep."

"All right."

"Right now I'm scripting a Marathon Miracular. When I finally get it done it'll run two days and nights."

"Um."

This time it was friendly billboard fiends, all eager to welcome him to their latticework homes. They all wore work gloves and long underwear of a rather common type, which surprised him somewhat. They seemed to enjoy patting his back. The one thing about them was that they had no heads, but soon even this peculiarity was outgrown. He even felt that he recognized one or two. But he could not visit long with any of them, for he was in a hurry to get somewhere. He came to a much larger group who lay in their holes blinking up at a very small set. Impatiently they motioned him to his hole and pile, where he obediently settled himself. He soon grew restless though, for the picture on their screen was of the moon. He got to his feet and stumbled forward in the dark, faster now because the biggest billboard of all lay ahead. He guessed it to be at least a city block in length, of proportionate height. Soon he had to stop: his way was blocked by an oversized travelers cheque and they had cleverly forged his signature on it.

"Where are we, Ed?"

"Let's see, Dick."

"City of Baltimore, state of Maryland," the large boy said.

Mr. Twombly leaned forward to look out the window past Behemoth and the boy. He imagined he should be feeling pangs, but all he felt was that they had added light. Oh, he could remember nodding and nodding his head, untold miles of asservation if laid on end, yes I certainly agree we must convert to electricity. That way we can see more sooty bricks of our factory walls, clear up to our fire escapes. Or was that one an apartment house: on a second-floor sill he thought he had seen a slanting, makeshift windowbox braced by wires, for storing groceries. He shivered to think of anyone asleep up there, for in an hour or two the alarm would ring. That sleeper would walk these grim treeless blocks, his belly flaccid with coffee and eggs, enter that factory door. Tonight he would walk back again. Mr. Twombly sank deep between Behemoth and the sleeping girl, drawing comfort from their warm backsides, three travelers passing through Baltimore.

"Nice little city, Dick."

"Um."

"I didn't mean little, Dick."

Mr. Twombly sat forward again. "Ed, there's my bank."

"Where?"

"Quick, the one with the clock in front!"

"Ah. I see it, Dick."

"The gray stone one?"

"Check." Behemoth turned to blink at him. "Dick, give you a pang to see it again?"

"Yes."

Together they strained to look back at the bank. The large boy looked too. When the bank was no longer in sight, he looked at Mr. Twombly and Behemoth almost openly. "You two guys are beginning to make sense to me."

Mr. Twombly got to his feet, for the large boy was smiling behind his mustache.

"One minute, friend."

"Better hurry, Ed."

"Friend, a word with you."

"Ed."

The large boy stood up and over Behemoth, so close that Mr. Twombly could feel the brush of his soft mustache, his hissed "You guys haven't come back just to tell them your watch has stopped." He drew off a little to catch Mr. Twombly's response to this. "Right or wrong?"

"Right," Mr. Twombly said.

"Ah then," the large boy said. "I believe we understand one another now?"

"I guess we do."

The large boy jerked his chin Behemoth's way, patted his very wide, his bulky lapel. "Use another bodyguard?"

"Thanks," Mr. Twombly said, patting Behemoth's swaying back as he gained his feet this time, with bag, "but two would be a luxury."

The large boy was certainly skeptical, but he did not persist. Instead he seated himself, drew out his ticket to jot something down. He even had the civility to wish them luck. Acknowledging this, Mr. Twombly took a last look at the sleeping girl. She lay with her silken legs sprawled out over the seat, her head tipped back against the sailor's cheek in the wild soft nest of her hair. Too dark for absolute certainty, but it almost seemed that her mutilated face wore a small half-smile.

"Fasten parachutes!" the driver yelled, as brakes caught hold. Watchful heads bobbed so hard that Mr. Twombly feared their thin necks would snap as he sped past in the

wake of his bodyguard, who ummed down the aisle out
of control. The alert driver threw out his arms in time to
save Hysteria. "Easy," he grunted, as Behemoth fell into
his wide embrace. The two big men were carried by
Behemoth's momentum against the instrument board,
and all lights went out. Without a word the driver rolled
Behemoth onto the floor, stooped to straighten his green
wool socks. Now he pressed a button and the door
labored open, snapped closed again. Nothing happened
at all the second time, so he stepped over to smack the
door hard with the palms of his hands. It did not budge,
and outside people were watching him. "Guess we'll have
to declare an emergency," he said. Helping Behemoth up,
he led his passengers past loud shrieks and knowing stares
to the rear of the bus. There was a shatter of glass and
cold air rushed in: the large boy had released the
emergency door.

"Guys, good luck."

"Pleasure to serve you gents," the driver said. "Tell all
your friends."

They made their thanks, jumping down, and hurried
abreast through the station doors.

"Your town, Dick. I'll follow you."

"This way, Ed," Mr. Twombly said, leading straight
to a door marked men. Alone inside, they dropped bags
on the floor and stood before mirrors straightening their
ties and hair. In the clear glass Mr. Twombly caught
Behemoth's questioning blink.

"Dick, how are we doing?"

"Fine, Ed, so far."

"I didn't mean to hit that driver so hard."

"Not your fault, Ed. He took it very well, I thought."

Smiling, he crossed to the stalls. "Got a nickel, Ed?"

Behemoth handed him one. "Keep watch, Ed." Entering a corner stall, Mr. Twombly closed and latched the door. He sat listening for a moment, then unlaced his shoe. "Ed!"

"Dick?"

Mr. Twombly came out of the stall waving his empty shoe for Behemoth to see. "It's empty, Ed!"

"Dick, that boy?"

"I thought you were guarding me!" But, "No, it's all right, Ed," he hurriedly reassured, for hopping back to the stall he knew that he carried his cheques in his right shoe now.

It cost them another nickel, which Behemoth willingly paid. They came out of the restroom so greatly relieved, so buoyant that they did not think to worry about what lay ahead until they faced the bars of the ticket cage.

"Hope we don't have any trouble, Dick."

"I hope not too," Mr. Twombly said, patting his watch and his pen. With false nonchalance he put down his bag and selected a bus schedule from the rack, one with a palm tree on front. "I've been thinking, Ed, bus travel grows a little tiring finally. What say we stick with Bloodhound till morning, then hitch rides or walk till night. We have lots of time."

"You choose, Dick."

"Let's see, here's Pith. Sun should be warm by 9:06."

"Pith it is."

Moving over, Mr. Twombly smiled at the girl in the cage. "Miss, we'd like two one-way tickets to Pith, if you'll accept this travelers cheque."

"Well, *hello* there," said the girl, her smile as bright. "How have you been?"

"Fine," Mr. Twombly said.

"I *thought* I didn't see you at your desk last week. You're on your vacation, I see."

"Yes."

"How's everyone over at old First Trust? You said Pith?"

"That's right."

"Sign right here," she said. "You have a pen?"

"Oh yes," Mr. Twombly said, filling out his cheque while the girl made out their tickets to Pith.

"There we are," said the girl, adding with a laugh, "I guess I better not forget to give you your change!"

"Ho, ho," Mr. Twombly said, as she counted it out. Patting his pockets, he picked up his bag and smiled at the girl.

"Have a nice trip!"

"Thank you," he said. Smiling, taking Ed's arm, he crossed the bright lobby at a leisurely pace.

"Dick, you're well known around here."

"Care to see something of the town? We have a little time before our bus leaves, Ed." Mr. Twombly guided Behemoth through a heavy door into a dark alleyway. There was light at one end of it, and he led the way down there, stopping when he found the street. There were no people, only two or three parked cars in sight. A horn sounded in the distance somewhere, but no car answered its mating call. Now a taxicab rounded the corner and they watched it cruise hopefully by, speed up to beat a signal turning red. They faced one another, for a sharp breeze cut across their chests.

"Little chilly, isn't it, Dick?"

"Yes, it is."

Turning about, Mr. Twombly led his friend back down the cluttered alley, found the station door on second attempt. They recrossed the lobby, sat with their backs to the smiling ticket girl. They had scarcely had time to unfold their schedule when an amplified voice announced a bus departing lane five, for the south. "This way, Ed, to the departure gate."

"Ah."

There was their bus gunning its motor in lanes five and six, already backing away as they climbed through its door propped open with boots. They had their same driver again. He held a cautioning finger to his mouth, for Hysteria had fallen asleep. Running past occupied seats, Mr. Twombly noted that the tireless couple still had not. The large boy was also awake.

"Guys get cold feet?"

Nodding, Mr. Twombly stood waiting for Behemoth to seat himself next to the boy. On Mr. Twombly's side, where the sleeping girl and the sailor had been, now sat a little man nodding and tapping his feet and tapping the seat next in front with his knife. "What happened to that girl who was sitting here?"

"She got off."

Mr. Twombly stared at the boy. "In Baltimore? She was going to Georgia, I thought she said."

"Oh? The navy's making history tonight."

Mr. Twombly dropped between Behemoth and the musical man. "Poor girl. She had learned her lesson, I thought."

"She didn't have a chance," the large boy said. "The

army did the dirty work, now the navy's mopping up."

Mr. Twombly, closing his eyes, "Did you notice her, Ed?"

"Fine looking girl," Behemoth said.

The music's tempo quickened perceptibly now, but it was not the little man who was setting it. The bus made the beat, he was simply the instrument. What he had was the ability to relax completely, so that his chin tapped his chest in time to his pointed toes on the floor and his knife, nicely balanced in his small slender hand, danced on the seat like a seismograph recording the end of the world. Over in his corner the large boy had picked up the beat, but he was trying too hard. He was stamping not tapping his feet, wagging his head instead of relaxing his chin, and his blade flashed maniacally before the old couple's spectacled eyes. Behemoth ummed, but Mr. Twombly was curiously soothed. He must have been tired, for the next he knew their bus was in traffic and Washington Monument was teeing the moon.

"Think I've got it down now," the large boy said, jotting something final on his ticket and tucking it away with his knife. "We'll start out with 100,000 copies, then see. I have high hopes for 'The Bloodhound Jerk.' Where can I contact you, c/o Basin Street?"

But the little man had grown, though incredible, even more slack, and while they watched his knife slipped from his fingers point-first to the floor. Otherwise he was still rendering pure Bloodhound Jerk.

"When he comes out of it," the large boy said, rising to his feet, "tell him he has straight half interest in the piece. I'll cut you guys in too. Just don't forget to mail your cards to your congressman, that's all I ask."

Now he was leaving and even the obsessed couple
turned briefly front in their seats to watch him stride
down the aisle, toss his ticket to the driver on the way out.
Mr. Twombly watched him stride up the ramp to the
gate, where he was greeted by a tall, dignified couple of
strong middle age. They stood one on each side smiling
down at the narrow-eyed look, and now it was the tall
man who wore the gray mustache. Mr. Twombly lowered
his eyes, for they were kissing that boy.

With a clatter of boots the bus started up, and all the
new passengers charged toward the rear. Mr. Twombly
drew in his legs to make room for the stoutest of all, whose
horrified eyes warned him to look after himself. She
mentioned the driver as she fell in a heap. But sitting up
with a sigh, she was thoughtful enough to assure herself
that Mr. Twombly was safe. She carried her backside
beneath a great coat, thus she had no way of knowing she
sat on his hand. Not returning his smile, she looked down
on the quivering knife at her feet. Her great elbow brought
a quick end to The Bloodhound Jerk. "Crazy man, pick
up your toy."

Scarcely troubling to look, or open his eyes, the
musician dropped his hand to the floor. His slender
fingers settled loosely over the knife, and he hung there
tapping his sharp toes counter to the free nod of his head.

"Pardon *me*," the lady said, on her feet. "I'm going to a
funeral. I don't need more trouble," she said. Taking
refuge in Behemoth's corner, she sat with her face toward
the window mourning softly under her breath. Behemoth
and Mr. Twombly looked at one another in silence, then
turned to look out the window on the opposite side. The
little man seemed lost in his music again, and under the

circumstances neither felt bound to relay the large boy's
contract to him. Their voices were low.

"Ed, no fade out in Washington?"

"Doesn't look that way."

"Or are these merely transients, Ed? Notice all the
New York plates."

"Hm. Where would that put the Washington cars, in
Arkansas?"

"Arkansas, I guess, or New York."

The district limits rocked by and in the seat next in
front bony fingers went up to jerk thrice hard on the cord.
No answering buzz could be heard, but already the bus
was settling with strong jolts to the pavement. The old
couple stood stiff on their feet, facing the rear of the bus.
Were they planning to use the emergency door? Mr.
Twombly drew his legs aside, but they only stared with a
wild curiosity at his shoes and his socks. Their magnified
pupils bobbed from his feet to his hands to his face, to his
bag, as though they despaired of seeing all that there was
to be seen. He noted that they warily avoided his eyes,
even when they dropped their heads intimately forward
to confide.

"We're leaving you now."

"Ho."

The lady had a great deal else to say, and her mate
encouraged her to with eager jabs at her side. Slapping his
hand, she lifted her eyes and waved out the window in a
slow, spiritual way. "Mayor, hadn't you better leave too?"

"I?"

"Night will be gone, it will be day very soon."

"Ah." Leaning forward into their whispering privacy,
he felt himself flattered by the real concern they

showed. "I've made arrangements to catch it at Pith."
"Ah, Pith." They nodded their absolute approval of
this, their relief. In a sudden spasm of determination the
lady twisted the top button from Mr. Twombly's vest,
with her other hand proffered her autograph book.
"Mayor?"
"Yes, of course." Drawing out and uncapping his pen,
Mr. Twombly covered her page with an extravagant Um.
The man made a bold play for his pen, but wagging a
finger Mr. Twombly held it out of his reach. He felt a
little sad at how meekly they thanked him and scuffed
out of the bus, especially with the driver beating his horn
so hard. But there was comfort in the sight of their little
white house alone at the edge of the highway, its cluttered
front yard well lighted and fenced, and at the door a
magnificent peacock stood waiting for them.
"Dick, what was all that?"
Patting his hand, "I thought surely you had the word?"
Mr. Twombly said.
At Behemoth's left the stout lady was grieving less
publicly now. She seemed to find her sorrow in the gray
light to the east. She stared out the window with great
watering eyes, which she dried at intervals with the sleeve
of her coat. Her huge face was naked, unsightly with pain,
and she made no serious effort to straighten her big hat.
"I'm going home to a funeral," she said. Her eyes fixed
toward the east, she passed Behemoth a card from her
purse. Behemoth passed it to Mr. Twombly. Large letters
read "MISSES STONE—THE SENITORES MADE—
WASHINGTON 6" with "Try Sen. Short" scrawled
underneath, and on the reverse: "CUM HOME MISSES
STONE ITS YUR CHERRYMAE." Mr. Twombly read

both sides over again before he asked who Cherrymae was.

"Cherrymae's my youngest," Mrs. Stone grieved, and unbuttoning the top button of her coat drew out a quantity of white ribbon and lace. With infinite delicacy she held the dress up by its straps, shook out the creases in its bodice and skirt. "Here's what Cherrymae will wear to her grave."

There were other questions which Mr. Twombly had wanted to ask, but listening to Mrs. Stone's dirge, seeing the pure white of that dress, he could not doubt what even the mailmen had known. Cherrymae was certainly dead. While Mrs. Stone tenderly refolded the lace, Mr. Twombly slipped the card back in her purse.

"It's a beautiful dress."

"The last time I saw her Cherrymae was wearing size ten. I hope she still does." With a sudden shuddering moan she dropped her head to the heap of lace in her lap, heedless of its freshness now, as though she saw it anyway already despoiled and indelibly stained by her tears. Looking away, Mr. Twombly saw that more than half the couples in the bus were turning backward to stare. It was Mrs. Stone's sorrow, yet he felt that they stared only at him. Their faces were haggard and pale, but their spectacles shone bright in the dawn. Feeling it somehow indecent for them to be looking this way, he held up his hand. "I've made arrangements . . ." he called, but their anger interrupted his words. "I knowed he had to be a yank," muttered one, and another, "What else?" He waited for most of them to turn frontward again, then closing his eyes allowed himself to be keened into a dreamless sleep so profound that he did not wake up until the driver shook his shoulders at Pith.

On his feet, Mr. Twombly helped the driver haul
Behemoth to his. Mrs. Stone and the musician were asleep,
but rancor kept the others alert. They did not draw in
their legs when the driver led his passengers out, nor did
they try to make room for Mr. Twombly and Behemoth's
bags. Even Hysteria, though giggling, sat stiff in her skirt,
well under control. The driver waited until the very last
step to mumble "So long."

But Pith was all Mr. Twombly had hoped it would be.
Its streets ran parallel to the new highway but a block
farther south, the thin strip of its pavement was lost in a
fine brown dust. A few very old trees hung over the street,
their deep blots of shade calling attention to the heat
everywhere else. People moved slowly, dogs not at all,
and lazy particles of dust hung warm in the air after the
bus. In front of the drugstore the Bloodhound thermometer read 82, even with its red belly in shade. Next door,
the long narrow movie house sat flat in the sun, the face
of the dime store beyond had faded almost to pink, but
across the street one fanatical house crouched freshly
painted, apart, on its green, shaded lawn. A lady in an
apron was wetting the grass, and whenever her way was
clear she wetted the street. On her left was the fire station,
the saloon on her right. The bank was of clapboard and
brick. Mr. Twombly and Behemoth turned to examine
the drugstore, the faded aspirin display, the dusty hairnets,
pipes, and balloons. With the aid of the show window Mr.
Twombly trapped a fat fly on his neck, but glancing
shyly at Behemoth he let it escape without maiming it
first. Cynthia would have been happy in Pith.

Behemoth needed a shave. His jutting chin was rough
and collecting dust, but what struck Mr. Twombly most

was how red and strong the whiskers appeared, seeming to
belong to a much younger face. He was shamed by the
sharpness with which he suggested they look for a washroom, and yet heading south past the theater he did not
take Behemoth's arm. Behemoth was for trying Mexaco
gas, but Mr. Twombly waved him on to a less familiar
brand. The washroom door was locked, and he had to
awaken the attendant to get the key from his belt. They
at last were inside, only to discover that Behemoth had
forgotten his razor blades, although it turned out that it
was he who had remembered the handsoap. The washroom was ill-equipped, at best. The sink had long ago
lost its hot tap, and the last of the toilet paper was choking
the bowl. A sticker on the mirror had formerly invited
suggestions to the management, but someone had bled
all over it. Mr. Twombly, insisting that Behemoth shave
first, waited outside.

The sun had quieted his nerves somewhat by the time
Behemoth emerged blinking and clean; he patted
Behemoth's back, and received in return a big-hearted
grin. Examining himself in the mirror, he found further
solace in the promising start of an all-white mustache.
Perhaps when he reached Phoenix he would let it grow,
at Christmas send a picture to little Gloria. He swallowed
an aspirin before he went out.

"Ed, could you eat?"

"Anything, Dick."

The station attendant looked after them as though he
believed their bags hid something belonging to him, say
his soiled paper towels, but continuing south they came
upon a friendly-seeming diner that still had all its wheels.
Sliding the door, holding it open for Behemoth, Mr.

Twombly felt better about the big man when he saw that
the set behind the counter was working. The coffee smelled
good, furthermore, and it seemed perfectly natural to
order the ham and egg breakfast de luxe for perhaps the
first time in his life. He had always been the continent,
soft-boiled type. Behemoth distractedly ordered coffee
and toast.

"Ah, Ed, you can't travel on that."

"Don't worry about me."

Quietly, spinning to Behemoth's ear: "Money's no
worry, you know."

"Nothing like that," Behemoth said, still facing front.
"Like to watch the old weight."

Mr. Twombly did not insist. When the cook served
their breakfasts, Behemoth shoved the breakfast de luxe
to Mr. Twombly, and Mr. Twombly shoved Behemoth
his toast. Although he took note, the cook did not ac-
knowledge his error. Withdrawing a little, folding his arms,
he watched Mr. Twombly devour his meal while Behemoth fumbled his toast. Mr. Twombly complimented Gus's
diner on its ham, the leanness and flavor of it. He finished
all his fried potatoes, then remarked rather loudly that he
thought he might order another of the same. Getting no
reaction of any kind from his friend, he made it official
with the cook. The cook remained folded, waiting for
Behemoth to say.

"Ed?"

"No, nothing," Behemoth said.

The cook went to the set. He did not turn it off but
slightly adjusted its dials, just enough that the eyes tended
to blear and the ears seemed to miss the significant words.
Behemoth looked from the set long enough to watch the

cook return to his grill, then sat stolidly facing the set on these new, rigorous terms until Mr. Twombly was served his second de luxe. His watering eyes blinked briefly at the laden plate.

"Ever been examined for a tapeworm, Dick?"

"No no, nothing like that," Mr. Twombly said, but added at once a good-natured laugh, for he thought he had noticed an edge on Behemoth's voice that might not have been caused entirely by the odious set. Nor did he further praise Gus's fare, was not in fact enjoying it quite so thoroughly. There was almost too much black pepper on his ham, too much of everything. His tapeworm was beginning to suffer from gas.

All were pleased. The cook, noisily scraping his plate, had proved an hypothesis of some kind, and Behemoth had lost all sense of the theme of the story he watched. Once outside Mr. Twombly loyally joined in denunciation of Gus, or of whoever was working for Gus. He took Behemoth's arm and they walked south, two buddies departing from Pith. Glancing back at the town he thought he would remember it with pleasure, although he could not say exactly what for. Perhaps for being the first town in his life where nobody had jostled him, or the first where he had not had to pretend he belonged. Perhaps for being 82 in the shade.

"It must be at least 85 now."

"Yes."

They took off their suitcoats and stood in their vests with their sacks upright at their feet on the edge of the road, their thumbs in the air. The new highway, straight-arming Pith, allowed cars to pass at full speed. Small cause for concern, the sun lay warm on their backs, and they

could see that the drivers were noticing them. Covertly
Mr. Twombly and Behemoth compared stances, facial
expressions, and thumbs. If Mr. Twombly found any
criticism to make, tacitly of course, it was that Behemoth
held his thumb a little too high, too stiff, obliging Mr.
Twombly to elevate awkwardly his own. Stooping for a
pebble, he aimed it across the highway at a rusty cola
sign. With pink pigs rummaging there, he felt himself
momentarily gaseous again. He heard Behemoth's pebble
bounce off the sign, and now the big man faced the
drivers with his hand held a trifle higher than before.

To pass time they made a little game of guessing which
drivers carried facial tissues on the rear window ledges of
their cars. At first they did poorly, missing four out of
seven, but they soon learned the determining factors
involved, notably make and model of car, occupants' ages,
and how closely wife cuddled spouse in front seat. If a
youngish wife touched her husband in a late model car
of average price, they could be sure the tissues were there.
Even if the couple were old and apart, the wise bet was
yes. But if it was the car that was old, it made small
difference how young or friendly the occupants were,
there would be something else on the ledge. The difficult
case was the new Caddy or Pack, for the owners of such
seldom touched, and here there was nothing to go on but
age: the ledges of drivers over forty were bare, but
guessing forty-and-unders was a matter of luck. Working
with such axioms as these, they ran their score up to thirty
and seven by the time a car stopped.

Well that it did, for this car threatened their growing
confidence in themselves. Longish, slightly higher, perhaps
longer than most, it had Greek letters where one would

normally have expected to learn its make. Yet it did not
seem to be a European car, not to say an Asian or African.
Pure yellow of three or four shades, mostly pastel, it
steered from the left, and the owners' gold-lettered names
on the door were in English, Tad and Dolores. Even the
gold hubcaps were monogrammed TaD. No, this was an
American car, a standard design subtly heightened, as
though its owners were anxious to be like everyone else,
but prominently. Dolores, no cuddler though youngish,
lowered her window to take aim with her camera, a big
one which pivoted menacingly on a blue steel stand
clamped somehow to the inside of her door. Were smiles
expected of the hitchhikers? Mr. Twombly and Behemoth
could not be sure whether they were her subject, or pigs.
They grinned, a last-second compromise. Tad, his eyes
looking straight down the highway under the peak of his
cap, allowed Dolores time to develop her photograph.
After a brief consultation she threw it away, took aim
once more with her camera. Mr. Twombly and Behemoth
were grinning less naturally, and this time Dolores did not
trouble to show her picture to Tad, who was not looking.
They could hear the ugly gnash of her teeth as she
screwed a new lens to her camera, several sizes larger than
the other. Mr. Twombly, feeling compassion, called
"Three's a charm," but Dolores was too busy aiming to
listen, or take comfort.

She must have got her picture this time: Tad nodded his
head and his car tossed gravel. He had bearings of some
kind on his hubs, for both TaD's remained horizontal no
matter how fast his wheels spun. Discarded photographs,
swept up in Tad's wash, settled in the dust at the hitchhikers' feet. Dolores had got a fairly good shot of their

bags, another of Behemoth's thumb. Mr. Twombly gave
the latter to Behemoth, but the former he tucked in the
pocket of his coat, nice souvenir of their trip. In surprise
they looked up, for Tad and Dolores were back. She
lowered her window again. "Did you want a ride?"

Smiling, mumbling pleased confusion at her thought,
they picked up their bags and stepped to Tad's car. The
back door had no visible handle, but it opened nonetheless.
Only a dog was in there, and he was curled in the middle
of the seat, apparently sleeping, rather small. Mr. Twombly
let the big man enter first, with his help. Once seated,
Behemoth sought to make room for Mr. Twombly by
sidling his backside, but the dog seemed to have his claws
planted well in the upholstery. With murmured admiration
Mr. Twombly climbed over them both. Settling on
either side of the dog, who even in sleep held his stiff
little tail straight up in the air, they made room for their
bags on the ledge by swiveling the monogrammed facial
tissue rack to one side. Perhaps the wash of Tad's car
closed the door, neither Mr. Twombly nor Behemoth had.
Dolores, seated sidewise with her yellow head propped by
a thin arm, was smiling. Her back was bare, and twisted
so in her sunsuit she showed herself up front like a chick
just stepping out of its shell. On the walls hung two pictures
of dogs, bone-framed. There were adjustable footstools,
and—"Don't turn that on!" Dolores warned. Her
whisper was as sharp as a claw, but now she sank her
chin to the back of the seat and, rubbing against it
placatingly, murmured, "It's Tippy. The light bothers
his eyes."

Behemoth, removing his hand, took umbrage at this
outrageous lie; it must have been particularly hard for

him to accept in view of the fact that Tippy lay with his tail to the tube. Dolores, though still smiling amends, had sunk back in her shell. She glanced cramp-faced at the rigid peak of Tad's cap, and away. A mistake had been made. Outside, landscape swirled by, and on Tad's dashboard a little box recorded his speed, 98, in restful green numerals.

"Got plenty of legroom? Those stools adjust."

"Plenty of room," Behemoth grunted.

Tad never took his eyes from the road, but he had a knack of throwing his words in the face of the man he addressed: "How about the back of that seat?"

Mr. Twombly said, "Very comfortable, thanks."

"If you're stuffy," Tad said, "you can lower those windows."

Mr. Twombly looked at the shining row of buttons beside him, their meanings in Greek. "Thanks."

Without looking Tad pressed one of his own buttons and his window lowered halfway. When he pressed another three or four times, the window started up in rapid inch jerks. A third button closed it at once, and Tad let it remain so. Mr. Twombly, tired of Tad's car, looked out at the fur-lined highway, at the cars eddying by, at a chicken nailed by one leg to the edge of the highway as though experiencing a stroke. Two incredulous cows opened their mouths, but said nothing, having just now discovered that light travels faster than sound. Looking back Mr. Twombly thought he saw a white patrol car swept up in Tad's wash, although he could not be certain. He kept his eyes from Tad's dashboard, for now his numbers glowed red. "How far have you come?"

"Thirty hours," Tad said. "I left Chicago yesterday

morning at five. We had a blowout near Pittsburgh, but I've just about made up for that. It's best to travel clockwise, you can take advantage of the main air currents that way. Of course, you're facing the sun your first morning out, but by the second you're headed west. You're in the shade of the Rockies by sunset. Harvard Mountain, at 14,399 feet, is 222 feet higher than Princeton, 227 higher than Yale. Too, you hit the desert several hours later by taking the clockwise route, sparing yourself a little of that heat. The normal high decreases .75 degree daily on the desert in September. Of course, I'm discussing here only late summer and fall. If you travel in spring you may want to move counter-clockwise, hit the desert on your second day out, that is if you set a higher value on comfort than speed. But you'll want to consider the various disadvantages involved—implicit, make that—and you've always got your air conditioner, of course." Tad paused, and a chill breeze passed through the car. "I hope I understood your question," he said.

"It was 103 in Phoenix a year ago . . ." Mr. Twombly said, but Tad was talking again under his breath. Dolores lifted a thin finger of warning, then pointed it downward at Tippy. This puzzled Mr. Twombly, for Tippy was still curled stiff-tailed in sleep. Up on her knees on the seat, Dolores surreptitiously scribbled something on a bit of paper which she passed silently to Behemoth. Behemoth, scarcely glancing at the note, passed it on to Mr. Twombly. "Tad's writing," it read, and "(Please destroy this)." Crumpling the paper, Mr. Twombly studied his buttons. He pressed number one and the lid of his litter tray flipped; he dropped the note in there, after quietly tearing it first. Now they all sat looking down at their hands,

while Tad kept on doing it, under his breath, so that they
caught only an occasional snatch: ". . . uninformed lay-
men . . . unmitigated fabricators—liars, make that . . .
crackpots . . . lunatic fringe . . . spurious info . . . crap—
make that shit . . . in this writer's opinion . . . standard
reference works . . . chambers of commerce . . . govern-
ment bulletins . . . maps . . . Gerhard Mercator—real
name Gerhard Kremer, 1512-1594, Finn. . . ." Tad
finished at last and hung his dictaphone back on the
dashboard. "Sorry," he apologized to Mr. Twombly,
tugging the bill of his cap. "You were saying, I think."

"I was just saying," Mr. Twombly said, "that the
temperature was 103 in Phoenix a year ago today, 104 a
year ago tom . . ."

"I've got the facts," Tad muttered, cutting in, "all I
need now is the goddam impression." He seemed to be
a man in love with his nerves, with a lover's concern for
their well-being and delight in their excesses, for his next
words, tentative, conciliatory, were addressed to himself:
"Let's try our best not to freak up an interesting project
like this one, shall we?"

Dolores let her smile flit from Mr. Twombly and
Behemoth to Tad. "Shall I tell them?" She awaited his
answer with her blue eyes very alert, her mouth also open
enough to show her sharp teeth, but ready to clamp shut
at Tad's word.

"Oh, why not?"

Released, Dolores pivoted to face Mr. Twombly and
Behemoth squarely. When she spoke it was with a new
purity of enunciation and timing, an almost insane sense
of duty to Tad and the language. "I can tell you something
of Tad's new project," were her words. "His tentative

title is 'Around the States in Eighty Hours.' " Now she snuggled looking back at them with a small, narrow-eyed smile, slowly nodding her head.

"Hm."

"I still don't feel quite right about bypassing Florida," Tad said to Dolores.

Swinging anxiously, "Florida would have thrown you off schedule," she said, with her air of being, with Tad, the last in the world speaking the language.

"I *could* have squeezed it in."

"Florida has been too much done this year."

"Florida is for ballplayers and clowns," Tad said savagely. "You can't make any time down there for the peanuts and bats. Circuses are decadent—atavistic, make that. Of course, baseball is a young sport, if it survives it could reach the level of art. It has human interest. God knows it has symbolism, *that's* been established. What we need is another Lew Wallace, 1827-1905. Meanwhile let's stop all this freaking talk about Florida. Of course, there's always Key West."

"Don't even think about that."

"I understand there hasn't been much activity down there," Tad said, "since that last hurricane ruined the fishing. I just hope those sons of bitches don't revive before I get these tapes off to the press. I don't want to be accused of writing regional stuff."

Dolores put in quickly, "The weather woman said Chloë has been spotted off Cuba."

Tad, tugging his cap bill, said gloomily, "She'll probably miss," but Dolores smiled reassuringly at Behemoth and Mr. Twombly, it was only those nerves.

"Probably I should have prefaced," Tad added more

calmly, "that I'm aiming this one primarily at writers. I admit that candidly. If you happen to follow the culture sheets, you may have noted that *The Apartisan Weekday Review* referred to me recently as 'a writer's author.' Well, if that's what the sons of bitches want, that they'll get. No skin off my ass, like they say, and I don't pretend to consider it bad business. If a writer could reach all the writers in this country he'd have an all-time best seller on his hands—let the lunatic fringe climb on if they will. And don't let anyone tell you we writers could have got where we are now without uniting our talents. The day of the ivory towerist is past—where would he build? Hell, we could elect the next President and three-fourths of Congress, if we'd just stay put for six months. Not that I have any political ambitions for myself, you understand. I simply toss that into the ring for you to perpend if you care to. Mull over, make that. I've been writing since I was five and a half. Hell, I was probably doing it in my diapers, if I could only *remember* . . ." Tad broke suddenly off to grab the dictaphone from the dashboard, and Dolores, Mr. Twombly and Behemoth looked down at their hands until he was through. Very little of it had been intelligible to them.

Tad did not at once resume speaking, but sat waiting for a moment as though for someone else to make a start. But then, "I've noted a certain uneasiness, constraint, among the laity in the presence of writers. That's pure crap! Aren't we all the same lonely, perplexed, rational beasts underneath?" he asked fiercely, tugging his cap. "When I referred as I did to the lunatic fringe a moment ago, I didn't in any sense intend that as commentary on present company. You must believe that. I don't even

know you men that well. And there's so very much more I
would like to know about you both, your names, how old
you are, where you are going. It's just that we find it so
freaking hard sometimes to make contact, to break
through. We see so much, so freaking *much* . . ." Tad choked
and, in a sudden paroxysm of frustration, his palm pounded
the wheel. They looked down at their hands, but Tad
surprised them this time by reaching for his emergency
brake and his tires gripped the pavement. Tad did have
good vision, for no one else had seen the three small boys
playing marbles on the soft shoulder of the highway. "I'll
want to include that," he said to Dolores.

Dolores lowered her window, taking aim, and the boys
looked up puzzled, then grinned.

"Wait till one shoots," Tad said, looking forward, but
Dolores had already taken her picture. She threw the
developed photograph away without consultation, quickly
screwed on her big lens. The boys, bored but still grinning,
had turned back to their game by the time she got them
in focus. Rather proudly she showed this her second picture
to Tad, who lifted the peak of his cap far enough to clap
one palm to his forehead. He took the picture in both
hands and held it before him, his hands visibly shaking.
"Christ," he said softly, "how symbolic can you get?"
Shaking his head he took off his cap to kiss Dolores'
cheek, and she smiled humbly, ecstatically as she filed the
photo away in the glove compartment.

"Christ," Tad repeated, and he was already doing it,
fervidly, by the time they had resumed normal speed:
". . . barefoot boys . . . crudely toed circle . . . 2 π r . . .
microcosm of the universe . . . prized marbles—agates,
make that . . . clack, clack . . . worlds colliding . . .

interplanetary clash . . . shocking view of the future . . .
in this writer's opinion . . ." Tad was panting audibly
when he finished, and they all looked up in silence now,
waiting. "Just don't let anything happen to that one,"
he said at last, rather wearily. "Just be careful of it, baby.
I'll want to use that one on my tour. We always hope to
parlay these projects into a lecture tour," he explained
to Mr. Twombly and Behemoth. "I think this does it. I
think they'll go for this one, especially in the South." His
palm smacked the wheel. "If it wasn't for that freaking
blowout we had, I'd take off for Florida right now, cut
in as far as Tallahassee at least . . ."

"Tad . . ."

"Relax, baby," Tad said, and they could almost hear
him smiling, "we're doing O.K., O.K. If you keep on
improving like this, I'll get you a movie camera."

The next few miles they drove in comparative silence,
Tad not doing it much now, and stopping only occasionally to point out to Dolores something he wished to
include. At one point he realized that he had been
neglecting the taverns and bars, and in a desperate attack
of nerves had Dolores snap some bad ones, but for the
most part they cut through the South without incident,
Tad's peak ever straightforward, the others looking out
their windows for glimpses of the amazed animals, back
quickly at those who had succumbed to amazement.
("There are 211 licensed taxidermists in the States, 1955
count," Tad informed them.) It took Tad almost fifty
miles to catch one bus, and he tooted his admiration as he
passed. Mr. Twombly and Behemoth looked up in time
to see their driver turn forward in his seat to toot and
wave. In Alabama a sharp yip and um broke the silence;

Behemoth had sought to ease Tippy onto the floor. They
hit Arkansas at two, where Tad had to slow down in the
middle for the capital, whose library had only 122,004
volumes, works of reference included. But soon they were
in the hills, cutting through dense timber so regular that
if you could see one you'd seen them all, and here Tad
was able to recover lost time. Here too the billboards were
less photogenic, smaller, less frequent, for there was little
vista and narrow perspective. Tad did not stop until he
got to the top, to a viewpoint. He did not pull off onto the
dirt with the other drivers, but left his car in the road,
and he waved Dolores' camera aside. "No picture," he
said. "This is a lunch-stop."

While Dolores rattled the thermos and cups, Tad took
a cigar from his pocket and, tugging his cap, got out of
the car. A little man, he walked stiff-legged past everyone
to the edge. There he stood with one foot on the rail, his
unlit cigar in his hand, looking straight out to nowhere
under his peak. His sportshirt was loose, and the breezes
tweaking at his shirttail showed sometimes the white
flesh of his firm, narrow back. Dolores had a cup of coffee
all poured and she carried it low, almost running despite
her high heels, among tripods and cameras to Tad. From
the car they could see, almost hear the tense suck of his
lips as he held the steaming brew to his mouth. Dolores,
loose at the ankles if nowhere else, smiled apologetically
at the photographers on her return. At the car she
propped herself with thin arms on the front seat, her yellow
hair drizzling over her cheeks as she hung for a moment
looking down at the upholstery. Some of Tad's most
trenchant writing could be read on Dolores' face. Looking
up bright-eyed, she smiled at the hitchhikers. "Don't

you want to stretch your legs? I'll bring you your coffee. Come on, Tippy."

Tippy, with no discernible transition from sleep, sprang through the opening door, his vulgar little rear hopping behind him. He was no problem. Mr. Twombly got out on his side. "Ed?" Closing his door, Mr. Twombly too walked over to the edge, where he stood a few feet behind Tad at the railing and waited for Dolores to bring him his coffee. Dolores was taking less care with his cup, or was less lucky, for on her way over she bumped twice into tourists, the second time violently enough to slosh Mr. Twombly's coffee over the front of her sundress. This man, instantly angry, relented somewhat when he saw all that had happened. He was going to apologize, but Dolores wringing her bodice laughed carelessly. "It's a throw-away," she said, tripping back to the car. She reached Mr. Twombly this time without accident; Mr. Twombly did not look at his cup as he took it from her, for it was only half full. He waited until Dolores had gone after Tad's refill. Tippy, having finally chosen a tripod, returned to the car, and now Behemoth decided to join them. The big man stood between Tad and Mr. Twombly at the railing, blinking moodily out at the view. Glancing briefly up over his shoulder, Tad slid a little farther along without removing his foot from the rail. He finished his second cup rather quickly and led the way back to the car, where Dolores was just pouring her own coffee back in the thermos. She fingered her camera tentatively. "No picture," Tad said, and they leapt away from the view-point.

Tad seemed anxious to talk about his project again, and perhaps to apologize obliquely for his nerves and whatever little discourtesies they incited him to. "When I said back there that I'm aiming this one primarily at writers," he said, with an air of having brooded uneasily and carefully about this, "I didn't in any sense mean to imply that the engagement of the layman is not earnestly, yes humbly sought after. Christ, I'd be the last man in the world to suggest that the layman isn't the very stuff of our freaking society. You only have to look around you to see that. It's just that we others have to take off, *soar* once in a while . . ." He stopped, flexing and unflexing his hands on the wheel. "I don't expect you to understand that," he continued, quietly, "but it needed saying. I said it. Perhaps I can illustrate. Let us suppose that man had continued so unimaginative, so complacent, so *groundbound* that he had never troubled to discover the wheel, where would we all be now, at this very moment? . . . That's right, on our feet. Well, some of us are not so easily contented, we set our sights higher. But that is not to say that we aren't glad to take the hitchhiker along, if he's willing to join us. . . . Of course, that's a figure of speech, a metaphor, from the Greek. Actually, there's much in 'Around the States' that should appeal to the educated layman, even the unschooled but intellectually curious, and those parts that escape him he can always pick up at my lecture. There's humor and pathos and charm, suspense and pornography. Nor do I overlook my historical setting—I take care of that in my flashbacks. I have a hero." Tad stopped now, grabbing, and they looked down at their hands for the next hundred miles, until he pulled up at a viewpoint.

This time Tad did not have to speak to Dolores, who already was rattling the aluminum shaker. He found his cigar and went straight to the railing, where he stood waiting for Dolores to bring him his double martini. Mr. Twombly and Tippy also got out, Mr. Twombly taking his place a few feet behind Tad. There were not so many photographers at this viewpoint, which seemed to disconcert Tippy but please Dolores. She was able to drink her own martini on her trips between Tad and the car, without jostling anyone; if she spilled a little it did not show for the coffee. Finishing his third cocktail, Tad tossed away his cigar and made ready to leave. Mr. Twombly, sucking his olive as he jogged beside Tad, thought to ask Tad what the make of his car was. "Buigk, of course," Tad answered with amusement. In the back seat Behemoth was laughing heartily at some joke, and Tippy curled himself meekly in the corner, but at a look from Dolores the big man turned it off and handed his empty glass to the front, still laughing and friendly. Tad complimented Dolores on her hairdo. They made it to the Rockies by sunset.

But when sometime later Mr. Twombly woke from a deep, unimaginative sleep, both Tad's hands were beating the wheel and his peak was turned to Dolores. Mr. Twombly's first thought was that the moon must be shining in Tad's eyes, but then he saw that the moon was directly behind them and the car was not moving. Tad's lips were protruding and purple. "I suppose you know what this does to my freaking title!"

"What could it be," asked Dolores, "one of our carburetors?"

"Stop talking nonsense!"

"Well, whatever it is," said Dolores, her voice dreadfully calm, "we'll have to go find a towtruck."

"Will you stop talking nonsense!" But he turned to face his red dashboard. "It's twentysix miles to the next town," he said furiously, feeling his pockets. "Besides, I haven't my wallet, and you know how those sons of bitches are about checks . . ."

He broke off panting while Dolores turned with glistening eyes to the back, shaking her head, trying to smile, *these writers*, but Mr. Twombly was already doubled forward unlacing his shoe. "Will this help?" he asked Dolores.

Tad looked savagely at the cheque in Dolores' hand. "What am I supposed to do with that, forge it?"

Uncapping his pen, Mr. Twombly took back the cheque. This time he gave it to Tad.

"I'll need some freaking identification."

Slipping his watch from his vest Mr. Twombly handed it over, back foremost.

"Well . . ." Tad put Mr. Twombly's watch in his pocket, looked around the car quickly and vaguely. "The heater won't work," he said, not looking at anyone, "but you can still lower those windows." Without looking back he got out of the car, muttering under his breath, ". . . I'll just freaking well have to invent," and in the high beams of the headlights Mr. Twombly and Behemoth watched Tad and Dolores walk off down the highway, Tad carrying his tapes and Dolores her camera, ugly little Tippy testily hopping behind.

"What time is it, Dick?"

"I don't know, Ed."

"Maybe I can find out," said Behemoth.

What Behemoth found was a travelogue, re-released for the Have You Seen This series, of interest to them because it showed them where they had been and where they were going. A pity Tad had to miss this, for it opened with hurricane Beulah savagely belaboring Florida. From there it panned, a travelogue of disasters, to the Mississippi flooding, small towns in Texas being swept off by tornadoes, New Mexico burning, Navajo sheep dropping dead of the drought on the Arizona reservation, Las Vegas, Death Valley. Behemoth had seen it before, but never in color. Perhaps it was the color that, sometime later, prevented their immediately noticing the flashing red light at their backs; too, Tad's dash was still glowing danger. But when light flooded the tranquil expanse of the Pacific as seen from the lofty hills above Hollywood, turning it purple, they did at last look behind them. Someone knocked at the window.

Mr. Twombly, studying his buttons, called "Just one minute." He pressed number two and his litter tray closed. Number three swung his door open. "Oh, sorry."

The policeman kept his full weight against the door as he stooped for his flashlight. "Having a little trouble in here?"

"Well, these buttons are in Greek," explained Mr. Twombly.

"Is that right?" The policeman, still holding Mr. Twombly's door, reached for the front one and it opened. Now he threw his weight against this door, pointed his beam at Tad's steering column. "Which one of you is Tad Bunyan?"

"Neither one," said Mr. Twombly. "Tad's gone after a towtruck."

"Is that right? How long ago did he leave?"

"What, Ed, an hour ago?"

"An hour or two," Behemoth grunted.

"Anyone ever tell this Tad it's against the law to leave a vehicle in the middle of the highway?"

"I don't know. I don't think so."

Releasing the emergency brake, the policeman attempted to push Tad's car off the highway, could not budge it. He straightened up gasping. "This Tad a relative of yours?"

"No no, we just met Tad and Dolores this morning."

The policeman held his flashlight on them. "You don't look like hikers," he said. He slammed the front door and went back to his car, where they could hear his radio harshly barking at him. He was back in a minute, rapping on their window again. "What make is this car?"

"It's a Buigk," Mr. Twombly called.

The policeman returned to his car, and now his radio was barking more harshly than ever. When he came back he did not ask them to open the door, but flashed his light briefly inside, calling, "They'll have a towtruck out here as soon as they can."

"Tad'll probably be back any minute," called Mr. Twombly.

"Is that right?" The policeman settled himself against the side of the car, looking in. The late feature had already started.

When the towtruck arrived forty minutes later, the policeman rapped on their window, nodded his head and pointed at it. He went to the front of the car with his flashlight, directed the drivers in their backing and filling. He had them raise and relower the hoist, and he played his light on them while they fastened their hook to the bumper. When they had everything right, he came

back to the window. "I'll follow," he called. Mr. Twombly
and Behemoth, thanking him, settled themselves for the
last half of the feature as the car swung away. Tad was
right, the seat did ride rather more comfortably so,
tipping backward.

At the carpound, several miles on the far side of town,
the policeman ordered Mr. Twombly and Behemoth out.
Number three did it. He helped them into the back seat
of the patrol car, snapped off his radio when it resumed
barking. The first miles he drove glumly reticent, but
then, "Wonder what happened to Tad?" he asked,
chuckling.

"Hm, I wonder."

The policeman helped them out of the patrol car in
front of the station; his footsteps, louder than theirs,
sounded lonely behind them. Inside, he stepped around
and in front of his charges to the desk sergeant. "Here's
that pair I reported," he said firmly, tossing his report on
the desk.

The sergeant had already examined the pair. He
continued his writing. "Ever find out the make of that
vehicle?"

The policeman stepped aside to hang his hat on the rack.
"That vehicle's been tampered with," he muttered.

There was real cruelty in the sergeant's glance at the
thick, exposed nape of the cop's neck. "Well, it's late, we
can talk in the morning," he said to Mr. Twombly and
Behemoth, his voice sounding pleasant. "No charges,
but you two can spend the night here if you want to."

"Well, if there's no charge . . ."

"You'll have to leave your bags in the safe."

Giving him their bags, they were led away, past their

cop now bent over the water cooler, by a frisky little
man with a head like a much used baseball, gray hair
cropped close to his hide, ears and nose flattened. He
climbed the stairs two at a time, despite the late hour, and
unlocking a gate swung it back with élan. "My pleasure."
Turning on lights, he seemed to enjoy too the rest of his
inmates, their groans and curses and grievances, even their
snoring.

"Who asked Clinker in here?"

"Does that mother-loving Clinker think it's the
mother-loving morning already?"

"He's likely to get fired for wasting the mother-loving
electricity."

"Where did he pick up those two—at a circus?"

"What kind of an hour is this for self-respecting mother-
lovers to be squiffed?"

Clinker led Mr. Twombly and Behemoth to their
bunks, chuckling, and on his way out he rapped protruding
feet left and right with his keyring, much enjoying the
howling. He turned off the lights and stood in the dark,
tenderly whispering, "Goodnight, sweet dreams, mother
lovers."

When their eyes had grown accustomed to the dimness,
Mr. Twombly and Behemoth peered at their bunk, each
bed neatly made up with a mattress, blanket, and pillow.
Clinker had turned back their corners for them. They
took off their shoes, and without discussion Behemoth
made a cradle of his hands and helped Mr. Twombly up
to the top bed. Mr. Twombly listened to Behemoth sink
sighing onto the lower, then slipped under his blanket.
But the air at this level was warm, vaguely urinal, he
could imagine bugs crawling, and he lay on top with his

face in the bend of his elbow, spreading the blanket up
over the pillow as a precaution. In the few hours left,
bugs might not find him. Now the full room adjusted
creaking, groaning, cursing to sleep, warmly human but
for a light steady tapping on metal, like a message.

"Who's beating the mother-loving radiator pipe?"

"It's my mother-loving wife," was the answer. "She's
got insomnia."

Mr. Twombly whispered "Goodnight," and hearing
Behemoth's guarded grunt fell asleep smiling. He awoke
stiff and uneasy, partly shivering, but the sunlight,
exotically striated, lay warm on his feet, a welcome, a
promise. The air smelled purer. Rolling to the edge of the
mattress, he drew the blanket over his shoulders and
stretched his stockinged toes to the sun, but stopped
suddenly short, caught twisted and awkward by the steady
gaze of the next man on his level. It struck Mr. Twombly,
he did not know why, that he had been watched for some
time, perhaps all night, shamelessly contorting and
grinning and bubbling. Although the man was rolled
snugly in his blanket, there was no sleep in his eyes, and
he held his flat cheek just off his pillow, above the
triangular green stone of his earring. The heavy, string-
bound plait of his hair lay rigid on the pillow behind
him. There was neither malice nor cordiality in his look,
pure observation. Perhaps he had simply been waiting
for Mr. Twombly to awaken, for now he slipped out from
under his blanket and swung his legs over the side of the
bunk. His look still on Mr. Twombly, he dropped easily
to the floor. He did not stoop for his shoes, but beckoned
to Mr. Twombly with both of his hands. Mr. Twombly
uncovered himself and swung his legs over the edge. He

looked for help, but the man merely beckoned again, stood back waiting. Mr. Twombly, fascinated by the man's calm audacity, dropped to the floor almost lightly. He looked in surprise at his legs, feeling pleasure in their tone and resilience, and he saw Behemoth blink wonderingly at him as he followed his stealthy guide past groaning bunks to a window in the corner. The man pointed to himself, then to the window. He raised the window a few inches, and tapped on it with a broad, calloused finger. "Tonight."

Mr. Twombly also pointed at the man and the window. "You? Tonight?"

The man, seemingly pleased to find that Mr. Twombly spoke the language, nodded his strong, slender head enthusiastically. "Me," he continued, opening the window a few inches farther. "You?"

Mr. Twombly peered out the window at the gravel drive two stories below. "How will you get down there?"

"*I* don't know," the man said. "I need more blankets."

"What about these bars?"

"*I* don't know," the man said. "I'm skinny." He grasped one of the bars, bending it sidewise; it was cut through at the bottom. Together they turned to look back at Behemoth, who lay on his bunk blinking at them. "He can hold our blankets," said Skinny. "When we get down we'll send him up a bottle."

Now Clinker was opening the gate to take them to mother-loving breakfast, and they went back to their bunks for their shoes. Behemoth, strong-whiskered again, jabbed Mr. Twombly's back furtively, but Skinny was talking. "You have to go to their breakfast," he advised, "but you don't have to eat it." He beckoned, and they followed him to the tail of the line.

"Everything satisfactory?" Clinker wanted to know on their way by.

"Fine, thank you."

"Well, just stay away from Skinny there, and you'll be out of here in no time," Clinker assured them.

If Skinny heard this, they received no sign from the firm, arching plait poised like a blackjack over his collar. There were about two dozen men and boys in the line, and on the way to breakfast they filed through the bathroom, bringing the stench out with them into the corridor. Their breakfast was already waiting on a scarred, palm-stained table, for each man a deep square pan with a handle, a beaten tin cup, and a spoon. Skinny, despite Behemoth's desperate try at evasion, sat between Mr. Twombly and Behemoth at the darker end of the table. "Don't eat those oats," he warned, "that's where they put their saltpeter."

"Why saltpeter?"

"*I* don't know," Skinny said, breaking bread. "That's how they take the man out of you. Watch out for that coffee—sometimes they fool you."

Whatever they put in their oats was not sugar, but Mr. Twombly nevertheless found himself hungry. Behemoth, though nervous, was starving. They emptied their pans, swabbing the last gray scum with their bread, washed bread down with weak, sour coffee. They even looked hopefully toward the kitchen for seconds, but Clinker called to them from the corridor. They were wanted at the desk by the sergeant. Skinny, his dry hands resting on theirs, detained them an instant. "You only have to give them your names," he whispered, "and your census numbers."

"Skinny, you talk too mother-loving much."

Skinny said nothing, nor looked, and hurrying ahead of them in the corridor Clinker was vastly delighted. "I always look forward to weekends and Skinny."

The sergeant looked up to wish them goodmorning. "This is Mr. William Russell," he said and pointed his pencil at a tall relaxed man, who nodded. "Mr. Russell's a budget counselor from Chicago."

Mr. Russell swung his briefcase from his right hand to his left. "William 'Bill' Russell," he said, shaking hands with them both. He transferred his briefcase, and his long gabardined sleeve, wrinkled but new, swung out with a card. Behemoth passed the card to Mr. Twombly; it confirmed all that the sergeant and William 'Bill' Russell had told them, also listing his telephone numbers.

"Mr. Russell had quite a time following Mr. Bunyan from Chicago," said the sergeant.

"He was a tough case," 'Bill' Russell admitted, his straight teeth flashing attractively. "But I guess it was my own fault for trying to do business with a writer." Well tanned, his hair sunbleached or graying at the edges and his bland handsome face just beginning to bloat, he carried his wide right shoulder somewhat higher than the other despite the weight of his briefcase. Actually the briefcase, strapped to the last hole, appeared at second look too empty to offer any appreciable ballast. "All I need to know," he said easily, "is what were Mr. Bunyan's intentions?"

"Tad's intentions?"

"What were his plans?"

"Well, I think he was writing a book," said Mr. Twombly.

"No, I mean what did he plan to do with that car? Did he hope to meet his back payments or did he just outright abandon that car?"

"Tad didn't say anything about that," Mr. Twombly said. "He said he was going to find a towtruck."

"Well, I guess that does it," 'Bill' Russell said to the sergeant, or to Tad and Dolores. But he was looking at Mr. Twombly and Behemoth. "O.K. if I speak to these gentlemen for a minute, sergeant?"

"Go right ahead," said the sergeant.

Tilting his head, 'Bill' Russell swung across the room. Mr. Twombly and Behemoth followed. Dropping his briefcase on a chair, 'Bill' leaned relaxed and lopsided against the wall, his hands in his pockets. "You boys doing a little traveling?" he asked, lowering his voice familiarly not surreptitiously.

"Yes, we are."

"Great country out here," 'Bill' told them enthusiastically. "The desert and the canyons and all. Ever think of seeing it by car?"

"Well, we've seen some of it by car . . ."

"No, I mean in a car of your own, your own car."

"Oh. No no."

'Bill' pushed himself from the wall, and now he did speak rather furtively, as if afraid that anyone overhearing might think he was losing his mind, or his profit. "I could let you have that car for fourthousandninehundred," he offered. "You could make small monthly payments out of your pensions."

"We don't have . . ."

"Save me the trouble of hiring someone to drive it back to Chicago."

"We don't drive, ourselves," put in Mr. Twombly.

Arching one eyebrow, his right, 'Bill' Russell spoke to Mr. Twombly. "Be a pleasure to teach one of you."

"No no. I'm sorry."

'Bill' Russell looked at them a few seconds longer. Then, shrugging his shoulder, he bent to sweep his briefcase from the chair. No skin off his ass, as Tad would have said, he wasn't the loser. "All yours, sergeant," he called with a wave and a smile, and pivoting shouldered his way out the door.

The sergeant was listening to a stout man in khaki and a conical hat, and otherwise anachronous, like an overgrown boy scout just breaking his pants. Warm and excited, he might have lost his troop in the desert, or found a new way to make fire. The sergeant listened sympathetically, sympathetically nodded, but the stout man was hoppy. As soon as he saw grinning Clinker march in with his grinning charges he hopped to the door stiffly, as though his plump knees would unbend just that far.

"All right, on the double, you mother lovers," Clinker cried. A gun flapped at his belt, and a blackjack. Chuckling, he prodded his men through the door, prodded Behemoth and Mr. Twombly along with them. "Into that lorry."

Stumbling into light, they scrambled blinking and cursing up on the lorry, its bed low and uncovered with facing wooden benches like a poor-class sightseeing bus, the license plate confirming an earlier suspicion of Mr. Twombly's. "New Mexico, Ed."

"I thought so."

The town was also slung low, as though down on its knees to the sun; all save the jail and the stucco bank genuflected. The houses, half-hearted without garages or chimneys, sat each on four bricks behind broken wire fences, their naked clay yards at first sight indecent. But nobody cared! Mr. Twombly, curiously excited, wished to see more, but now the leavetaking sign waved on its nails, the five gas stations were passed, and there was nothing. There was the highway: it cut west without pause through strange country, an intruder heading for cover. On either side, the land lay knobbed and rubbed over by time, like old knees and elbows; what growth survived was ingrown and kinky. Even the thinly wired telephone poles appeared stunted. Sullen horses and cows kept their eyes to the ground, while overhead a more prosperous buzzard swung at ease on proud wings, a potatochip bag in his beak. Everyone laughed, where was the party? The wind jiggled the stiff grins on their faces.

"What are we going to, Dick, an uprising?"

"*I* don't know, Ed. I doubt it."

"I suppose these are friendly scouts," Behemoth whispered, "but let's watch them."

The scouts all kept together on their side of the lorry, never looking at the others seated opposite. Neither did they look much at Skinny, who rode half-seated on the back end of their bench. They laughed whenever he said something amusing, but always they added some comment, in their language, and laughed more at that, as though cutting out the others while discouraging Skinny. It almost seemed that they felt ashamed of his riding on their side of the lorry, felt that he belonged across with the others in point of age, conversation, and disreputable clothing. Their shirts and their jeans were newer and brighter, their boots higher heeled, their belts more elaborately carved, and they did not wear earrings. The smooth backs of their necks, round beneath their black hats, looked as though they had all been clipped by the same barber a few hours before. They seldom spoke English, preferring their own more equable language; it went well with their soft, full-fleshed countenances, from which Mr. Twombly imagined fine faces like Skinny's would someday be carved. Skinny, observing Mr. Twombly's interest, slipped over between Mr. Twombly and a gray-bearded man who was sleeping. "This is a break," he told Mr. Twombly and Behemoth, "we get out of jail and they pay us."

"Where are we going?"

"*I* don't know," said Skinny, "wherever it's burning."

They turned on the bench to watch the cars passing, the pale women and children staring up through their windows. Skinny raised his hand to a yawn, or a war-whoop, and three small boys ducked their blond heads to the seat. "They think I'm a longhair," Skinny said, rather loudly. "I just keep my money up there." He looked around the lorry as everyone laughed, the scouts laughing again at some comment.

They tossed on their benches as Clinker swung the lorry onto a dirt road escaping north from the highway, but thick, acreous dust muffled their laughter. Even Skinny was quiet. Here the prostrate land was more than ever deformed, humpbacked, and tumorous, while ahead in gray clay prodigious hippopotami lay basking. The road, discreetly bypassing gray backs which appeared to be breathing uneasily, followed the edge of a small, narrow canyon. A few old grasses and shrubs cringed in the dry wash at its bottom, but halfway up its sheer side a gnarled juniper leaned out horizontally, strongly green-needled. Someone long ago had somehow climbed up to that tree, or down, and chopped off two of its branches. To the north, flat cliffs rose in dense haze, like empty pasteboard boxes stacked carefully for burning, and low in the south hung the sun, sullied and anxious, half delirious with love for this land. The scouts alone seemed untroubled. Dusty, perspiring, they sat in their row less self-consciously now, looking quietly ahead with whatever thoughts and memories, as though the slowly moving lorry were bringing them home from a dance and at any minute now they would be parting. A gun cracked, cracked again, and they watched a tin can hop twice on the desert.

"Split pea soup, mother lovers," cried Clinker.

Grinning they drew their eyes back from the desert, sat looking down at their dusty boots or their hands until the plump man in khaki rapped the cab window and shouted. His other hand he held outside, widely gesticulating. Ahead they could see what excited him, someone had ignited those boxes and they were not empty but packed with explosives, sending up a tight brown cloud to fill the empty sky. As they looked the lorry made two sharp turns, throwing them forward and backward, backward and forward, and they straightened to see their guide's excited face already pressed flat to the cab window and knew that now his catastrophe was behind them. They did not look but clung to their benches with their hands and the backs of their knees, for the lorry was spinning again. They waited for their guide to turn forward.

"What is it, Dick, a mushroom?"

"No, Ed, more like a melon."

In just those few seconds the brown cloud appeared to have hugely expanded, or they had climbed higher and could see it more clearly. Surely they were not very much nearer. Whenever the lorry seemed aimed for a minute toward the cliffs, the road would turn to the left or right, and they would be shying away, if not leaving, so that it seemed only the stout man's determination and Clinker's innate giddiness kept them trying. Yet they were climbing: a few junipers and cedars were growing, in possible places, and soon a taller, more regular tree which Skinny called piñon. "You'll want to pick about fifty pounds of those nuts before you go into town next week," he said. "I'll tell you where you can get seventy cents a pound for them."

The scouts leaned far out over their side of the lorry trying to snatch cones from the trees, which now grew much more thickly and closed out the view in every direction but up, where the dark haze of the sky could be seen through their top branches. There was a new density to the air, a sudden congestion of odors, partly of the dry earth and needles under the trees, partly of the trees themselves and their clear, running juices, perhaps their nuts too, but more disturbing to the men was something foreign being brought to them by the wind, pressing warm against their faces even though they were in shade. It was as though they were being pressed down and sealed off from the sky, if that heavy brown above the tops of the trees (much taller now and with cones the size of potatoes) was truly the sky; for they came suddenly into a clearing and found it no brighter, the compressed air around them

as unnaturally dark as before. Birds shrieked, horrified.
That was no clearing but a fleeting view of a cremated
world, its charred skeleton still standing in the tidily
heaped ashes of its still smoking vitals. The man up front
shouted, and everyone looked ahead to a hot red glow
among the trees, all cheering as Clinker with a whoop
aimed the lorry full speed toward hell. In the murky
distance between, singed men lay with their heads propped
against trees, looking up at the lorry without curiosity.
Other men, less weary, waving, stood nearby with axes,
and Behemoth mumbled something about Indian
prisoners.

"No no, Ed . . ." but just then a uniformed man stepped
onto the road in front of the lorry, and everyone rocked
toward the cab as Clinker jumped on his brakes.

"Are you crazy?" Clinker and the uniformed man
yelled it together, and the uniformed man stepped up to
the lorry to say it again, "Are you crazy?" Then he walked
around to the other side of the cab, where their guide had
already hopped to the ground. He looked at their guide,
and he looked at the back of the lorry. "Just what exactly
the hell do you think you've got in there?" he asked, and
under his breath he asked something else.

"You said to bring everyone."

"I didn't expect you to lose your little brown head!"

"I thought maybe we could use them for cooks."

"We don't need any half-assed cooks," cried the
uniformed man. "We need fighters! You can trot right
back for some more," and to Clinker: "Don't run away,
I have some brown-drawered prisoners for you." Turning
about he stalked off in the general direction of hell,
Clinker trotting after him eagerly.

Their guide walked around the lorry, slowly and with scarcely any hop in his stiff knees, beckoned to Mr. Twombly and Behemoth. Skinny helped them climb down, whispering to Mr. Twombly, "Be with you as soon as I can."

As they approached the stout man in khaki, he turned and walked a few paces away, tugging at the tight parts of his pants. When he faced about he did not look either Behemoth or Mr. Twombly in the eyes, but looked somewhere in the middle distance below and above. "I guess this burn isn't as bad as we thought," he told them, scratching himself. "You two men can hang around and drive back with Clinker and me." He started to leave but spun and came back. "I'm sorry," he said, eyes to the ground. "Thank you for being ready to help us." They accepted his apology and his thanks with earnest nods of their heads, and shyly he nodded back. "All right, everybody down," he called. "There's some fighting to do."

The men climbed down from the lorry slowly, coughing, and gathered in two separate groups, the scouts beneath a tree, the others in a clear space a few yards away. Their guide moved over and stood awkwardly between. He made some comparative remark about breakfast oats and the fine lunch they would have, but he had little heart for humoring them and no one on either side seemed to hear. Mr. Twombly looked away to see Skinny lurking alone among some bushes behind their guide's back. Skinny beckoned, and Behemoth reluctantly followed Mr. Twombly over there.

"This is our best chance, before they ask for our numbers," Skinny whispered, crouching low. "Follow me." He crept a few feet away, but looked back in surprise

at Behemoth's um. Creeping back, he took the big man by
the sleeve, drawing him down. "Listen, friend, I know
this ranger from last time," he whispered. "That fat
boy's all right, but that ranger's a man that will keep you
fighting four sleeps and then throw you in jail for taking a
nap. Anyway, you can make better money picking nuts.
It's easier too. That fighting's hard work. You might have
a heart failure," he said. "Follow me."

They followed among bushes, away from the road,
hurrying to keep Skinny's faded jeans in their view. From
time to time Skinny would stop, crouching low with one
arm and hand extended stiffly behind him, and they would
wait without breathing until he waved them on, veering
away from the sound of a voice or an ax. Sometimes he
would not turn off but would point with his finger, and
they would sometimes look back in time to see the
disappearing tail of a deer or a rabbit. Skinny seemed to
know exactly where he wanted to go; whenever caution
forced him to the left or right, he would turn back at first
chance. Soon it did seem a little less dark up ahead,
gasped air passed the throat less searingly, and except
for the crunching twigs and cones underfoot all the
noises of man were behind them. The cries of the birds had
lost a little of their terror, they sounded now broken and
garbled, as though shock were setting in. A black and
orange butterfly sat pursing its wings on a wild orange
flower, while a few feet away a colony of ants made a
home with no more than usual haste, as though for
eternity. Skinny himself drew up in a stand of young
pine, straightening his back. Smiling he waited until Mr.
Twombly and Behemoth were breathing more easily,
and then he took their right hands one at a time in his,

holding them with a gentle, lingering pressure. "Joe Tsosie," he said.

"Dick Twombly."

"Um, Ed Brown."

"I'll show you where the good nuts are," Skinny said. "They're on the way to my hogan."

"Which way are you going?"

"North," Skinny said, pointing. "Over north toward Shiprock."

"Hm, we were heading southwest," Mr. Twombly said, nodding his head in the general direction. "We were going to Phoenix."

"Phinix?" Skinny said it absently, as though he misunderstood or did not believe them. "Do you want me to show you those nuts?"

"Well, we probably ought to be getting on our way pretty soon. What do you think, Ed?"

"Yes."

"Maybe I'll see you next week again?"

"Well . . ." But Skinny was already moving away, the easy swing of his body under the faded shirt and jeans somehow indifferent, sadly private.

"Thanks for your help," Mr. Twombly called, but Skinny did not look back and they watched him trot off to the north, keeping to the bushes and trees.

When Skinny had passed out of sight, they climbed up on some rocks to see where they were. They could not tell much, except that they were in forest. They determined that the darkest brown was west of them, judging by Skinny, and agreed to walk south for a while. They could veer southwest when they got to the desert. Their way was downward, among tall trees and a shiny green under-

growth that made their throats ache with the promise of a
brook. Every few steps they stopped to look on each side
and listen for bubbling water. But the earth everywhere
was as dry as the rocks, drier, and the only sounds they
heard were of the birds and the warm wind in the trees,
or occasionally a cone bounced on branches, hit the ground,
and rolled a short distance on dead needles. One fell
close to Mr. Twombly, spilling some of its tiny nuts at his
feet. Heedless of the trouble he knew it could cause, he
cracked a nut with his teeth, half munched and half
sucked its soft flesh up front in his mouth. Behemoth,
seeing his pleasure, cracked one himself. After sucking
awhile, they spat out the bony bits that were left. They
ate three or four more in this way, the sweet juices soothing
their throats, their desperate thoughts of a brook. They
decided to take along a supply; it might be some time
before they reached water or lunch. Mr. Twombly
collected the nuts that had fallen, while Behemoth took
his from the tree. In half an hour of picking and munching
they each developed a little bulge in one pocket, though
not big enough for the other to notice. Patting their
pockets they went on, for above the smaller piñon trees
ahead they could see that the sun was already moving
toward the west.

The cliff, where it broke so suddenly before them that
they found themselves leaning forward five paces from its
edge and teetering, had no road going down or even the
possibility or need for such communication. Its wall
dropped crumbling away to where the desert caught it a
thousand feet five hundred years below, the past uncovered in the prodigious dig of future archeologists who,
workdays, would take you to the bottom with their flying

time machines. Even from the top through the haze a sightseer could make out their findings, a few roughly rounded clay hogans, scattered but inextricably related by their small eastward openings and the thin trails which bound them together, here and there interlacing other more prominent trails that led as crookedly from nowhere to nowhere else, a few slanting stakes stuck at random in the sand, bearing no visible wires or present purpose, like so many arrows left in the hide of some tawny beast abandoned by careless or frightened hunters, one hopeless white windmill amid a sprinkling of petrified horses or cattle, dog-sized, and several more reassuring objects that seemed to be the picked-over carcasses of black, or blue, sedans. The sightseers walked along, not near the cliff until they came to a recess in its wall where collapsed rock and dirt made a less precipitous drop to the flat below. Hoofed animals had traced a path down this, and one old-shoed man had used it coming up. Behemoth went ahead, a sturdier buffer in case the follower slid. They soon discovered reasons why that man had not returned the way he had come, their path was lost in a great heap of fractured rock so that they found themselves climbing backwards down higher and higher steps, onto ledges that slanted narrowly away from dark caves and cracks. Looking down before they dropped, they often saw small brown lizards with their tensely nodding heads raised high above poised front legs and visibly beating hearts, staring glittery-eyed into a crevice or cave. Usually when feet hit their ledge they would duck into these dark places, but sometimes they chose to escape instead to a lower ledge.

"What was that man saying at the zoo about Gilas, Dick?"

"He said we'd find them in Arizona, Ed. This is probably still New Mexico."

Choosing a widish, crackless ledge, they sat down to rest and eat some nuts. From this halfway point they could see smoke rising off a hogan thinly, as though the occupants were warming mid-afternoon coffee or tea. Before another they made out a darker smoke, perhaps a squatting mother and child, and in the distance the brown, inquisitive whirl of a dust devil such as Behemoth had seen one Sunday in his livingroom. Still farther off another column of dust moved not quite so fast, but more directly and flashing sometimes in the sun, toward them in a line parallel with the cliff.

"Ed, could that one be a car?"

"I think so," Behemoth sucked. "I think I saw some blue on it."

"Where could they be going or coming from? Just look out there."

"I'm looking."

"Wherever they're going, they've got a long drive ahead of them."

"I suppose they could get somewhere, if their gas holds out."

Mr. Twombly laughing patted the big man's back. "Maybe if we got down in time to meet them we could find out where and how far it is."

"Let's try it, Dick. That's the only car I see down there that runs."

So, spitting the last uneatables of their nuts, they climbed again, down ever more difficult stairs on which in the growing heat ever warier lizards sat watching deeper and gloomier caves. But a last high, monsterless step dropped them onto a hill of dirt and gravel that sloped several hundred feet to the desert, like tailings from the richest sand mine in the world. Now they slid and jogged downhill, into the hot wind, stopping once to take off their coats and their flapping neckties, roll up their sleeves. Their blue car was moving faster than they had thought above, but the distance was also greater, and they reached the dirt road below the cliff five or ten minutes ahead of it. They sat waiting, their coats folded beneath them on the hot sand, until their car drew near, then stood up and brushed themselves and raised their thumbs. Their car, a new pickup truck, shiny blue, clanked and sputtered hoarsely as it rushed by, and the three men in front faced straight ahead as though thus they hid their sidewise eyes. The women and children behind stared back more openly. Mr. Twombly and Behemoth watched their truck speed off, turn into dust, and then they dropped their hands to look at one another. But even before that harsh motor had passed out of hearing they heard another one and turning saw a much older truck sliding down the slope behind them, not far from where they themselves had come, its brakes fiercely biting steel and its red fenders still flapping a little in the wind, as though it had flown down from the edge. They did not raise their thumbs this time but stood watching this pickup slide screaking to their road and howling stop. They made no move until one of the grinning men up front waved them to the back, then quickly throwing coats inside Mr. Twombly climbed up and somehow hauled the big man aboard as the truck took off.

Settled facing on the sandy bed with the tailboard rattling under their bouncing arms, they peered through heavy dust at the other occupants. The two women looked far away when they found that they were watched, but most of the children traded level stares until one felt that he had been singled out especially. Thus it was best to look in a general way, at hands and hair and colorful clothes. Mr. Twombly cleared his throat, and the older lady looked woefully aside at him. She had five or six dollars in quarters sewn to her blouse around the neck, while the younger lady had almost as much in dimes. There must have been some rare ones there. "Phoenix?" Mr. Twombly called.

Both women and all children, even babies, looked at him.

"Phoenix?" Mr. Twombly asked again, pointing up ahead, and the old lady looked out there. "You go to Phoenix?"

"Oo."

"This truck?" He pointed down to the truck this time, and then ahead: "Phoenix?"

"Oo."

"This truck . . . to Phoenix?" he asked, pointing several times.

"Oo. Oo. Oo." The old lady was nodding her head with impatience now, and repeating it loudly and rapidly, "Oo. *Oo.*"

"Phoenix? This truck? It does?"

Shaking her restive head she raised one corner of her blanket to her mouth with a wrinkled hand, for she was giggling and her bright gums showed. She ducked her head down to the young woman's shoulder, giggling, and some of the children ducked giggling too.

The young woman was still serious; there was a note of anger in her voice. "What you want to know?"

"Ah, are you going to Phoenix in this truck?"

"Truck? Where is truck?"

Pointing, "Here. This red truck. This *car*. This *pickup*."

She nodded dubiously, "Oo."

"Is it . . . going . . . to . . . Phoenix?"

"*I* don't know," she said. "I guess so. Truck! Truck! I never did hear so much words before!" Shaking her head she looked out to the desert, the old one too very sober now, and silence settled on all of them, with only veiled, indignant glances that jumped away when caught. The older children scooped sand and watched it trickle from their hands, while one of crawling age explored the wildernesses of the women's skirts, performing with the ponderous movements of all fat babies and elephants. The two smallest were mostly hidden in cradle boards. The old lady's was dark and meager-armed, but the younger woman's had immense biceps and elbows that folded into rosy rolls of flesh. The old lady must have owned the one she held, at least she was suckling it. Whenever the pickup hit a good rock or dip she would pound the cab, and the driver and his son would look back to wave and laugh. The driver wore an old felt hat and an old mustache, like that Bloodhound boy's blown thin and wild. He had turned the pickup onto a fainter road that strayed from the cliff, most often to the south and west, and behind them they could see the ominous brown melon vastly swollen in the sun, but intact again and separate, a thing to view, its disturbing pressure easing off even though its odor still clung to them.

Mr. Twombly soon learned this driver's ways. Whenever he had a choice he took the narrower, fainter road, sometimes if roads were equally poor he made his own

until he came upon one that suited him. Once briefly
they were on a highway with white posts and signs ahead,
but their truck was staggering, steaming frightfully and
they turned off before the writing became legible, onto
a narrow sheeptrail winding up a rocky hill which their
quieting truck attacked with joy. Mr. Twombly glanced
uneasily at his friend, but Behemoth was sleeping soundly,
so soundly that he was unaware that his glasses had
jiggled from his nose into his partially open mouth. Mr.
Twombly reached over to replace them on his nose, but
at the next good bump they jumped off again. He
adjusted them once more, and now everyone was watching,
not with smiles but solemnly, really interested to see
whether those glasses could be properly secured. Nor did
anyone smile when they jumped off a second time. Gently
Mr. Twombly removed Behemoth's glasses, bent their
earbars carefully into tighter loops before replacing them.
Everyone waited for the glasses to be tested by three or
four resounding bumps, and at the fourth or fifth they
looked at one another and to Mr. Twombly in a con-
gratulatory way.

But now he heard a titter, the old lady behind her
robe, and turning saw Behemoth grumpily awake and
feeling for his glasses, removing them, adjusting their
loops more comfortably. The big man replaced his
glasses and closed his eyes. There was a short tense wait
for that next bump, then Behemoth was sitting up and
blinking hard at tittering. But he laughed good-naturedly,
taking his glasses from his mouth, and now everyone was
silently shaking and pressing forward over tightly folded
arms. It was a deep, deep laughter that threatened to
burst the sides or choke the throat before, at last, with pain,

it reached the mouth, and it died as hard, in scarcely
lessening explosions that until the very last seemed about
to return in greater force and overwhelm them all, the
old lady most of all out of control and dabbing frantically
at each of her eyes by turn as though hoping to save at
least one of them from being washed away.

What finally sobered her, thus all of them, was watching
one of the little boys crawl over to Behemoth and, with
the support of the big man's knee, grab at the glasses on
his nose. She said something to the child, but seeing
Behemoth remove his glasses for the child's inspection she
smiled and sat drying her eyes with slow, elaborate dabs.
A little girl was making O's and X's in the sand, and Mr.
Twombly showed her how to play ticktacktoe with them.
The rocking pickup sometimes shook their sand, so he
got out his pen and they played for a while in his pocket
notebook. When she tired of this, he drew a turtle for her;
she took his pen and drew him a horse, a leaping horse
that tossed its mane and tail for joy. By signs he let her
know that hereafter the pen was hers, and he gave her a
few pages of his memo book to practice with. The ladies,
who had been watching in silence, now uncovered their
babies for Mr. Twombly and Behemoth, jiggling their
boards to wake them up, and they even permitted Mr.
Twombly to examine their coin displays. The younger
woman's collection was a common one, but the old lady
had a fine 1896S. He was trying to explain her good
fortune to her, with small success, when the pickup hit
something big, hit it again, and slid broadside to a
screaking stop.

When dust had settled they could see a black and white
heap beside the road, and the women got to their feet

and excitedly remarked. The driver trotted back and stood over the animal, watching it writhe and thrash the ground with its sharp hooves. He looked helplessly at a flock of sheep and goats making noises at him from a hill above. After a final, lingering shudder the dying animal stretched its legs out stiff, front and back, and now the driver turned to the truck and grinned. "Atin," he called, stooping to cut the throat with his big knife. Grinning he dragged his goat back to the truck by its hind legs, and hung it so to the tailboard, where Behemoth had liked to prop his arm, while all remarked. A little goat, its broken neck lay limply on the slanting bumper a few inches off the ground, at which it seemed to stare longingly. Some of the blood dripped over the license plate, but the driver sent his son up front and wiped that off with the rag he brought, giving special attention to the 1940 numerals. Then he stood up and patted the animal's back, grinned at Behemoth and Mr. Twombly. "Klizzie," he said.

"Klizzie?" Mr. Twombly said.

The driver nodded approvingly. He smelled even more strongly of smoke then they. "You speak Navajo good," he said, and patting the goat once more he returned to his place behind the steering wheel.

The brown melon was no longer visible. Either that burn was under control by now or it was hidden behind the last hill they'd climbed. Mr. Twombly worried only a little about where they were going, for unlike Tad this driver seemed to like to keep the sun always in front of him. He even pushed his hat back on his head, welcoming blinding light, and drove on contentedly so with his front fenders flapping and his goat bumping hollowly behind. Once he stopped on the giddy lip of a narrow

canyon so high that they could not hear the family wagon
splashing across the stream below, nor the colt splashing
doggedly after it, but clearly heard an axle squeak and
the driver shouting encouragement to his team, the
distant past restored but imperfectly. Inverted next, as
from the bottom of a draw they looked up at a stone two-
storied dwelling built snugly into a concave cliff, about
midway up, almost completed now but for front steps,
front door, and window glass. It looked out at a grand
red mesa and lesser rocks eccentrically carved and
windowed by the wind, a view not sought by the trading
post where they stopped for gas and pop. This square
stone building crouched heavily beside its pump, with
gray-paned windows barred and kitchen yard solidly
fenced against blowing sand, brown grass, brown sheep,
brown men. If there were any larger settlements, their
driver avoided them. He did not stop again until a high
mountain stood in his way and the sun had sunk behind a
quickly forming cloud that grumbled quietly to itself as it
prodded the mountain top with tentative lightning forks.
The camp he chose was in a grove of four dead white
trees with bare, crooked limbs that looked as if the lightning
had planted them.

Everyone climbed down, the women by turn taking
both cradle boards while the other climbed. Everyone
watched the driver cut down the goat and cut its stiff
belly with his knife, then all got to work, the children
collecting firewood from the ground, the women rolling
rocks into a pile, the grown son chopping forked branches
from the trees with vast energy. Mr. Twombly and Behemoth helped the children pile their wood. By the time the
driver had his goat prepared, they had a good fire going

for it and a sturdy rack for him to hang it from. While
they sat around the fire waiting for the meat to cook, the
women cleared the sand in front of them and fished
knotted cloths from their bodices. Untying knots they
spread their cloths upon the sand, and arranged the
spoons and babyfood on them with care, critically
examining the pictures on each of the sample packages.
They fed their babies zwieback and apricots, from time
to time offering milk to wash these down. Presently the
driver rose to turn and test his goat, prod it with his
knife, and he seated himself a little closer to Mr. Twombly
and Behemoth on his return. "Klizzie," he said, and
smiled.

"Klizzie," Mr. Twombly said.

"Ve-ry good Na-va-jo." He took one of the sample
packages from the old lady's rag, and his battered thumb
pointed out the words on it, pausing at every word for
Mr. Twombly to repeat it after him, "Klizzie . . .
Klonnie's . . . Oldest . . . Wife." They went over it once
more, "Klizzie Klonnie's Oldest Wife," and then he
pointed to himself. "Here's my name," he said. "Klizzie
Klonnie—Many Goats." He returned the old lady's
sample and took another from the younger lady's cloth.
He read it over privately once with his broad thumb
before showing it to Mr. Twombly. "Here it is," he said,
pleased to see that he was right. "Lu-cy Ma-ny Goats."
He held the tiny box in both his hands, read it occasionally
while he talked. "My old wife is a fashioned one," he
said. "She likes to keep the Navajo. We use the Many
Goats. I'm Many Goats, my wife is Lu-cy Many Goats.
Here's Alfred Joe, Robert Joe, Bobby Joe, Minnie . . .
A-da-line . . . Kee Joe, Tom Mix Joe, Woody Joe, Betty

Jane, Johnny Joe . . . Lu-cin . . ." He broke off to say something in Navajo, and the young lady answered him. "Lu-cin-da, Thomas Joe. All, all Many Goats except that afashioned lady there. She's fift'five," he said. "That's her first kid she got for ten year ago, her first afore since Woody Joe. She had this Lucy Many Goats since almost thirty year ago when she had her husband number one. She give me twelve kids afore this Thomas Joe, four atin. I don't know how many she give this number one, maybe two or three." He looked up from the little package suddenly at Mr. Twombly. "That's a damn good old lady, isn't it?" he asked, smiling but with a new brusqueness in his voice.

"Yes, it is," Mr. Twombly said.

Nodding, Many Goats lifted his hat to smooth the strong gray hair beneath, and from sitting position he raised his stocky body to his feet with his hands still above his head. "Lucy Many Goats already give me six kids, two atin," he said. He dropped her sample box on her cloth, stooped brusquely to tousle her baby's hair. He tousled the old lady's baby too. "And that's how it is with me," he said, going over to test the goat.

"Your wife has a fine 1896S on her blouse," Mr. Twombly said, nodding at the old lady, "worth plenty money," and Many Goats turned to smile and nod with pride, he knew, he knew. "She's fift'five," he said.

Behemoth cleared his throat. "Are you going to Phoenix in this truck?"

"Phinix?" Many Goats turned to look at laughing Lucy Many Goats, said a sharp word to her.

Lucy dabbed her eyes, shook her head a little bit. "It make you crazy to think of with so much words," she said.

Many Goats said something else, and now the old lady replied at length while he listened patiently but with some surprise. "My old lady say she hear Phinix burn up afore some time ago," he said, glancing at Mr. Twombly and Behemoth doubtfully. "I don't know where she hear for a thing like that. We go to Los An-ge-les. You want to go to Los An-ge-les?"

"No, we go to Phinix," Mr. Twombly said.

"My brother Notah live in Los Angeles," said Many Goats, "with his wife. They relocated him out there afore three times ago. Notah always come home pretty quick afore, but this time he stay out there since five months ago. He like to work for the airplanes. Lots of pesos and beer out there. I tell them to relocate me out there, but too much kids and wives, they say. So I guess I take my family out there myself this time and wait to them send this check of this fire to me. And that's how it is with us."

"Do you go through Phoenix on your way to Los Angeles?"

"Phinix?" Fumbling in his back pocket for some papers there, Many Goats nodded at Mr. Twombly absently. "I go pret-ty close. Pret-ty close. I drop you out there. This card I get from my son, Billy Joe. I send Billy Joe to school in Utah, you know where Utah is. This is the first letter he send from there. He write pretty good for Navajo." Mr. Twombly took the grimy card and unfolded it. The neat printing was addressed to "Mr. Many Goats, Lukachukai, Arizona," and "Dear father," the message read, "I like school and I like the teachers pretty good. I like to play basketball. But I don't have much money for pop and candy as the other kids. I hope you can send me my money right the way. I hope I won't have to

remain you a can of this. I love you mother and father.
Your ever son, Billy Joe Many Goats."

When Mr. Twombly had finished, Many Goats took
the card from him and read it over with his thumb. " 'I
hope you send my money right the way,' " he read, still
proud but much annoyed. "He know I don't get money
right the way. Billy Joe know that. He know that since a
long time ago." Refolding and tucking the card away, he
turned to jab the goat crossly with his knife. "He know
how slow it is," he said.

The goat being ready, he cut it down with quick
backhand flicks, caught it before it hit the ground by
plunging his blade into the rump. His son stuck a stick in
the open mouth and swinging carefully together they laid
the goat on other sticks. Now it was time for Klizzie
Klonnie's Oldest Wife to do her work, and Many Goats
stood, arms folded, watching her divide the meat with
the ax and knife. Lucy Many Goats served the meal,
handing the men their portions first, the children next. Mr.
Twombly and Behemoth got mostly ribs, some flank, with
jutting bones to hold in either hand as they picked off the
lean smoked meat and the crisp smoked fat, all delicious,
every bite. They paused to watch the head passed round,
each member of the family reaching in for a bit of warm
brain and other things which they licked off their fingers
and washed down with pop. When his turn came, Mr.
Twombly took sparingly of this delicacy. Behemoth
watched him lick. "It's good," Mr. Twombly said, but
seeing Behemoth gray in the fading light he passed the
sadly staring head to Many Goats. Many Goats offered
it nose-first to Behemoth, who put up his hand with
fingers widely spread. "Hand too big, you eat mine," he

said, and watched wretchedly smiling while Many Goats reached in, scooped out, licked. Many Goats got the last of it, and Behemoth watched the head roll off across the sand, lean finally against a pop bottle to nuzzle a trim black leg bent at the knee above nicely pointing hoof. Other bones lay scattered all around, picked out now by a flash of light from the mountain top, now glowing in the brief dark it left. Many Goats stood up, using his hands this time, and looked at the black sodden cloud. "We better go afore it get too wet up there."

Even as they ran hooting to the truck a damp wind swept down on them, huge drops splashing their faces freshly and dotting the white sand they sank onto, harshly slapping the truck as it lurched off. They still threw up thick dust behind, but soon the narrow, winding track ahead shone in their lights like two wet strips of isinglass. Many Goats attacked the first steep grade with throttle out, as though hoping momentum would carry them all the way, but before they had climbed a hundred yards their tail was swinging freely from side to side like some big-hipped woman swaying to voluptuous music among the trees. Many Goats rapped on the window violently, and everyone crawled to the rear of the truck, huddling against the tailboard between Mr. Twombly and Behemoth. Now the truck did not sway so much, but their speed was lost and their wheels dug deeper and deeper into the mud running beneath them like heavy mucilage, until soon they seemed to be creeping backward on spinning wheels. Many Goats shifted to a lower gear and they fought on, inch by inch, digging one for every two they climbed. Pelting rain had almost snuffed out their lights, but every few minutes a lightning flash showed them a little of the steep way ahead, a little of the empty space on the near edge of it. Exclaiming underbreath they huddled closer against the tailboard, shivering, drenched, all of them, except perhaps the quiet babies beneath their mothers' blankets in their cradle boards. The grade was suddenly steeper and they knew by the frantic way Many Goats raced his motor and by the way the wheels slung mud that they were fighting to a certain standstill, sliding sideward if anything, and they listened to the motor fade, spark up, fade again as Many Goats tried to rock the truck back on the road. Finally the motor died and lights blinked out. They groaned as Many Goats climbed down. Almost they would have wanted him to keep on trying, settle the question one way or the other, now, rather than leave them hanging on this ledge all night. What could he do with his right rear wheel sunk to the hub, with all that water coming down, the crackling, almost constant lightning showing him how it was with them?

What Many Goats did was stand stiff-armed in the rain, with lowered head, discussing the problem with his son in shouts. Now his son ran to the cab and the motor raced while Many Goats leaned against the tailboard with all his grunting strength. This did no good. He yelled angrily to his son, banged the tailboard with his fist; when finally the wheels stopped spinning he stepped back scooping mud gingerly from his face and shirt, shaking it like wet turds from his fingertips. Now the two men stepped heavy-footed across the road, crawled up a greasy bank and out of sight, came skidding back with armloads of brush. They lay down in the mud and spread their branches beneath the truck. Next they trudged up the road for rocks, making many trips before they had a foundation that would hold their jack above the mud. Their jack was an old-fashioned one and they had to change its position frequently, laboriously reinforce with rocks each grudging inch it raised the truck. At last they had the right wheel free enough to work their chain into the slimy groove beneath; with their shovel they scraped off the mud-clogged wheel, but still had to wire up a six-inch gap between links on top. They wedged flat stones beneath the wheel before letting down the jack, then dug up those larger rocks driven into the mire by the weight of the truck. These they spread before and beside the wheel, dropping another in the sucking mud as soon as one sank out of sight. They did not pause to look at their handiwork, but tossed their filthy tools in back and stamped into the cab. Many Goats got his sputtering motor going, assaulted his pedal criminally while he found his gears. They had two feet to go until the edge, and they felt themselves creep sidewise about half this far, before their spinning chain gnashed rocks and bucked them forward to the road.

Many Goats, taking advantage of his good start, drove hard ahead, not slowing or giving way to rocks or curves or branches or anything, until a floundering pickup blocked his road. This pickup had been coming down the hill, but now it was heading up: water ran in the deep groove it made when somehow it spun around on this narrow trail and came to rest with right rear wheel in space. The driver had placed branches in front of his other wheels, big rocks behind, and now he sat half inside his cab with his door flung wide, toeing his throttle faintheartedly. He seemed glad to come back and discuss his situation with Many Goats. Now he ran forward waving, laughing, hallowing as Many Goats cautiously

nudged up behind his truck. With pleased gestures he
indicated how well their slanting bumpers matched, then
climbed inside and gestured for Many Goats to bash him
one. Many Goats did, and the frontmost truck sailed
across the road. Now Many Goats was stuck, but he had
a towchain under his seat and the man he'd helped gladly
pulled him out, a fair exchange. He shouted jovially as
Many Goats untied the chain, and waving spun off fast
the way he had come. Many Goats, heaving his slippery
chain into the truck, also laughed and waved. "Mark
Twain," he said, the kids exclaiming and the old lady
cackling beneath her robe.

The mountain was dry on its other side. At least the
rain had stopped and the road was firm, only sweating a
little in the hot blast of air that seemed to rise from a great
stove below. From time to time they dipped into foggy
hollows, puddled and clammy like giant pores that
sheltered them briefly from the heat, but mostly they
drove on top among weak thin trees, and quickly dried.
Mr. Twombly, resting his head on the roughly blanketed
shoulder of Klizzie Klonnie's Oldest Wife, seemed to ride
on a sandy, turbulent cloud far above a piteously smoldering world on which he could only look down helplessly,
having left his paper bag, his aspirin, and his surgical
instruments, behind in the sergeant's safe. He had thought
to sprinkle wet sand on the world below, had leaned over
the edge to take good aim, when somebody shoved his
head back up. It was Klizzie Klonnie's Oldest Wife, she
was waking Behemoth too. They had come to a highway
with white posts and lines on it, and Many Goats stood
on his runningboard. "Phinix down this road," he said.
"We turn off here."

"Phinix down this way?" Mr. Twombly asked.

Pointing, Klizzie Klonnie's Oldest Wife prodded Mr. Twombly and Behemoth from behind. "Oo. *Oo*," she said.

They climbed down giving thanks, saying goodbye to everyone, and stood at the edge of the highway watching Many Goats bounce up a rocky trail on the other side, his old wife standing straight in back and pointing out the way to them with slow, sweeping gestures to the right.

Soon the truck was gone and the only light they saw anywhere was from the moon, but they started down the highway as she had directed them. They walked slowly, taking off their coats, for although it was late, midnight at least, the air was as hot and close as if still heated by the midday sun.

"I wish we had your watch," Behemoth said.

"Ah, Tad needed it more than we did, Ed. Besides, it didn't work."

"That wasn't what I was thinking of."

"What? That down payment, Ed?"

"Um."

Patting his back, "Don't worry about anything, we still have a sound foundation," Mr. Twombly said.

"Look, Dick! Lights."

"Lights . . .?" Behemoth could see them around the bend before Mr. Twombly could, streetlamps scattered thinly over the steep hillside and swinging high in the heat, very old and white. They stood out starkly because there was no neon anywhere, nor one glowing orange window shade. Windows, if not boarded up, were dark cavities in faulty, forward-tipping walls which the swaying streetlamps stained unevenly. Yet most doors were on, and black and silver shingled roofs looked tight beneath the moon. Mr. Twombly and Behemoth, walking as softly as possible on the cobblestones, heard their footsteps pounding ahead of them through the tall, crowded houses on either side of the narrow streets. Other sounds became prominent when they stopped, vines scratching dryly on old latticework, small animals hurrying on boards, unthinkable creaks. They went quickly past an empty, sidewalked block, its cement and plaster buildings crushed in heaps, past the barbershop, the barefaced movie house, the gravestoned bank with its glowing night deposit slot. A few prewar cars with inflated tires were parked carelessly along the curb, their backsides protruding into the street.

"Ed. Where is everyone?" Mr. Twombly whispered.

"*I* don't know," Behemoth said.

They stood behind a gray hotel four stories high, its front door swinging open in front of them. Without touching the heavy door, they peeked inside. Its lobby was empty, dim, its rocking chairs and cuspidors pushed to the wall. Slipping in, they crossed on tiptoe to the creaking stairs, paused halfway up, went on abreast. They did not try the first door they saw but tiptoed along the hall until they found an open one, number 25. There were three beds lined up inside, two with mattresses, a bureau, and a rocking chair. They left the door open after them and stood whispering encouragement before they tried the other doors. One was locked, but the second opened to wooden hangers and folded comforters. They crossed to the window next, stood looking through that blasted hole at the empty block, the tight streets on the steep hill beyond, where nothing moved but the sparse, swinging lamps. Returning to the closet for comforters, they piled them on the tipsy rocking chair. The unmattressed bed was between the other two, and they carried a mattress to it from the farthest one. Now they spread out their comforters, lay down fully dressed but for their shoes. Probably they could have found sheets somewhere, but they were too tired to look. They settled on their backs, looking around and whispering. Enough light came in the window for them to see all walls, and now and then a coolish breeze came in to stir the heat.

"We left our bags in New Mexico," Behemoth remembered now.

"No matter, we can grow beards," Mr. Twombly said, and felt his chin.

"Um."

Mr. Twombly turning on his side, toward Behemoth, tucked his legs more comfortably, and closed his eyes. "You already have a nice start," he said.

It was the sun that woke them in the morning, not so much the brilliance of it as the heat pressing in on them. Their comforters were soaked, their iron bedsteads hot, and they could feel the plaster wall without touching it. Even the floor was warm to their stockinged feet. There seemed to be a little activity below, no visible people but a few newer cars, a dog, an occasional garbage pail in front of a house with an antennaed roof. They put on their shoes, folded their comforters, and went into the hall. Their room was next to the ladies' room, and they wandered through the dim corridors until they found the door for men. The cold water ran, a little brown, but there was no electricity. In a shower stall they found a sliver of yellow soap, and they lathered themselves from head to waist, drying with their handkerchiefs. Behemoth's whiskers still were red, although the hair of his chest was white; he was beginning to look like a buffalo. They went downstairs feeling much refreshed, the air in the lobby almost cool against their damp cheeks.

Someone was passing their hotel, a stooped old man hobbling along with a fancy folding rule in his back pocket. He had already passed the door when they came out, but he turned to look at them. Mr. Twombly raised a hand. "Pardon me, is this Phoenix here?"

"Phoenix?" the old man said, fingering his long gray beard. "Phoenix is a hundred mile further down the road. This is Harding here."

"Ah, where is everyone?"

"There hasn't been but a few of us around for the past fifteen years," the old man said, shuffling toward them a step or two, "not since the mine gave out during the last great war. We're just staying around to keep the city up, waiting for the people to return. Harding will rise again," he said, assured. "Meantime a man can live for sixty-seventy dollars a month. Food is high, but rents are cheap. The climate's nice, and we've got our shelters ready-dug all through this hill. That's the hospital up there on top, they'll open that again someday. That was the high school, the grammar school, the church, the theater there, the mortuary, the barbershop—they'll open that someday too." His crooked finger pointed out everything there was, finally getting around to the one remaining restaurant. Thanking him, they started off. He wanted to shake hands with them. They shook his hand and walked on to the restaurant.

The lady inside watched them until Mr. Twombly grasped the knob, then turned away to rearrange her big home-made donuts in their bowls. "Hello," she said, her back to them. Her heavy brown hair was rolled in big donuts too. She faced around when they had chosen stools. "What will it be this morning, hot coffee or cold soda pop?"

"Hot coffee, please."

She served them donuts automatically. "I didn't see your car drive up."

"We came in last night," Mr. Twombly said, "by pickup truck."

"Visiting friends in Harding?"

"No no, just passing through."

"Sleep in your truck?"

"No. We stayed at the hotel last night."

"At the hotel?" She took a donut from a bowl, examined it for flaws. "Are you going to open the hotel?"

"No no."

She put the donut back, saying, "I keep thinking someone will open the hotel again. The floors and walls are sound, all it needs is a little windowglass."

"Oh, I don't know. Those windows let in the heat, let in the breeze at night."

"That's right," she said, but she watched them a little queerly while they ate. They ordered two more donuts, and now she didn't watch so hard. She spoke to them when Mr. Twombly paid. "Those donuts all right today?"

Delicious, they both assured, and she smiled as though she were used to that. "Is it all right if we prowl around town a little while?"

"Prowl all you want. Nobody'll mind but the ghosts," she said.

They knew she watched them cross the street, pass the

theater and the bank. Inside, the door of the vault was open, and there was dust on the tellers' stools. Already it was 99 in front of the barbershop. Avoiding the ruined block they climbed steep wooden stairs, a shortcut to the next street above. In the daylight they could see that some people were trying to keep Harding up, cobbled streets were clean, behind one painted fence an old woman cut dead hollyhocks in her tiny yard, green grass grew around the mortuary. Climbing past the brightly windowed church, they came to a more abandoned street with no antennas or garbage pails. Here lizards rustled in tall dry grass, and Mr. Twombly and Behemoth picked their way through thorny vines that made a wilderness of the dangerously rotting stairs and the broken, unpainted porches. Some houses were partially furnished behind locked windows, almost livable, with beds and animal pictures and phonographs. Many had large fireplaces and spiral stairs. In one bedroom closet they saw a child's pedal car, like new but for one scratch on its blue paint, but too large a toy to travel with. It looked still in style. But in other places the mountain had slid through open windows, or caved-in walls, so that they looked into a wallpapered kitchen or diningroom half filled with rocks.

They found a house with the kitchen door unlocked. This was one of the furnished ones, with even a few dusty groceries like salt and baking powder on a shelf above the sink. The pretty calendar on the kitchen wall was almost all used up, its one remaining page for December 1943. There was a fireplace in the livingroom, a bookcase, and an easychair. They tried a Rudy Vallee record on the phonograph, but it played too loud and they quickly turned it off. Mr. Twombly went first up the circular stairs, in case boards were weak. He waited at the top for Behemoth to catch up with him. All the upstairs doors were closed, and Mr. Twombly opened one.

"Ed!"

A man stood inside the door, holding a board in both his hands above his head. Trembling he held it so, staring with bright eyes at them, and in that instant of uncertainty Behemoth crouched and lept. There was swift, almost joyous willingness in the big man's leap, wonderful to see. His big left arm swung first, next his right, two grunts were followed by a double crunch. Blood flew, the heavy board clattered to the floor, and the man settled slowly on top of it.

"Nice work, Behemoth!" Mr. Twombly cried. Circling the man, he got to his knees behind. Grunting, Behemoth too sank down. This man was a heavyweight. His hair was curly, rather long, and even comatose he had a vital, impatient face that would not hide behind his golden, bleeding beard. Hastily they bound his limp arms with his belt behind his back, bound his feet with Behemoth's belt. Now they sat down to rest and wait, Behemoth smiling rather tranquilly, as though some long rankling hurt were at last allayed. He stood up when the man began to stir, and took his board from under him. Opening his eyes the man looked up at Behemoth, who blinked down steadily.

The man turned his head aside, shaking blood from it. "I should never have let you get the jump on me," he said. "I thought maybe my wife had sent you here." He lifted his head to look at Behemoth. "She didn't though."

"No, she didn't," Behemoth said.

"I didn't think so," the man said, sinking back. "She

would have been here by now, if she gives a damn. I wrote her three days ago."

Behemoth asked, "Why are you hiding here?"

The man flashed him a bright, bloody smile. "Because I'm a murderer. Don't look surprised. I murdered twice," he said, hunching his right shoulder to his nose. His dirty white shirt came down red. Now he tried to wipe his eyes, but he could not reach them, and neither Mr. Twombly nor Behemoth made a move to help. "I might as well tell my story," he said, smiling his vivid smile, "since I've got such a breathless goddam audience. It was a stinking night like tonight will be, exactly one month ago. . . . Hell, I might as well begin with the first act," he said. "I've been married twelve years, I had three kids. When I first saw my wife I was John Barrymore at twenty-three, with a dance-on part in a musical. My wife, poor wretch, was on vacation from Wichita. Her father, being a slightly deaf old bastard, bought front-row seats. Well, five years later I was still John Barrymore at twentythree with another dance-on part. My wife had given me five full years of it, and she was just a little weary of waiting alone in the apartment at night, or coming to the theater and scarcely seeing me. I won't pretend that I was loath to leave the Great Gray Way, hell, I was fed to the throat with it. We had little Joan by then, two more on the way, although at the time of course we were only expecting one. So we ran away to Phoenix—I had some friends in the little theater there, and it was almost as far as New York from Wichita. I went to work for the telephone company, the first work I'd done since my army days. I rather enjoyed it for a while. That first year they let me climb around in the sun, but then those pastel phones

came in and one of the vice presidents heard that I was
playing Macbeth in a local show. A pity to let that gift
for gab go to waste, he thought. Oh, he was a canny
executive, as you can see. Still, they gave me a little raise,
Adele seemed happier than she had been for years, and
we still owed the doctor two hundred dollars for the
twins. Besides, they let me have my evenings free, and I
was a big-assed star down there. Most of the male leads
out here have asthma and sinus and are unreliable. When
they get excited they're liable to have attacks. I don't
mean to knock myself. I'm an actor, I know that. That's
what makes it hurt so much. I'm an actor, I can act!
Christ, I even sound like one—John Farraday." He
flashed his smile at them. "Say that name out loud just
once."

"John Farraday."

"See what I mean?" he asked. "Well, Mr. Martin
Muir saw it too. He happened to catch me in 'The King
and I' while vacationing, came back three nights in a
row. The next week he came back to see me in 'Private
Lives.' Hell, I'd been propositioned by plenty of crazy
scouts and agents in my day, but Mr. Martin Muir is a
big-time producer with soft pigskin shoes, and he strokes
his horny glasses when he talks. He can make you feel like
Apollo of the Belvedere. I couldn't say no to him, ruin
him, let his quarter-million dollar musical go on the rocks.
But I did have the prudence to wait until I received his
second airmail letter from New York before I made plans
to move. Preliminary plans, I still didn't give notice to
the company, but told a few close friends. We didn't tell
the kids. I waited until I got two more letters, both
airmail, both urgent and a little desperate as though Mr.

Martin Muir feared some other producer would buy me up before rehearsals began that month. A final meeting was to be held any day, to settle salaries and dates, and of course I would hear from him immediately afterward. It goes without saying, I was delirious. Adele seemed transported too, as though she'd been suddenly relieved of guilt, a guilt I'd imposed. I gave notice to the telephone company and my landlord; we were already mostly packed, but now we could bring suitcases and boxes out from hiding in the closets and beneath the beds. We had been renting the same house for seven years at an exorbitant price, always finding reasons for not buying, I guess waiting for this chance. It came just in time, even Adele admitted that, another year might have been too late. My hair was falling out. Here, lift it up in front. Go on, lift it up!" They did, and saw how beneath the heavy curls his hairline receded sharply to a peak. There was a little grayness too, although they would not have noticed this if he had not mentioned it. "You see . . ." he said, but stopped to play his tongue across his teeth. Twisting sidewise he turned to look down at the floor, and he was laughing quietly. "Look what you did, you broke my tooth," he said. They could see it on the floor.

"It doesn't matter," John Farraday said, letting his head sink back. "Don't bother to apologize. That last letter was mailed on July 3rd, at 5 p.m. Almost sixtynine days ago. I don't know what happened to Mr. Martin Muir. At first I was afraid he had fallen sick, but I think even a sick man would have asked someone to write by now. Maybe a firecracker blew him up—I could forgive him that. Maybe I should have written him on printed stationery, like his, maybe my typewriter ribbon had grown too old for him. Maybe I should have signed my name in green ink, I don't know. Whatever it was, I don't want to hear. Not *now*." He had been staring up at the ceiling while he talked, but now he closed his eyes as though the dim light were blinding them. "It wasn't really so bad, I guess, those first weeks. I was still expecting to hear from him immediately afterward, I was looking for a letter every day, a telegram every night. I went back to work—at least I was near the telephones. I just didn't talk to anyone. The really black days started on August 1st. My doctor thought I was working too hard, he suggested phenobarbital. I preferred whisky though. I wouldn't take a drink until I got off work at five, but then I'd take them as fast and many as I could. I drank mostly away from home, because it drove me nuts to have Adele sit and watch me with that crushed look on her face that said she couldn't blame me for doing it. That's how it was that night a month ago, I'd been drinking at home, not very much because the kids were having an 'entertainment' at summer school and Adele couldn't go. Joan was a sunbonnet babe or some such thing, but John was a poppy and Betsy was a buttercup. I'm sure of that, because they wore clever paper hats that made them look surprisingly like the flowers they were supposed to represent. The auditorium was stinking hot and I slept through most of it. I felt terrible. But I was sober by the time the lights went on—the entertainment was much too long—I was just feeling sick. That's why in the stationwagon going home I made the kids shut up. They were full of exciting things to say about the entertainment, but they shut up when I told them to. I remember waiting for one of them to start talking again, so that I could shout, but not one of them said a word. We were driving along that way beside the canal, without even the radio. I still don't know what it was: maybe I hit a rut in the dirt, it had rained the night before and the road hadn't been scraped. Maybe one of the kids jostled my arm, but I don't think so, they were so awfully still. Maybe I fell asleep . . . I still don't know. What I remember is seeing the brown water suddenly under us and how loose the steering-wheel was, and then how surprisingly cool the water felt. I can't remember the kids saying anything, or crying out, but I can remember turning to them as we went down and seeing them already starting to kick. All the windows were open and the water came in at once. Joan was beside me on the front seat, and I had to fight to make her come out past the steeringwheel. She hadn't held her breath, and she was choking when we reached the top. I swam with her over to the bank, and rolled her onto it. The current must have been stronger than it seemed because when I got back to the middle and dove I couldn't see the stationwagon anywhere. I had to come up for air. I swam upstream about ten yards and dove again. I was still almost ten yards away from the stationwagon, but I swam to it underwater rather than go up again. John had locked the back door earlier, as I'd taught him to, so I had to go in my door and reach in over the seat to the kids. They weren't kicking anymore. I had to hold Betsy down on the front seat with my knee while I groped for John, to keep her from floating back in again. John's foot was stuck, and by the time I got him my air was gone. I thought surely I would have to breathe before I could get them both over the steeringwheel, but I wrenched hard with what strength I had and they both came free. On the way up I finally had to take in water, but when I reached the surface I still had hold of them. It seemed a terribly long time before I had the strength to turn their faces to the air. Somehow I pulled them both over to the bank with their faces up, and Joan helped me pull them out. I laid them on their stomachs, side by side. I gave them artificial respiration, straddling both of them and pressing down on them one at a time, for more than two hours before I gave up. Joan was on her knees yelling at me and she tore my shirt, but I shook my head. I'll never forget her crawling over to them, snatching the twins up by turns, and shaking them."

John Farraday had been watching his audience eagerly, seeming always ready to stop if they once looked away, but now it was he who averted his face as though he suddenly hated them for sharing his pain. But they had not asked him for anything, and helplessly they waited for him to go on. "They call it manslaughter," he said, "of the second or third degree. My lawyer says they wouldn't even call it that if only one kid had died, maybe even if they hadn't been twins. I disagree with all of them —it's murder or it isn't anything. I'm not a butcher, whatever else I am. I swore I wouldn't stand that charge —let them give that to Mr. Martin Muir. So here I am. I thought Adele would follow me. I wrote her three days ago, thought of course I would hear from her immediately afterward. Well, I give her until this afternoon. If she isn't on today's bus, she doesn't give a damn. I'll turn myself in and the hell with it. Five lives will have been lost, not two. . . . But I suppose they already are. I suppose it's too goddam much to ask any woman to come up that hill with one kid beside her, the kid a little taller and quieter but otherwise as though everything were just as it was six years ago. I don't imagine Joan will ever forget that quiet ride. I know I won't. But what really hurts is remembering all the times I made cracks about there being too large a crowd, in front of all the kids. You know the cracks you make when you have twins around . . ." John Farraday stopped and now it was as though the disturbing vitality in his face were being drowned by the water that flowed down his cheeks from his staring eyes, into his ears, and he would do nothing to save himself. Almost they would have liked to see the terrible flash of his smile again, but his lips were too slack for use. Gently they turned him over, untied his arms and legs. They watched him sit up to put on his belt, and Behemoth put on his.

"What can we do for you?"

He almost smiled at them. "You can get me something to eat. I can't go on much longer on water and radishes." He took his wallet from his pocket and handed a dollar to Behemoth. "Get me a can of clams and a half gallon of milk. No, skip the clams. A can of meat—be sure it has a key. You'll find the grocery down past the grammar school."

Outside, the sun hit them like a heavy blow on the head and shoulders. They stopped to remove their coats, continued on. They found the grocery, in better days a Saveway store but now bare-shelved behind. Mr. Twombly cashed a cheque, and they bought lunch for themselves as well. They climbed back up the hill by a different street, Behemoth carrying the groceries beneath his coat. John Farraday had closed the door, and this time Behemoth opened it. He was still sitting where he had before. He did not speak while Behemoth drew the groceries from the bag and lined them up in front of him. They watched him tear open the milk carton and drink the cold milk chugalug. He scarcely touched the meat, nor did they themselves have much appetite.

John Farraday took out his watch. "It's two-thirty," he said. "The bus comes in at three. Will you go down and see if she's on it?"

"Of course."

"She won't be," said John Farraday, "but if by some chance she should happen to be, don't mention my name. Just ask her if she got the map."

"All right," they said. They rose to leave.

"She'll have black hair," he said after them, "if it isn't gray. . . . The same with Joan."

The heat seemed a little less intense this time, they were better prepared for it, and going down the hill they walked in shade wherever possible. They stood near the bank, across from the restaurant, the lady inside watching them until the bus stopped between. It seemed a very long time before any passengers got off, and then there were only two. They could not tell the color of their hair beneath wide hats, but they recognized Mrs. Farraday and Joan by their black clothes. They waited for the bus to pull away before they crossed the street to them. Mr. Twombly spoke. "Did you get the map?"

Mrs. Farraday had been looking up the hill, but now she looked at them. She would have been a lovely woman, with just a little makeup on. "Oh, yes," she said, and felt inside her purse.

"That's all right. We know the way."

They led them up the hill by yet another route, a longer one that took them around the mortuary and behind the church. When they reached the deserted street, Mrs. Farraday touched Mr. Twombly's arm. "Is he all right?"

"Yes, he's been expecting you."

"I didn't get his card until yesterday. The mail from here must be terribly slow, and they have only one bus a day."

Mr. Twombly nodded. He and Behemoth led them across the porch, pointing out the dangerous boards, and up the winding stairs. The door at the top was open wide. They stood aside to let Mrs. Farraday and Joan enter first, but already they knew that the room was empty now. They stood behind them at the door. John Farraday had packed the groceries away, and he had torn a corner from the bag and left it beneath the board. Mrs. Farraday stooped to pick up the note. She read it over to herself, and then she handed it to Joan. "I'm going to give myself up. I love you both."

Mr. Twombly took a step into the room. "Where will you go now?"

"I don't know."

Mr. Twombly picked up the grocery bag, and he and Behemoth led Mrs. Farraday and Joan down the stairs. They led them back down the hill, this time taking the shortest way to the hotel. Behemoth held the door, and Mrs. Farraday and Joan went in. They stood uncertainly inside, but then they crossed on tiptoe to the desk. There was a sign above the desk which Mrs. Farraday read aloud, and smiled. "Beds $1.00 each. 2 for $1.25." She took two dollars from her purse and Mr. Twombly, behind the desk, made change. He selected a key from the board, and he and Behemoth led their guests up the noisy stairs to the third floor, showing them to room 35. Mr.

Twombly went in first, dropped their key on the bureau
top. Mrs. Farraday and Joan crossed to the window, stood
looking out.

"You'll probably want to rest awhile," Mr. Twombly
said. "The ladies' room is just next door." He and
Behemoth stood at the door, and Mrs. Farraday turned
to smile. Joan still hadn't said a word. They closed the
door quietly after them, walked to the stairs, but Mr.
Twombly went back again. He tapped lightly on the door.
"Mrs. Farraday?"

"Yes?"

"Did John ever hear from Mr. Martin Muir?"

"No."

Mr. Twombly and Behemoth climbed to the fourth
floor, passed along the corridors opening doors and
peering in. These rooms were much like the others, a
little dingier perhaps, with uglier wallpaper and older
paint, but most of the beds had mattresses. They climbed
a wooden ladder, and Behemoth pushed back a trapdoor
leading to the roof. The sun hit them solidly, but they
climbed out on top. All of Harding could be seen from
here. The bank lay immediately below, and the barbershop. Above, the hospital stood up boldly against the
sky, a little lower the grammar school, the church, the
mortuary, a cluster of lesser buildings clinging to the hill,
like a latter day acropolis partially resurrected, wired,
and antennaed here and there.

"We could stay here, Dick."

"Yes," Mr. Twombly said. "I knew a Mrs. Kroll back
in New York, nursemaid to those Alegard twins. She
would like it here, but I don't think I'd better write to her.
There was a man at that home the other day. Jack

McKnight, I think he was. We probably shouldn't invite both him and Dad Ingalls though. I wish we knew the name of that girl from Georgia we sat next to on the bus."

"The pretty one."

"Or even that boy with the gray mustache."

"Hm. I don't suppose Skinny Tsosie would be interested?"

"Skinny? No."

"There are others, Dick."

"Yes, Ed, lots."

They climbed back down the ladder and the stairs, passing the third floor quietly, stopping by their room to leave their coats. They stopped at the desk to find their key, tuck it in their pigeonhole. At the front door they parted, Mr. Twombly going left for groceries and Behemoth right to see about turning on the electricity.

Printed December 1995 in Santa Barbara
& Ann Arbor for the Black Sparrow Press by
Mackintosh Typography & Edwards Brothers Inc.
Design by Barbara Martin.
This edition is published in paper wrappers;
there are 200 hardcover trade copies;
100 numbered deluxe copies;
& 26 lettered copies
handbound in boards by Earle Gray.

Photo: Donald Braman

Douglas Woolf was born in New York City in 1922 and he died of cancer in 1992. He attended Harvard with Norman Mailer and JFK and then served in World War II as an ambulance driver in North Africa for the American Field Service, where he first learned a passion for the desert. Later he was a navigator for the Air Force. In 1955 his first novel *Hypocritic Days* was the capstone publication of Robert Creeley's The Divers Press. In his postwar life Woolf was constantly mobile, earning money as a migrant farm worker, ice cream man, groundskeeper, hawking beer and hot dogs at sports events and filling candy machines. In 1959 Grove Press first published *Fade Out* which enjoyed great success. Grove then published another acclaimed novel *Wall to Wall* in 1962.

Other books by Woolf appeared regularly after that. Black Sparrow published his novel *On Us* in 1977 and in 1993 brought out a complete collection of Woolf's short fiction entitled *Hypocritic Days & Other Tales*. Additional novels and collections are planned for the future.